Dear Mav

THE FINAL SCORE

Thanks for
Saturday night.
Happy reading
and don't get
too horny!
Give Jesi a kiss
Love
Chris.

THE FINAL SCORE

Chris Marton

New Edition © Chris Marton, 2021

First Published 2015

Published by Christopher Marton

A CIP catalogue record for this book is available from the British Library.

ISBN 978-0-9932940-1-3

Book layout and cover design by Clare Brayshaw

Cover images © Konstantin Yuganov | Dreamstime.com
© Wisky | Dreamstime.com

Prepared and printed by:

York Publishing Services Ltd
64 Hallfield Road
Layerthorpe
York YO31 7ZQ

Tel: 01904 431213

Website: www.yps-publishing.co.uk

Chapter One

The purple on the woman's lipstick had struck Kevin as been vaguely obscene, though he had never known why. It was only when he brought her lips down around the helmet of his cock that he realised why. Resembling two lean cuts of quivering kidneys, they were the same colour and their sheen even reflected the light in much the same way.

Druggies about to undergo the dank horrors of an acid trip for the first time could not have been more anxious. There was something intimidating about the total sense of focus the woman gave the act of sucking his cock. Those purple lips engulfed the rigid member in their sticky maw. A fugitive flash of a television documentary intruded into his thoughts like a furtive whisper – a ravenous lioness eating a still-twitching antelope, vulgarly tucking in whilst toying with it like a kitten.

It was nearly too much for Kevin. Clenching his eyes shut as he lay back on the bed, he realised why a blind man's other senses compensated for sightlessness. Kevin's felt heightened to unbearably superhuman levels. Small currents of electricity coursed from his fingertips, his brain, his toes – all surging to the base of his scrotum. They merged into an expanding miniature sun that crawled its way up the stem of his cock.

"Fuck!" The hissed exhalation took Kevin by surprise. It took seconds to realise it was his voice. He felt his cock would melt like candle wax. The woman finally withdrew her mouth from around it and left it fisting upwards like some organic egg secreted by an alien goddess. With a last mocking lick from her tongue, she drew herself upright with the easy grace of a ballerina to settle on her haunches over his rock-hard penis.

Her moist cunt enveloped his member like some B-movie monster engulfing its prey. Once enclosed in her sticky maw, the tiny sun burned anew and ascended. Kevin somehow found the courage to open his eyes and found them locked on hers. Those bright-as-button orbs crinkled with mocking amusement under long eyelashes. Those purple lips pursed themselves into an expression more obscene than anything going on underneath. Kevin felt excited and repulsed at the same time. Was this normal? This impossible demi-goddess was acknowledging him as a person in the midst of this carnality.

"Fuck me, bitch! Fuck me hard, you cunt! You pussy! Harder!" Her gasping exhortations hardly seemed to emanate from a human larynx. Closing her eyes in exquisite pleasure, she arched her head back and started to syncopate herself in rhythm to bring her dance to a brutal climax. Obscenities bubbled forth from those purple lips like a breached dam – that same mouth that had engaged him in banal ice-breaking chit-chat a few minutes ago. Relentless was the only word for those vulgarly large breasts – as relentless as the prow of a battleship bearing down upon a vulnerable frigate. Despite a few telltale hints of sagging age, her nipples were still pert – overseeing the purple galaxy of the aorta around them. They flapped about in a grotesque pseudo-life of their own as if independent of the bucking body. It seemed scarcely credible such vulgar splendour had lain hidden under the crisp white shirt of the schoolmistress outfit she had been wearing – lying in wait like the Trojans – waiting to be unleashed and lay waste.

'Oh, fuck!" Kevin gasped as the miniature sun reached the helmet of his prick. The woman's cunt had virtually massaged it ever upwards. The interior of her vaginal walls seemed possessed of a thousand tiny muscles throbbing with life. His cum virtually punched its way out in relief. Kevin's cries blended in with those of the woman into an atonal chorus.

Down, down, those relentless breasts flopped to envelope Kevin's face, like a carnivorous plant engulfing its prey. He could have stayed locked in the blissful embrace of that post-coital limbo for all eternity. Life's myriad problems and frustrations, its snubs and slights, evaporated into insignificance. Outside, he heard the faintest gasp of a breeze, the haphazard clacking of a pair of high heels on the pavement, the low rumble of an unidentifiable vehicle driving past.

Three forty five pm. The rest of the world was sweating away in unsatisfactory low-paid work cowed down in soulless, steel-and-glass offices, staring at the same PC screens and sat in the same poky cubicles until put out of their misery by redundancy. The other lads he knew would be lying under faulty tractor engines, sat for pile-inducing eternities in cabs, risking brain-damage from bucking cattle, or sweating away in the artificial infernos of garages.

"Good boy," the woman breathed into his ear. It wasn't just the outfit she had recently been wearing that brought back fledgling, erotic memories of a firm-breasted student English lit teacher and the approval he'd sought in subconscious rivalry with the other boys in his class. One occasion, a short ghost story he'd half-copied from a Marvel Comic back-issue for an essay had earned her praise. While she'd gushed about his originality and story-construction abilities, he'd been more concerned about the hard-on taking root in his boxer shorts. It was all he could do to avoid drawing attention to it while standing up in front of the class.

"And, cut!" The Director's imperious voice rang out like a pistol shot. Kevin's bliss was cold-bloodedly cut short. The wall-eyed teenage lad holding the boom microphone sighed with relief as he could finally cease balancing it over the bed.

A dry click announced the sound-recordist switching off his tapes. Rosemary's painted fingernails expertly flick off the DVD camera trained on Kevin and the woman. It drooped on its tripod like a depressive vulture in the desert.

Kevin had lost his virginity. It had been recorded for all eternity on digital video and would soon be available to view on a website for the right fee. It would ultimately earn him two hundred pounds in pay and back-royalties. It had been with an experienced hard-core porn actress in her mid twenties from somewhere near Bury named Sascha, who was moonlighting from her regular post as a salesperson for a microfiche company. Kevin once again thanked that white van driver who had damaged his motorcycle and nearly cleaned him up on that country road one night.

Chapter Two

Failure can form its own cycle of dependency. Playing two years for Thormanton Under-18's football team had taught Kevin that much. In the end, like a stagnant marriage or an unfulfilling job, it had become a dangerous narcotic. All ambitions were crushed for fear of even greater humiliation and failure and the sheer effort of having to rouse yourself.

On and off, the club had been running in one form or another – depending on local birth patterns – for nearly forty years. Entirely dependent upon a shallow pool of willing local talent, their best-ever season had seen them finish fifth from bottom in a league of twelve with a grand total of seven points back in 1973. Three years later, they had temporarily ceased to exist owing to a lack of local youth, only to resume an unremitting diet of mediocrity at the turn of the decade. The local cup competition they entered only lasted four rounds. Thormanton had very rarely got past the first – and only then when their scheduled opposition had gone out of business.

Kevin had moved to Thormanton with his Mother three years ago in the midst of a painful and acrimonious divorce from her red-brick University Lecturer husband Chris. He had been her Lecturer at Hull and eight years into his previous marriage when they met. Kevin had seen his Father's first wife only rarely – she was a small almost child-like woman who never seemed to smile. She had remarried shortly afterwards to a local council worker.

Kevin had grown accustomed to his father's long absences growing up in a comfortable commuter suburb on Humberside. He had identified with his Mother whilst his Father had been away on theatre trips and organising staging stage shows in his Drama Department, as well as attending the student parties afterwards and staying overnight at a girls' accommodation. He became a bit-part player in Kevin's life – his Mother's brave face and laughter grew more forced and hollow until the inevitable. Kevin holding the pillow over his twelve-year-old ears to blot out his Mother's shrieking and his Father's unconvincing expostulations heralded the arrival into his life of Lynne.

Lynne was a type Kevin had grown accustomed to on the scant occasions he'd been allowed into his Father's world. Most academic years – especially in a Humanities class – had a Lynne. Supervising her in a tutorial, his Father had taken superhuman effort to keep his hands off her and pay the superficial lip-service to Political Correctness popular certain among louche intellectuals.

Lynnes existed in countless artistic environments down the ages. Their common position was invariably kneeling in wide-eyed awe at the feet of some male authority figure many decades her senior and perhaps slavishly washing their brushes. Lynne had been in such a posture when Kevin first clapped eyes on her. She had all the poses down pat – the saucer-eyes stare of rapt awe under a tight cap of dark curly hair, the inoffensively-assertive body language, not to mention the tight designer jeans to maximise the appeal of her pert arse and the zip-up leather boots. Her natural state was to be the Pilot Fish to the shark of his

Father – a minor satellite bathed in the reflected glow of a larger planet.

Regardless of her physical charms, she was not drab exactly, but inconsequential. The thought of his Father slaking his sexual appetites on a girl seven years older than him gave Kevin the dry heaves.

Lynne was young, pert and available and his father regarded the effort of bringing him up and providing for a family as an onerous chore compared to fucking this professional nymphet.

Once she'd graduated, Lynne had married his father. On the few occasions Kevin had visited them recently, he'd sensed a hint of desperation in Lynne. Her eagerness to serve her Master was in danger of becoming a parody of itself and Kevin reckoned he'd give it another two years before his Father's gaze strayed across the lecture hall to another saucer-eyed young student.

For a clean break, his Mother had moved out to a semi-detached house in the North Yorkshire village of Thormanton. Village was a trifle generous term for a glorified hamlet of around 300 souls and even the bulk of the footballers came from the outlying farms. It had grown up around a narrow stone bridge and was little more than a drab little street on the main road between the market towns of Salton and Norbury. Too small to possess even a village hall, the social life revolved solely around the local free house pub The Spotted Cow.

The youth football team had started off as an offshoot of an adult club that had withered away through chronic indifference. It competed in the Salton and District under-18 league that currently consisted of eight sides – Salton, Norbury, Colstone Celtic, Wellthorpe, Denbymoorside, Nunthorpe Athletic, Thornton Westborough, and Thormanton.

Losing heavily by two figure goal tallies to the likes of Norbury, Denbymoorside, and Salton was palatable since they were market towns – or as palatable as being thrashed twenty-nil could be. But the remaining four were villages little larger than Thormanton. Kevin could even recognise their counterparts in those teams. They seemed immune to the crippling lack of confidence that infected Thormanton. The sole difference between them and the town teams was that they usually won by six-nil instead of twelve.

Kevin had never mixed much with the other lads in the village, nor had much inclination to. His background had been primarily suburban middle-class and, mixing with his peers in the top stream at school, not mixing with the local yokels as he termed them reduced them to the level of background noise. There had been one occasion where – among a lunchtime gathering – they had been talking about the relative merits of various makes of tractors – the John Deere as opposed to the David Brown – only for one outside the charmed circle to remark; "Fuck! Don't you sad fuckers talk about anything else?" Kevin sniggered involuntarily but he remained haunted by the mutely resentful looks some had shot in his direction. It was like he had thrown a dead pig into a synagogue or had defaced a statue of the Virgin Mary before a group of Sicilians.

Although never considered good enough to be a regular in the school eleven for his year – he'd amassed a paltry six appearances in over four years – Kevin still felt slighted when he'd failed to make the cut for a week's training at Ipswich Town. Their sadistic P.E. teacher had once been on the club's books and still had connections with it and arranged for one select Year's players to attend coaching sessions there. Although, in his heart of hearts, he knew he never stood a realistic chance of travelling down to Suffolk with the rest, it still hurt and he felt diminished by being left behind.

Football had taken priority over academia in his latter years at school. He felt a new force surging through his body that could only find expression on the sports field – although not in the static regimentation of a cricket pitch. Confined to the sweaty sterility of the class room, he mind sauntered into twenty different places at once – none of them wherever the teacher wanted.

Kevin had barely scraped by in his GCSE's and failed to make the cut for the top Universities. Re-sits had enabled him to qualify for a place on a three-year Humanities course at an obscure red-brick university that had only recently discarded Polytechnic status – though hardly the dreaming spires his Mother aspired to.

However, this left a gap-year in between leaving school and attending his First Year. Having heard countless horror stories from acquaintances about five-figure debts accrued by students, Kevin had decided to use the idle time to build up a bankroll to sustain him.

Kevin had started playing for Thormanton aged fourteen. He had rapidly become a regular in the first team though this was due more to a lack of material and a willingness to turn up for games than any talent on his part. Most games consisted of ninety minutes running about to little effect.

After the comfort zone of school, this was a crude throwback to being an infant kicking about with older lads from his early years on Humberside. Their middle-aged manager, Eric Skilbeck had always praised him for his effort and commitment but Kevin knew it was more to buck him up and ensure he turned up to make up the numbers for the next game.

Thormanton's sole trophy during those long, pointless years was invariably the Glenn Hirst Fairplay Shield. Named after a former youth player in the league who had died in a car accident back in the 80's, it was little more than a patronising clap on the shoulders for being obliging cannon fodder. Kevin felt that playing dirtier might at least show that they had some backbone and would not meekly accept their downtrodden status. But it was obviously too deeply ingrained into the psyche of his team mates to shift.

There was something faintly pathetic about watching their customary macho swagger off the field dwindle away to passivity when confronted by marginally superior opposition on the pitch. Stocky-built farm labourers who had spent entire summers in back-breaking work Victorians might consider excessive immediately mutated into emasculated wimps against opponents who had completed nothing more strenuous than a paper-round. Loud-mouthed boors who verbally bullied themselves into the centre of attention in school playgrounds and pubs withered away into submissive bit-part performers.

The previous season had gone much as expected – nil points, twelve goals scored, sixty seven conceded. Fourteen of these had come in their final game at Norbury Town.

Norbury was a market town of five thousand souls that advertised itself as the gateway to the Yorkshire Moors. It still held a weekly cattle market – though not for much longer if local planners had their way – but the growing profusion of new companies sprouting up, or stillborn in the new economic climate, on its outlying industrial estate signified the town's growing estrangement from the surrounding agriculture. The High Street threatened to be a morgue of closed-down shops that bore bleak testimony to the proliferation of identikit supermarkets taking root.

Norbury Town played at a respectable level in non-league circles and their senior players – many of whom had skirted the fringes of the professional game without ever threatening to break through – received a basic part-time wage plus travel expenses. They shared facilities with the town's cricket team which ensured a three-sided pitch. Modest, utilitarian stands resembling bus shelters with ideas above their station in life had been erected over basic tip-up plastic seats painted an unbecomingly tacky blue to match the club's colours in an attempt to meet FA standards – but it hadn't a prayer of even staging Conference football let alone League.

Even Kevin felt they were out of their depth in this arena where real-life professional footballers at York City and Scarborough had performed whilst going through the motions in trifling local county cup-ties. The width of the pitch sapped their strength and the muscular running and quick-passing game of Norbury under-18's crushed their spirits.

Thormanton were quickly reduced to chasing shadows – bit-part players at their opponents hour of glory, for they had already claimed the league championship two matches ago. Without leaving second gear, Norbury's final game took on the atmosphere of a stately procession.

"Champions! Champions!" In lieu of a crowd, Norbury provided their own triumphal chants. Kevin – gazing forlornly at the presentation of the championship trophy by a blazered and red-faced local league official with his greying, receding hair Brylcreamed severely back – bleakly pondered the homogeneity of soccer culture. The Norbury Captain – at 18 a stockily-athletic figure with a low centre of gravity in his final year at the club – self-consciously hugged his plump girlfriend. Kevin had known him vaguely at school in the year ahead of him and recalled the acne-infested dullard he'd been. Now he swaggered about with a newfound buoyancy

"Where was our fuckin' defence? You wor' leavin' Sammy's goal wide open every time!" Steven Cooke's whiny petulance cut into Kevin's reveries as Norbury embarked on a mock-lap of honour.

"Mebbe if you got back to help out now and again, we'd have some cover." Even by local standards, Robert Swales' North Yorkshire accent could be incomprehensively broad. Kevin did not need to turn to wearily turn his head to know these two diametrically opposed old foes would be eyeball to eyeball.

"I can't score if I'm back defending!" Delusions of grandeur were nothing news from Steven Cooke. His Mother had come from a lower-middle-class terraced house in Salton to marry a two-hundred acre tenant farmer. She had imagined she'd wed into the middle classes proper but had merely aligned herself to the great unwashed with money and responsibilities but none of the prestige. Steven's elder sister was deeply into show jumping and her parents heavily subsidised her by buying two horses. A cattle wagon-driving acquaintance of Kevin's once said that if he ever pulled into a farmyard and saw one horse in a stable, they'd be a delay in payment, but if there were two, you might as well turn around and leave.

Having being brought up to be a member of the upper middle classes, with the appropriate voice, Steven had had to perform a hasty volte-face and coarsen his vowels throughout adolescence in order to blend in. Football – being agreeably proletarian – also helped, and, by his late teens, his North Yorkshire accent was slipped into as naturally as a second skin. But his class-conditioned reflexes ensured he saw Robert and his ilk as one step removed from extras from "Deliverance". His Mother – like many who venture far from the security of their class – adopted a near-parody of upper middle-class values and failed to comprehend why its genuine members (who knew an inferior imitation when they heard one) snubbed and excluded her – which further fuelled her resentment.

Robert snorted. "You couldn't score in a fucking Whore-house." Robert was the second eldest of six children – four of whom played for Thormanton. This was elder brother Keith's last season before he was overage. Keith tended to be more withdrawn and obsessed with farming, a common ailment in this area – but Rob more than compensated. His parents had sent him to a private school to improve his coarseness but it had been like trying to teach a dog to stop urinating on your car wheels.

"Now then, lads, watch your language." Eric Skilbeck's prissy tones fluttered around their guttural oaths like a nervous butterfly. Like many well-spoken middle-class men who adopt a regional accent to fit in, the effect was effete and unintentionally camp.

Thormanton were in various stages of undress in the Norbury away-team changing rooms. Although it offered the unaccustomed luxury of piping hot showers at this level of football, the majority of the lads were changing straight back into their clothes. Eric had half-heartedly urged them to avail themselves of the facilities, instead of stinking the place out with sweat, but few were willing. Many wanted to put this day behind them as soon as possible.

Rob and Steven's row quickly petered out. It was becoming a well-worn routine between the earthy grafter in defence and the pseudo-glamour boy at centre forward. Its words were set in stone – as were those of what followed.

"Couldn't we get some bigger lads in?" Colin Adkins was something of a football purist. Kevin had read – and occasionally borrowed – the weighty tomes on football he owned. Colin had used a gift voucher to purchase a bumper book on football tactics that boasted a foreword by Howard Wilkinson. They had even tried to impress Skilbeck and some of the other lads by trying them out at a rare training session one Sunday afternoon. Inevitably, it had petered out into self-conscious half-heartedness and forgotten by the next match, apart from one free-kick routine.

It had been intended for John Swales to run up to the stationary ball as if to blast it at the defensive wall, then jump aside to chip it to lurking Steven Cooke for a clear shot at goal. Unfortunately, in the actual match against Wellthorpe, it ended in high farce as they both jumped over the ball, leaving it for each other. For sheer comedic effect, a silent routine from Buster Keaton could not have improved upon it as demonstrated by the guffaws from the Wellthorpe players who had just realised what had happened. After that, John Swales settled for blasting the ball impotently against the wall and tactical nous was silently laid to rest.

Colin was deep into a particular hobby horse of his. "There's one or two decent players can't get a game for Norbury," he implored Eric Skilbeck. As he lived with his family on the outskirts of both Thormanton and Norbury – just within the latter's catchment area – Colin was keenly aware of this. "Andy Blackburn. Jim Pinkney. Garry Smith. They're all decent players and can't get a game for Norbury to save their life! They're looking for someone to play for. If I have a word wi'...."

Eric Skilbeck's thin lips tightened as he stamped on the idea at birth. "No, Colin! I've told you before. We organise this team for...."

"...we organise this team for the youth of Thormanton, not for the benefit of those who can't get a game for Norbury or Salton!" Steven provided a half-decent simulacrum of Reg Skilbeck's discreetly-camp accent. It was an oft-repeated phrase that made allowances for pettish mimicry.

"Fat lotta good it's doing us getting slaughtered every week!" added Colin, turning his back in disgust.

"We're just a little village," whined Skilbeck. "You can't expect us to compete with town's like Norbury and Salton."

Kevin could stand it no more. He felt like an adult breaking up a crowd of fractious infants. "Salton's a town! Norbury's a town! Rest of 'em are fuckin' villages! Not much Bigger than us! Fuck me! Wellthorpe's a sodding hamlet! They do alright!"

Everyone seemed stunned by this outburst. Robert and goalkeeper Sammy Patterson exchanged a mute glance that – if intended to refer to a woman – would have indicated "time of the month!" Even the steam from the showers seemed to hang still in the air for a moment.

Kevin pulled his shirt over his head and stepped out of his shorts. As he lumbered into the showers, he heard Rob say "Bet we could beat the fuckers at fighting!"

"You do! Do you?" That was Darren Colclough, the team's Captain. A stocky-tending-to-portly eighteen year old who worked in Salton at an agricultural suppliers, this had been his final season. He wrenched at the black armband signifying his status and flung it carelessly to the sodden floor. "And thank fuck I won't be doing this next year. I've had more fun at the fucking dentists."

The sound of the exultant Norbury players getting changed and singing obscene victory chants buzzed like a migraine through the thin partition walls. Exhausted with the match, with the effort of life itself, Kevin trudged into the showers. Only Sammy Patterson was there. Diving in the mud of a light, pre-match shower had stained his body – although he had all but given up making a token show of effort for the last three goals conceded. Kevin could have sworn he had dived out of the way of a thunderbolt volley rather than save it. Kevin idly wondered if Sammy's sister Emma had been among the smattering of spectators.

Kevin basked in the fine warm spray. He sensed, rather than saw, someone's eyes coldly boring into him.

Eric Skilbeck managed to avert his eyes in time and made a show of talking to Sammy Patterson. But Kevin nonetheless finished his shower self-consciously shielding his genitalia and made it hastier than he otherwise would.

Nobody else was around in the changing room when Kevin finally emerged. Darren Colclough's armband lay abandoned on the damp floor like a discarded condom. Kevin reverently picked it up, brushed it off and tenderly placed it in his sports bag.

★ ★ ★

Kevin had fallen for Amanda Richards in a big way from the moment he heard her curiously affected "ickle girl" voice across his classroom in his final year. In time, he would recognise it as the affectation of a born prick-teaser but, at the time, it stood out very pleasantly from the sullen, studied indolence of her contemporaries. Nobody could eat a banana more provocatively than Amanda. Her lips were not full and sensual but somewhat pinched and, nonetheless, enticing. If caught in the act of cunillingually devouring a banana, she would adopt a look of mock-offense under heavily-lidded eyes.

This constant intake of fruit (for Kevin never saw her eat anything else) must be what ensured her trim figure. Whereas most girls who dieted strenuously looked ghoulishly anorexic, Amanda was sexily slender for Kevin who normally preferred a more voluptuous form. Her breasts were small but insolently pert and high while her buttocks were two collar-studs. No doubt about it,

Amanda Richards had been the girl of his dreams. Alas, she was going steady with an anaemic-looking monosyllabic worker from York. This was a crime against nature. His demigoddess deserved better. But she was still going steady with this wanker!

And he was going steady with Keeley-Anne Humberstone. She was lathe-thin without the compensation of interesting breasts. Her lean face was comely enough, but perpetually disfigured by a disinterested blankness. Kevin would see dozens like her in his lifetime. For her type, the period in between school and marriage was a treacherous and uncertain limbo best rendered safe by been as brief as possible. They invariably married young – often in their teens – and would make great play of remarking that they were always mature for their age. It was hollow bravado. Physically, they remained much as they were mentally – frozen at 16 like flies in aspic. Other women developed hips and tits in unison with adult personalities. The likes of Keeley-Anne remained sexlessly stunted.

Kevin and Colin Adkins had cadged a lift from a mate. This was Bert Dale – a youth in his early twenties who owned a second-hand Vauxhall Crossland X. Keeley-Anne and her friend had arranged to meet them in Salton at a pub that would still turn a blind eye to anyone under eighteen. Kevin owned a motorcycle, but that rendered snogging and copping a crafty feel on the back seat a distinct no-starter.

Kevin had been getting nowhere very fast with Keeley-Anne. It had started on a note of false optimism at a barn dance in one of the nearby villages and an exchanged smile. Colin had scored with her friend Mary so Kevin felt asking out her friend was a calculated gamble. They seemed to click and, having dropped her off home in

Bert's car, he barely slept that night in anticipation of the sensual pleasures ahead.

What lay ahead was what Kevin would deride as a simpleton's attempts at mind-fucking. Striking up a carefree conversation with her proved nigh impossible. Kevin was sufficiently mature to conceal his carnal instincts beneath a veneer of polite interest in her personality but it was difficult to gain a foothold on the icy slopes of her chilly exterior. A few desultory words would pass between them followed by a half-hearted snog and grope on the back seat of Bert's Crossland X. He'd thought he had struck gold when she she had invited back to her parents semi-detached house. The evening had passed in an air of heavy patience while he had feigned interest in some glitzily-vacuous TV talent show with Keeley-Anne, and her Mother.

Her Father had disappeared to the pub at around nine p.m. and the Mother had trudged upstairs to bed at eleven. There had been a discreet wait until he was sure she was in bed before a furtive hand snaked around Keeley-Anne's shoulders to begin hostilities. It proved a phoney war as a clumsy banging at the front door heralded the return of her Father with Kevin's trousers at half mast. Kevin was amazed at the speed and agility he'd pulled them up in time – as he was at regaining his composure to maintain an air of decorum while her father idly flicked through the TV channels before stumbling upstairs.

Kevin peeled off quickly. Keeley-Anne followed suit with all the eagerness of a dental appointment. They snogged passionately – well, Kevin had – French-kissing her in a manner picked up at a school dance. It had been like snogging a corpse. Inevitably, after much frenzied breast-fondling and nipple-suckling, he tried to penetrate her – uncomfortably aware that such a momentous event deserved to be less demeaning and sordid. But Keeley-Anne had expertly held her thighs tightly together and refused to flinch. Kevin had tried every position he'd known without looking too desperately-virginal before quitting.

With no real excuse to stay, they had got dressed in a stilted silence and Kevin trudged his morose way outside to catch a taxi home. Unexpectedly, Keeley-Anne had abruptly brightened and kissed him with something approaching genuine pleasure.

This had been the remorseless pattern to his social life for the past three months. Kevin was starting to suspect there was a degree of calculation to her actions. Keeley-Anne could chastely withhold herself throughout the course of the evening with something approaching contempt, then brighten up on cue and bid him farewell as if silently promising him better luck on his next visit. "Treat 'em mean and keep 'em keen."

Only once had she volunteered any information. Her previous boyfriend was a squaddie named Peter who was currently stationed abroad in Germany. The suspicion had formed in Kevin's mind that he was a convenient time-filler and this night was to confirm it. She had been more sullen and stroppier than usual as they ping-ponged between the sparsely attended night clubs and pubs, laid waste by the economic crisis, in Scarborough.

Kevin felt tense and priggish among the shrill shrieking of the going-to-seed office workers. It tended to be the fatter women making the most noise, as if determined to show they were having a good time. There were shaven-headed ugly brutes who defied conventional wisdom through pulling gorgeous sophisticated-looking women by being ostentatiously loud and boorish in lieu of self-confidence. Kevin found himself becoming a lay-expert on body language. Self-defeatingly awkward youths jauntily tried to impose themselves into circles of blank-faced girls only to be silently excluded by discreetly turned backs.

The OK Karaoke bar lightened his mood a little. While everyone else was having a go at what Colin termed "slapper-fodder" – Robbie Williams, the Spice Girls, etc – Kevin screwed up his nerve to attempt Hi-Ho Silver Lining. Standing out like a sore, throbbing thumb, Kevin caught a glimpse of Keeley-Anne exchanging disparaging glances with Mary. He channelled his cold fury into his singing and was gratified by the smattering of applause he drew and one or two girls jiving to it. One unshaven, haggard, wall-eyed loner had even taken the opportunity to drunkenly compliment him on his performance, in an offensively-assertive way, and his balls on getting up in front of an audience in the first place. Any elation he felt soon ebbed away afterwards.

In one do-or-die attempt to salvage something, Kevin and Keeley-Anne had eventually drifted outside the club and down a darkened alley. Kevin's mouth was soon locked in a savage vacuum with the girl. After what he felt was a decent interval, his right hand commenced its preliminary reconnaissance by awkwardly fondling the pert young breasts thrusting against her tight top. Kevin's trembling fingers kneading them back and forth like dough.

Though her mouth seemed responsive, Keeley-Anne's face remained provocatively dispassionate throughout. To judge from her face, she could have been weathering a mild case of indigestion. Kevin tried sneaking his hand up underneath her top but found it too tight for easy progress. Further progress was forestalled by the girl abruptly pulling apart with a sharp "No!"

It was like a slap in the face. Kevin withdrew his hand from her top as if stung. "Why not?" Kevin attempted a suave, seductive tone but his voice sounded an octave too high.

"Because! That's why"

An eternity of moments elapsed before he formed a retort. "Is it Peter?"

Her silence spoke volumes. There was not an ounce of fat anywhere on Keeley-Anne but Kevin was beginning to wonder if it denoted denial of fleshy sensuality rather than photogenic beauty. "Christ! What the fuck do ya' see in that twat?"

In the past few weeks, Kevin would normally have asked what he had done but he was growing weary of assuming it was always his fault.

"I'd like to go home now."

Kevin sighed heavily. Peter had been in his year at School – an obnoxious youth of medium height who made great play of his violent older brother always been in the background in case of trouble. His desire to enlist had come about during the uncertain two years his brother was no longer a pupil.

In silence – the tension between them a palpable entity – Kevin escorted Keeley-Anne back into the club. The drive home maintained a distant politeness with neither in any great rush to advertise their split. Kevin felt a sadistic urge to take advantage of this and force himself on the girl, but something made him hold back and nurture the black venom in his soul that he had promised himself to spit upon the world.

Chapter Three

" Watch yoursen', Kev! She's an awkward bitch!"
Tom Fenwick's shout came a fraction too late as
the hoof of a pregnant Friesian cow stamped indifferently
on the corn on Kevin's left toe.

"Awww, fuck!"

It was getting on for two in the morning. Outside the
cattle shed was pitch black except for a smattering of
stars against a cloudy sky. The neon lighting in the shed
illuminated the building's interior in a harsh artificial day.

A fortnight on from the definitive split with Keeley-
Anne and Kevin had reluctantly been dragooned into
aiding Tom Fenwick at calving. Normally, Tom's younger
brother Harry would be in attendance. But, tonight, was
the annual Darts team outing for his pub, the Spotted Cow.

Kevin had been enlisted to sacrifice valuable drinking
time for often a fruitless night standing attendance on
expectant cattle on the three previous weekends and was
going stir-crazy as a result. Given his current emotional
state, Kevin astonished himself at how indifferent he was
to giving up a Saturday night for, what could be, another
fruitless wait.

Normally, a cow delivering a calf was a straightforward
process. But, recently, the Fenwick's had been having
more than their fair share of over-large calves being

born deceased. This resulted in the miracle of natural birth turning into something resembling a repair pit on a Formula One race track with the brothers and Kevin acting as midwives cum mechanics. This latest example had proven no different as an exploratory grope from Tom inside the expectant cow confirmed his worst suspicions that the calf was the wrong way around in the womb. Having herded the animal away from its fellows – cows contentedly chewing on their cuds, newly-born calves gambolling stiffly on uncertain legs, the lone bull patrolling his harem in an ominously proprietorial manner – Tom and Kevin eventually harnessed it to a rope halter and affixed it to a wall.

In spite of the chill night air, Kevin sweated as – stripped to the waist – he and Tom tied two short lengths of stout rope to the calf's protruding hooves. These, in turn, were fastened to a long retractable metal pole contraption that used a hydraulic lever to jack the calf out of its mother. The whole operation queasily resembled changing a tyre.

Time and again, the cow nervously shifted position forcing Tom and Kevin to swear oaths and refit the jack to the cow's haunches to start the whole laborious business all over again.

It was a grisly experience. Kevin winced as the jack grew harder to crank as the inexorable creak of its mechanism was pitted against the stubborn flesh of the cow. Something had to give – painfully. Ultimately, all that submitted was the calf's resistance as it was unceremoniously yanked outside the fetid warmth of the cow into the bitter cold of the shed.

Kevin noted with relief the absence of a lolling tongue thereby indicating it was still alive. It gave a plaintive moo and staggered drunkenly to its uncertain feet. Tom rubbed its damp body down with clean straw to massage its circulation going, then nodded to Kevin to untie its Mother.

Tom's open, fleshy face beamed an awkwardly toothy grin. It was the sort of face that looked congenitally incapable of malice. "Tha'll miss this when tha's at college."

"Like a hole in the head," Kevin felt like saying but did not. Farming bored the living crap out of him but Tom was a fair employer and alternative employment was at a premium in this region.

"They're always a bugger if they're born back to front," said Tom.

"Reckon it'll live?"

"If it survives the night, aye!"

Kevin had already learned from school that gaining an animated conversation about anything other than agricultural matters from the locals was a fruitless task. Typically tacky teenage subjects like sex, music, and sport were given scant attention. Kevin found this bleak and off-putting. Would such an obsession with work be the norm if they were bus drivers or accountants?

"There was summat' on the News about foot-and-mouth up the North-east somewhere," offered Kevin.

"Aye," Tom grunted. "As if BSE weren't bad enough, it's getting like the Plagues of Egypt."

By Three a.m. Tom was satisfied there would be no further developments – or if there was, he could not be bothered to wait up for it. With a last glance at the herd, he flicked off the cattle shed lights and he and Kevin ambled wearily back to the farmhouse. It was a white-painted two-story building that resembled a child's painting of a house with a door centrally set amid five windows.

Kevin forced himself to linger for a farewell cup of tea in the kitchen. While they wound the morning down small-talking, a low rumble and the glowing orb of head lamps heralded the return of Harry Fenwick.

One could detect fraternal links facially between the two brothers, but the differences bore testimony to the dominance of nature over nurture. Harry's features were those of a once-handsome rogue going prematurely and cheerfully to seed. His beer belly strained against his imitation leather belt and his receding curly hair still retained the vague outline of its youthful style. Like many men who wed young (he was barely eighteen when it happened) he treated marriage as a secure base from which to operate as a still single teenager behind his family's back. Rumours still abounded about a fancy woman somewhere in Salton he visited on Market Day.

The faintest whiff of cheap after shave preceded Harry's swaggering entrance into the kitchen. "Ey' up, lads! Busy night?"

"How was t'darts dinner, Harry?" asked Tom.

Harry played every Friday home and away for the Spotted Cow team in Thormanton – currently becalmed in mid-table in the Salton and District League. His surname usually appeared in passing mention on the penultimate page of the Salton Gazette. Tonight had been the usual annual jamboree in Scarborough – usually consisting of a friendly match in town, a meal and a night club.

"Biggest laugh wor' watching old Dennis Earnshaw trying to chat up this lass wi' her husband stood by her." Somehow, with Harry, the conversation invariably came around to sex.

"Some fit-looking lasses about. Make's me wish I wor' twenty years younger again. Is it me or are lasses tits getting bigger?"

Tom shifted uncomfortably and put down his half-empty mug of tea. "I'll just check on 'em again before I turn in."

Harry was suspiciously quiet as Tom lumbered outside. Then he fumbled inside his pockets for a glossy pamphlet which he held under Kevin's stunned eyes. A pair of tanned, solidly-siliconed breasts dominated his eyeline.

"CLUB SKINEMATIQUE – for the sophisticated and discerning Man" read the title. Kevin was amused how often hardcore porn simulated a veneer of upmarket elegance – PLAYBOY, PENTHOUSE – never SOCIAL INADEQUATE or SAD BEDSIT.

"Fuck me! Where didja' get this?"

"Little place I know in York. 'visit it same nights my Missus thinks I'm playing dominoes at t'Spotted Cow."

Kevin thumbed through the eight page brochure. "No need to travel to see these things. Have you got a computer?"

"Aye, but kids need a bucket o' cold water to be seperated from it. I'm not one for queueing. Besides, I wouldn't know how to cover me' tracks, if you catch my drift."

Kevin came to one particularly prominent pair of silicone breasts attached to the Amazonian body of an auburn-haired model adopting the regulation issue mouth-open eyes–heavily-lidded "come hither" look.

"Reckon you could do her a favour. She'd eat a little boy like you alive."

"Chance'd be a fine thing."

Kevin eventually came to the last page. "Keep it if you like. Plenty more where that came from," said Harry.

"Ta!" Kevin gingerly pocketed it. "Tom know about this?"

"Him? Nah'. First time he ever had a hard–on, he ran downstairs to mi' Mother that his knob had died and got rigor mortis." Kevin spluttered at the mental image this conjured up. "Any road, he come's back a week later an' says "it's alright, I've worked out what the problem is. It had got bunged up wi' this white puss. But don't worry, I've found a way to pump it out. I reckon another week an' I'll have itclear." Kevin's ribs were starting to ache. "Twenty years later, he's still at it!" Harry mimed the act of wanking while pulling a grotesque face of sexual satisfaction. ""Bugger me! How much more o' this, is there? I'll never be rid of it!""

Kevin's shoulders were still rocking when he mounted his motorbike outside and started it on the short ride home. The mental image of Harry's mime artificially buoyed up his spirits even as the onrush of chill air froze him to the bones through his riding leathers.

He might have been more alert to the white van hurtling towards him with an ominous speed down the one-lane country road. The driver made no attempt to dip his headlights and Kevin slowed down. The van had passed the reasonable point where it would be expected to reduce its speed and panic gripped Kevin's throat. He swerved into the grass verge at the last moment as the van bore down on him.

It caught the motorbike a glancing blow that spun the smaller vehicle around. Kevin was flung from the bucking seat and his next sight was of the ground hurtling towards him. The impact seemed to knock all the wind out of his body.

Kevin could not say how long he lay by the roadside. The motorbike puttered on even though it was stranded on its side like a tortoise on its back. Any crash you can walk away from is a good one, Kevin remembered someone saying. It was of little comfort as he wheeled the motorbike – its frame slightly bent out of shape and no longer roadworthy – back home.

★ ★ ★

""Fuck me!" he says. "I'll never be rid of it!"" Harry Fenwick's jokes usually made the rounds of the local lads via Kevin. Satisfied by how comically he had exaggerated the facial expression for comic effect, Kevin saw Colin Adkins convulsed with malicious merriment a few days later as they furtively scanned the porn brochure in Kevin's bedroom, with a CD of "One Night Only" playing in the background.

"You reckon Tom's ever done "it"?" ventured Colin, giving voice to the unspeakable – that void-like state that every teen male virgin feared.

Kevin shook his head like a spastic robot. "Mebbe in the dim and distant past. Sometimes, in my worst nightmares...."

"Shite! Doesn't bear thinking about." Colin paused. "How's your trusty steed? I heard about t'accident."

"The bike? Frame's bent out o' shape. Spent most o' this week ringing around garages trying to get a cheap quote. It'll fucking clean me out to get it fixed."

"Someone sitting on a feather?" The hesitant falsetto of Kevin's Mother preceded her self-conscious entry into her son's Inner Sanctum bearing a tray with two glasses of lemonade. Kevin inwardly thanked himself for taking the precaution of concealing his stash of porn between the pages of a hardback football annual.

"Thought you'd be thirsty." The two lads helped themselves to a glass. Colin adopted the time-honoured pose of the adolescent male guest more polite than his host.

"That was your Father on the phone, Kevin. He's engaged. He's set a date for sometime in September."

"Oh, I thought Kev told me he'd already married," queried Colin.

"He did," answered Kevin. "This is another one."

"I need a scorecard," said Colin.

Kevin's Mother paused on the threshold on leaving. "Kevin's Father is like a lot of men in his profession. He views being a University Lecturer as a dating agency-cum-massage parlour for sad, middle-aged men." Her bitter laughter hung in the air long after she was gone.

Kevin saw Colin's face building up under the weight of questions he was dying to ask. "Perk o' the job," he offered by way of explanation.

"Fuck me," said Colin. "All my Uncle Norman gets is his travel expenses and a subsidised canteen. He'd say he was in the wrong job."

Kevin downed most of his lemonade in one gulp. "He's not the only one."

Chapter Four

Kevin had always felt self-conscious squiring Keeley-Anne around. He felt as if he was exposing some innermost part of himself to all and sundry. Did those observing them together makes notes on the girl and judge him accordingly – whether his preference was for her lathe-thin figure and small breasts, long straight hair and wedge-like face. Now he felt the desolate vacuum a twin must experience when its sibling dies. Where once there was a human appendage to one side, now there was nothing.

Ironically, Keeley-Anne had not been exactly what you would call a soulmate. The only time he saw her smile was when he was kissing her goodnight. The relationship had been distinctly balanced in her favour and bristled with too many snubs and slights for his liking. A dread of rejection and ending up alone meant he had stolidly endured them. He had often tried to force himself into a pose of masterful indifference but had felt too self-conscious and trapped in an existing image to try it.

Now, as he glumly chugged down a pint of lager and lime in the main bar of The Spotted Cow, he wondered by what miracle he'd been able to pull a prize bitch like Keeley-Anne and whether he would rise so high again. The darts team playing away at The Sun Inn in Denbymoorside ensured that the pub was host to half a dozen flaccid souls on a Friday night.

Several of his mates on the football team were among their number. Kevin could scarcely credit that his mates would engage in such a patently uncool activity redolent of sweaty, beer-bellied losers that still hadn't grasped that the seventies were long over. Now he envied them being able to occupy their time so mindlessly. More importantly, there was nobody around to give him a lift into town.

The following day, Kevin felt an invisible hand firmly push him back into the depths of his seat as the "snake" plunged into darkness. The posters promised, "THE RIDE OF A LIFETIME. EXCITEMENT AND DANGER BEYOND YOUR WILDEST DREAMS – AND NIGHTMARES. ARE YOU MAN ENOUGH TO RISK IT? THUNDER CANYON!!!"

Ostrich Park Zoo had started off as with wildlife the centre of attention in the 1950's. Dolphins, performing seals, a killer whale, and a chimpanzee's tea party initially featured strongly in its repertoire. All had gradually faded away during the eighties, like tired, outdated Music Hall turns, and the zoo now functioned as little more than an adjunct to the funfair with ever more spectacular rides added every year.

It said a lot for the area that Ostrich Park was the largest local employer outside agriculture. Slumming students and gap year graduates could be found manning the car park or the rides in addition to the resident staff. The slave wage standard of living resulted in the nearby village off Dunthorpe having a distinctly downmarket, housing estate air that militated against the cosy middle class Tory atmosphere of the surrounding area.

Nonetheless, it was the unimaginative site of the annual Thormanton F.C. outing. A cursory attempt was made to add variety to the choice by a voting system that included trips to Bridlington or Scarborough as options. But the overwhelming choice was invariably Ostrich Park and those who voted otherwise bowed to the inevitable. The attraction of a brand new nerve-shredding ride was dangled before them as an incentive.

Kevin, Robert, Sammy, Steven, Colin and several siblings staggered out of the ride as it juddered to a halt. Giddy with excitement, they tottered drunkenly out of the embarkation bay. Robert and one of his brothers had already nipped around the front for a second ride. The others dispersed to the rest of the Fair and – inevitably – the Dodgem cars.

Kevin had completed three violent circuits of the track and had just rammed his car into the rear of a middle-aged man and his eight year old son when it happened. A shuddering blow to the back of his car sent a shockwave through his unprepared body. His swung around in his seat – an oath on his lips – only to be greeted by a mocking giggle.

"Catch me if you can, Kev!"

Emma Patterson blew a mocking kiss and arced her car in a tight circle away from him. Her passenger, Belinda Turner – an overweight, ginger-haired sixteen year old – held on for dear life as Kevin sharply reversed to pursue them. Time and again, Kevin was on the point of striking Emma's car only to be thwarted by the girl's nimble manoeuvring. He managed a feeble thump on her left-hand bumper before his money ran out and his car abruptly ground to a halt.

Kevin lingered by the ride for a minute or two until Emma's car stopped dead and both girls disembarked. "Pity your Sammy isn't half as nippy on the field," he remarked.

Emma had no tits worthy of the name (unlike the impressively plump-breatsed Belinda) in Kevin's eyes. Her brown, mousey hair was cropped and boyish and she wore remarkably little make-up. She had a natural, open face and a moderately interesting body kept in reasonable shape by being a first-team regular for her school's girl soccer side.

"Glad you're impressed." There was an inner excitement about the girl that went beyond the giddiness of the dodgems. "Has Mister Skilbeck told you yet?"

"Told me what?"

"She's playing for us!" It was like a knife in the bowels.

Eric Skilbeck normally had a habit of holding his face too uncomfortably close during conversation. There could be something over-familiar about his manner. He had the nervous air of a man expecting to be lynched at any minute. Emma's Mother – Olive Patterson – provided support.

"My Emma's played for her school. She was their captain last year."

"Aye," rumbled Kevin. "Against girls her own age. With us, it'll be hulking great buggers from Salton and Norbury."

"My Emma knows what to expect. She's quite prepared to pull her own weight."

Kevin grasped for straw. There was no reasoning with these two losers. "What about the League? Aren't there rules against girls playing with us blokes?"

"They've agreed to make an exception in our case. What with being so short o' players," said Skilbeck.

"They would!"

Mrs Patterson and Skilbeck whined away an increasingly unconvincing line in excuses as to why this was a good thing. Their imploring rang increasingly hollow and desperate. Kevin eventually found a feeble excuse to wander off and try the other attractions, but his heart was no longer in it. On the way out, he caught sight of a selection of DVD's as prizes on a hoopla stall. One title stood out. "DEAD MAN WALKING."

Chapter Five

" "It's true. Elsie Sleightholme saw it all. She wor' washing up at her sink, an' her house looks onto Skilbeck's."

The whole drearily repetitive pattern of domino night that Wednesday at the Spotted Cow was rent asunder by the gossip. In a village hermetically sealed off from the 21st century as Thormanton, such news had an anarchic, disruptive force similar to a carnival. All normal routine was suspended as the village buzzed with speculation.

Kevin was aware of an alien vibration in the Main Bar as soon as he stepped in. It was too light-hearted to be a death and it carried the air of a schoolboy sniggering at a porn mag behind the bike sheds, made all the more grotesque by the fact these were middle-aged men and women.

Wednesday morning was the local council's Refuse Collection Day. Without fail, a platoon of green plastic Wheelie bins and attendant cardboard boxes stood sentinel outside their respective houses. The Council lorry would pull slowly into a central area and a handful of overalled workmen dispersed to both sides of the road and cart the bins to be emptied into the crusher.

Elsie Sleightholme had noted the newcomer to the refuse team a fortnight ago. Sandy-haired, thickset turning to fat, ruddy-faced and with an gold ring in his left earlobe, he looked a good decade younger than his mates. He had swaggered with an easy confidence into the Skilbeck's front yard to collect their bin and the boxes of newspaper to be recycled.

She had seen Eric Skilbeck converse with the man for a few stilted moments on the past two visits. The refuse collector had smiled with an easy familiarity as Eric almost tiptoed out of his semi-detached house. A few words had already been exchanged though Elsie saw Eric was standing significantly closer than previous. There was less than two feet between them when it happened.

Eric made a half-hearted attempt to brush the man's hair. The man's face darkened with outraged anger and he floored Eric with a meaty left hook. The refuse collector looked poised to follow up with a boot to the prone man only for his workmates – alerted by the ruckus – to intervene as fast as their portly figures would allow them.

As Eric Skilbeck clambered pathetically to his feet, the offended refuse collector explained volubly to his colleagues. The lorry had remained parked for nearly an hour – long enough to register as out-of-the-ordinary and arouse attention. Several villagers hovered nearby to observe.

Eventually, Eric Skilbeck was seen to offer what could be described as a limp apology to appease the workman and he scuttled back inside his house with as much dignity as he could muster. The openly abusive refuse collector allowed himself to be calmed by his mates and led back to the lorry to half-heartedly resume the morning's rounds.

The news emanated outwards like ripples from a stone dropped into a stagnant mill pond. Kevin's Mother had received the Chinese Whisper at around six thirty that evening thanks to a phone call from a friend.

"Tried to chat up this lad on t'refuse lorry and got a gobfull of fist! Dirty old sod!" Robert Swales was holding court secure in the limited horizons of his machismo. Kevin reflected that his ostentatiously open-necked shirt, deep tan, and plaid jeans would probably have got him a centrefold in GAY NEWS Special, Rough Trade Edition.

Sammy Patterson wondered aloud how Eric Skilbeck's wife had not suspected. "Maybe she had," laughed Kevin. "Mebbe she was puzzled as to why the only way he's fuck her was if she shaved her head, wore a false moustache, and took it up the arse."

Half the pub rocked with shocked laughter. But the anxiety remained of who would coach and manage the football team. Two weeks later, an emergency meeting was held in the pub to discuss it. The players' parents decided to perform the paperwork themselves but leave the team in the hands of whoever was Captain for now – the obvious inference was that it would die a natural death in due course, especially with a bunch of players in their final eligible season and no replacements on the horizon.

Kevin attended the meeting and assumed the mantle of player-coach with mixed feelings. Having recently bought a book on soccer tactics on ebay, he was bursting with ideas but realistic enough to appreciate how his sullen charges would respond.

Although the nets had been taken down for the Summer break – to avoid being vandalised by the cattle that grazed there – the stanchions still stood erect when Kevin called his first midweek practise session. Five players turned up, Emma, Steven, Sammy, Nick Cammack and Peter Russell – the latter two both fifteen years old and young enough to take these rituals seriously. At least Sammy's presence meant that they had their first choice goalkeeper. Emma betrayed the unaffected enthusiasm of the newcomer and she eagerly threw herself into the fitness routines Kevin had culled from the book. Several odds and ends were lined up in lieu of bollards for them to dribble around.

Robert and his three younger brothers had the excuse of being in the midst of harvest – both corn and silage. But Colin's family farm was smaller and Kevin had seen that their ninety-plus acres were now bare stubble.

Peter Russell – still at school and running to plumpness – was a newcomer. Kevin and Steven exchanged worried glances as struggled to trap a long cross field ball from Emma and tripped over his own feet. Steven helped him to his feet.

"You say you played for your school?" he asked Peter.

"Well, sort of. I was substitute once when there was all that flu going about," volunteered Peter. "They even brought me on for the last ten minutes when we were four-nil down."

The session commenced at seven in the evening and petered out around just after eight. For Kevin, the short walk home stretched unendurably.

★ ★ ★

In farming, harvest was the F.A. Cup Final of the season with all its attendant anxieties and sense of anti-climax. Tom Fenwick tended to hog the combine harvester, cocooned in its air-conditioned cabin from the world outside. He would sit there for hours amidst the ear-grinding rumble of the powerful engines mowing down endless rows of wheat and barley with the coldly-glabruous expression of a seasoned executioner.

Harry tipped the grain into the storage barn and operated the diesel-powered drier. He looked, for all the world, like a futuristic bank robber behind his white face-mask to protect his lungs from the dense clouds of dust that hung ominously in the air. Harry's roguish air seemed diminished by this lone, mute role.

At least there was some variety in his labours as he drove the JCB to shovel corn into the bed of the drier, attended the dials and instruments to ensure all was okay on the drier, sampled occasional handfuls of grain for their temperature, and tipped the corn – once properly dried out and cooled down – into the main storage shed.

Kevin filled in the gaps. After a wait of one or two sunny days, the rows of cut straw were baled – tightly packed into heavy rolls bound with plastic twine. Neatly packaged, they sat haphazardly on the bare stubble like a child's discarded toy bricks. With their resultant collection and stacking in the farm yard, a sense of relief settled over the Fenwick's farm. They were on the home stretch and it was all downhill from here. The next implement to scour the face of these fields would be the plough or the power harrow to signal the start of the next cycle.

Kevin luxuriated in the artificial draught of the cab's air-conditioning as he drove the tractor down the lanes of straw which the bailer noisily devoured and periodically halted to excrete a full bale. Stripped to the waist, Kevin strained the catch the football commentary in the cab's radio over the din. The plateau-like farm land baked in the broiling mid-August sun though Kevin was as hermetically sealed off from it as any office worker. Partly it was the dust – irritating clouds that hung in the dry air and prickled the skin like energised mosquitoes. That was bad enough, but a more insidious threat was breathing them in. Several years continual exposure could bring on the dreaded "Farmer's Lung" – and for someone who had no ambitions agriculturally, that would be an ironic fate.

Kevin caught sight of the busy holiday traffic rushing past on the road running parallel to the field. Nuclear families with restless kids in the back, aggressively-patient Mothers keeping calm in the front, and stolidly sun-glassed Fathers at the wheel were the norm. But Kevin would catch glimpses of something more promising – office-bound career women with dyed blonde hair, dark tailored jackets and hot, tanned bodies kept taut by gym-work. He imagined the black or purple underwear holding firm, bulging breasts against crisp white shirts. They were probably going home to lonely TV Dinners in soulless flats.

This would give Kevin all the motivation he needed to plough through intimidating volumes of Shakespeare and Joseph Conrad. The Holy Grail of a degree would ensure admittance to the promised land of sexy, sophisticated and uninhibited career women who would ride him like Willie Carson on Speed.

One particularly uneventful Saturday night out at the pubs in Salton resulted in a welcome lie-in the following Sunday morning when a light drizzle ensured there would be no harvest work that day. The distant crack of a single gunshot somewhere nearby broke into his slumbers. He soon relapsed into a booze-fuelled snooze. But the incident would have repercussions.

Chapter Six

The lyrics to Meatloaf's perennial karaoke favourite "Paradise by the Dashboard Light" sounded alien when sung in a broad North Yorkshire timbre. Keely-Anne's steady boyfriend Peter stumbled over his word and sang them about a beat too late as he awkwardly vamped on stage alongside her. The girl's saucer eyes remained riveted on him and seemed not to acknowledge Kevin's presence in the crowd in the pub.

Even a masochist cannot endure forever. Kevin took advantage of Colin's impatience with the pub to silently indicate it was time to go. He had been unusually withdrawn all night, as if holding something back.

Scarborough usually had a thriving night life but the recession had denuded it of all energy in recent times. The pubs they frequented had often been reasonably full on a Thursday night. Now they resembled sterile waiting rooms on every night except Saturday.

A few blocks down the street was a cluster of fast food outlets side-by-side. Colin complained that a chicken kebab at the nearest one had given him "the shits" and rendered him shaken and feeble the following morning so Kevin allowed his mate to direct him to a more favourable choice.

"Hello, sir. Have a good evening?" The Asian man behind the counter was somewhere in his mid-twenties. Kevin reflected how those of ethnic origin retained what they thought of were traditional English manners due to their tenuous hold in society. Two of the four helpers behind the counter tending to the rotating trunk of indeterminate meat on the skewer were new to him. He couldn't help idly wondering by what means they had arrived in the country. There had been at least two occasions where his time in a kebab shop had been disrupted by tattooed, barely-coherent yobs demanding of the owners to "see your passport".

"And some chilli sauce and garlic on mine," Colin finished his order. He turned around and stared over Kevin's shoulder. "Now then!"

While they had been making their order, Robert Swales and Sammy Patterson had drifted in. Pleasantries were exchanged and the two newcomers revealed they had been to a Billy Fury Tribute Act at another club in town.

"Big deal!" teased Colin. "I wouldn't like to make my living impersonating a dead man."

"Me neither," replied Robert. "Jimmy Savile would've been up my arse like a rat up a drainpipe."

Their smutty sniggers ebbed away to an awkward pause. Mention of the disgraced celebrity carried extra weight around here due to the fact he had an apartment on the sea front. As their talk wandered into gossip about mutual friends of no concern to him, Kevin's gaze drifted around the shop interior.

Later on, he would reflect of the slender chain of events that led to what ensued. Nothing was pre-ordained. It was like an elaborate chain of dominoes toppling. At any time, one misplaced piece could have brought it all abruptly to a halt. The catalyst to set it all off lay strewn across the bench seats lining one wall.

It was a dusty, discarded copy of a free newspaper – METRO. Kevin picked it up for want of something to do. He'd barely scanned the news articles but, while looking through the small ads near the back, he alighted upon the link that reduced everything around him to a faint murmur.

Guiltily, for he was sure the other three lads would notice, he cannily folded up the paper and crammed it into an inside pocket. Colin had talked the other two into giving him and Kevin a lift back to Thormanton in Robert's second hand car.

All through the journey home, he was uncharacteristically muted. He contributed his share to the conversation, but it was background noise in the light of what he had unearthed. Everything had changed. The world had tilted on its axis. The tectonic plates shifted. Kevin felt the others must suspect something about him, but none paid him much heed.

Robert dropped him off outside his house and Kevin fairly sailed up the stairs to his bedroom. He laid the newspaper out on his bed as reverentially as an ancient manuscript. The advert was scanned and reread as if to confirm it was no illusion.

"FULFILL YOUR FANTASIES. PERFORMERS REQUIRED FOR ADULT FILMS. MALE AND FEMALE. GOOD RATES OF PAY."

Chapter Seven

Kevin had waited until he was alone in his bedroom and his Mother had been out of the house on early Monday evening before calling the number on the advert on his mobile. The phone rang several long seconds before a woman with a nasal Estuary English accent answered. Kevin had somehow stuttered out his query and the woman had taken down his particulars – age, height, build, prior experience. She had given him a choice of weekend dates and times to attend an audition at a prestigious hotel in Leeds city centre. So it was that one Sunday morning, Kevin had skipped lunch to travel by Northern Coast Rail in time for a Noon appointment.

Kevin apologised to his Mother for missing Sunday Roast and caught a taxi into town. He worried if she suspected why he looked so uncharacteristically well-groomed for a weekend – even down to the mouth wash and discreet dab of cologne. The Trans-Pennine he caught at quarter past eight brought him directly into Leeds Station with thirty three minutes to spare. Marching briskly through the barriers past the usual unshaven beggars cadging spare change, BR Police, students, and away football fans wearing the red and white of Brentford F.C. converging on Elland Road for a Sunday match, he hailed a white taxi from the rank and asked its Pakistani driver to convey him to the address he clutched like a lifesaver.

He knew his purposeful stride looked anything but casual and nonchalant. Surely there was someone here in this teeming throng of stateless humanity who suspected what he was up to. Kevin looked too well-dressed for this early in the morning. Every stranger indifferently glancing at him seemed privy to his innermost thoughts and darkest secrets. The woman at the other end of the call had stressed the need for secrecy.

Kevin stood dwarfed by the towering building. He had half expected some sleazy, downmarket establishment so this had taken him aback somewhat. He was a good twenty minutes early and he hoped this would make a favourable impression. If it paid off, his money worries, motorcycle repair bill, and the stagnancy of his sex life would be solved in one fell swoop.

The woman on the phone had told him to report directly to a room on the fourth floor. Kevin had assumed there were good reasons for not asking at reception and, doing his best not to look too conspicuous, bounded up the stone steps into the lobby and into a lift.

Kevin emerged on the fourth floor and stepped into what looked like a bar. A lone, pimply-faced bartender was polishing a wine glass. More intriguingly, five women all roughly in their mid twenties displaying artificial tans sat around one corner table chatting animatedly. Kevin felt they looked as if they snacked off little boys between meals.

Kevin took a deep breath and rapped twice on the door the woman on the phone had mentioned. There was a ten second pause, then it slowly swung open.

A languid pair of heavily-lidded green eyes scanned him. "Yes?" The low, calculating tone emanated from a sensuous pair of thick lips. There was an unhealthy, excessive air of sensuality about them that both excited and repelled Kevin. They formed the base of a symmetrical triangle with the eyes and a pair of high, aristocratic cheekbones. The face was that of a woman of indeterminate age, though Kevin estimated her late twenties, early thirties. Her auburn bob of hair looked too vivid to be natural.

"Er, it's Kevin Troughton. On the phone! I had an appointment for twelve thirty for...." As low as his voice was, it still sounded too loud within the earshot of the woman at the table.

The face brightened, something about the act lifted Kevin's spirits. "Ah, yes!" The door opened wider and she beckoned him inside with an almost courtly gesture.

Kevin almost stumbled inside. The interior was little more than a large double room into which the woman and her associates had erected a digital camera mounted on a tripod and several filming lights and umbrella canvas reflectors. These were trained on a bare corner of the room. A balding, grey-haired man in his mid-fifties in casual clothes fussed over the controls. His face was running to a double-chin that a sparse goatee beard did little to alleviate – looking as if it had been clumsily stuck on, rather than grown.

An overweight brunette girl in her twenties with a deep, artificial tan and a short skirt lay reading a magazine on a nearby sofa.

The woman who had greeted him sauntered over to a table where several sheets of printed paper lay. Kevin could hardly take his eyes of her. A pair of, graceful dancers' legs were encased in a tight pair of leather trousers. When she bent over, the muscles in her arse seemed to expand like a pair of miniature balloons. There was a practised precision about her every otherwise banal movement – as if she was constantly aware of an audience and playing to it.

Kevin had been given a sheet of paper with the lines to memorise and enact. Given ten minutes grace, he had committed them to memory and spat the lines out in a semi-convincing impersonation of Dennis Hooper in BLUE VELVET, even down to the manic staring of the eyes. There had been a moment's uncertain pause that seemed to last hours, then the brightening of the woman's face alleviated his tensions.

"You like that, don't you, fucking bitch! On your knees, fucking whore! Suck harder! You can't get enough of it, can you!"

One video camera lens and four pairs of eyes fixed Kevin. The hotel's central heating was full on but Kevin still felt a chill air swirl around his bare buttocks and genitals. Kevin cursed his limp penis. Here he was giving his all spitting out the lines he had memorised and trying to convince his tiny audience he could be a star porn performer and this was the best he could muster. The fact that he had so much riding on this desperate gamble probably did not help.

"Very good," she commented. "That'll do nicely." Only now did he notice the heavy American twang that mutated her vowels. "Now, there's just one more thing."

Kevin felt that pulling the T-shirt off over his head and stepping out of his jeans felt uncannily like getting changed for football. Most of his team mates cast sly glances at his genitalia out of curiosity − or amusement, he often felt − and he frequently found himself making comparative looks at his near neighbours. Now, he felt more naked than he ever had before as he pulled down his boxer shorts and felt the shock of the cool air around his exposed nether regions. An image flashed into his mind from his childhood of a baby elephant with its trunk hanging limply wandering around a herd of its elders.

The woman directed him to stand with his back to the wall in a pool of light from the spot lamps. The middle-aged man whom Kevin realised must be a director squinted down the lens of the camera and trained it up his body from toes to head.

"You look in pretty good shape," the woman remarked. "You work out regularly?"

"Er, I play football every Saturday. I'm Captaining them next season."

"Can you stand facing the left just to catch your profile," the Director was saying. Kevin complied. He cursed himself that his penis hung limply down like waste skin waiting to be clipped off.

"Must be a great honour," the woman continued. "Captain?"

"You haven't seen us play," Kevin was grateful for her to be making the lead in the conversation, and ensuring it was about a subject he could talk freely about. Still, he was aware of nervously gabbling his words and defeating all hopes of sounding suave and cool. "Losing twenty-nil is nowt' to us!"

The woman gazed blankly at him. "'Nowt?'" she echoed.

"Er, nothing. Sorry."

"Don't apologise. Not familiar with the word, that's all." To Kevin's relief, her full lips contorted into a smile. "Kinda' cute."

Kevin was aware his cheeks were burning a deep red. "Why bother?" she asked him. Was it too much to hope she was taking a genuine interest in the mundane little life?

"Good question. Nowt', er', nothing else to do 'round where I live."

"And where's that?"

"Thormanton." Her gaze blanked over again. "Small village about forty miles from here."

"So, you're a hick from the sticks!" The harsh tones were all on one level with no attempt at putting any feelings in it beyond a patronising sneer. Kevin had heard similar voices many times before at school from youths in lower streams with massive chips on their shoulders who were anxious to pounce on any perceived sign of ignorance for them to proclaim "stupid cunt!"

The newcomer had strode into the room while Kevin was facing the opposite way. The obvious fake tan and blonde dye of his hair had failed in their attempts to improve his looks and merely made him grotesque. He led with his nose – either walking or talking – which was upheld with an ostentatious sneer. Kevin was familiar with this look from braggart lads at school squaring up for a fight. The cut of his shiny suit and the gold jewellery on his fingers and around his neck accentuated, rather than offset, the man's essential cheapness. He sidled over to the woman and placed a proprietorial arm around her shoulders.

The woman seemed to squirm slightly at his touch. "Must be something to keep you out of mischief?"

Kevin quailed at having to reveal his life in front of this unsettling interloper. All intimacy he flattered himself at having enjoyed with the woman crumbled but he bravely soldiered on. "Pub. Travel twenty miles to a night club in Scarborough, or York. Darts or domino nights are the highlight of my social calendar."

"Somebody sounds as if he feels wasted here," interrupted the man. The man's errant hand stroked the woman's shoulder but she remained frozen in place.

"Aye. But once I've been accepted at University and I've got my degree, you won't see my ar... er, me, for dust."

"What are you studying?" The woman still sounded genuinely interested in him.

"Gonna be a teacher, touch wood. Anything's better than farm work."

"Don't fancy all that fresh air and healthy exercise," she smiled.

Kevin shuddered. "Don't get much stuck on a tractor all day."

"I dunno. You look in good shape for it." Kevin grew a few inches metaphorically at her words.

"What part of the States are you from?" asked Kevin, silently glowing that he hadn't used the gauche-sounding to his ears "America".

"LA. Los Angeles."

"I hear they're really into keeping in shape there."

The woman gave a dismissive wave of her hand. "It's not the same thing. It's artificial, manufactured. Desk jockeys working our all hours and pumped up on steroids."

"Most guys your age over there are snorting coke the minute they're off the breast," sneered the man. It had only just struck Kevin that the man had a London accent.

"I'm flattered," said Kevin. "Why leave?"

The woman arched her eyebrows. "You mean, why come here?"

The man snorted. "LA's porn stars might as well be walking around ringing a bell shouting "unclean, unclean" nowadays. And the cops over there have to pretend to work for a living."

Kevin took this as a coded reference to AIDS and this, plus the reference to being arrested, suddenly struck home.

"I'm finished here," the Director called out.

A heavy pause, then the woman's face and voice assumed a clipped, business-like note Kevin recalled from a teacher at school was about to take him to one side to discipline him.

"Now, we have one more thing to do. You can say "no" if you want and we'll understand, and you can leave now. But we need to get a good idea how you perform. So, whenever you're ready, and in your own time, can you jerk yourself off in front of the camera."

Kevin felt the butterflies fluttering even more manically in his stomach. His mouth felt suddenly dry. He somehow managed to nod assent and faced the humming video camera with all the trepidation of confronting a firing squad.

He drew a deep, shuddering breath and limply grasped his flaccid penis as if expecting it to give him an electric shock. Kevin had anticipated some sort of sexual performance on the day and had deliberately withheld any acts of masturbation or heavy drinking days beforehand. Now, he fretted impatiently as it stubbornly refused to react to his touch as readily as it usually did – like a recalcitrant soldier slouching on parade.

He felt the eyes of his four watchers boring into his head – into his very soul. The man's face had a sneer as always, the Director had the mien of someone inspecting tins on a supermarket shelf, the girl (what was her role? He was half-disappointed he wouldn't get to perform with her.) seemed engrossed in her fingernails, and the woman.... She pursed her lips, and her eyelids adopted a heavily shuttered look, as if perusing a choice meal.

Desperation focussed Kevin's mind. Concentrate on the woman. With superhuman effort, he locked eyes with her and made her the centre of his immediate universe.

Kevin imagined those red lips nibbling hungrily at his penis. He could scarcely imagine how many cocks she had sucked in the past. He visualised her going down for deep throat on him. The embryonic crow's feet at the corner of her eyes crinkled in amusement. Was she reading his mind?

His flaccid member showed some signs of stimulation. It stiffened in his hands and expanded. Kevin's measured jerks pulled the foreskin completely back from the tip to expose his glistening helmet. He relaxed into a familiar routine and – apart from the woman – everyone else in the room and the camera faded from his consciousness. Kevin relaxed and closed his eyes. The memory of the woman was imprinted on his mind and now he gave full vent to his fantasies.

The woman was riding him, head arched back, sweating, panting like a thoroughbred race horse. Her breasts throbbed with unearthly life and expanded in all directions like air bags. They filled the room and engulfed him – absorbing him into their warm spongy depths. He was floating for eternity – lubricated by their sweat – as a familiar tingle crept up from the base of his scrotum to the tip of his helmet where it spewed a steady stream of viscous white onto a conveniently laid towel in front of him.

Kevin opened his eyes. He felt a strange, depressed feeling curdle up inside him. Now it was over, even the colours of the room seemed drab and dowdy. The man was stifling a yawn. The girl glanced out of the window. The Director was checking his camera. Only the woman seemed to acknowledge him

"Well done." Kevin tried to think of a cool retort but could only nod and smile goofily. "Some we've had in this weekend couldn't even manage that. You can get dressed now."

Kevin laboriously clambered back into his jeans and shirt. They seemed superfluous now, like rotting skin on a peeled apple. He allowed the woman to lead him across to the table where several piles of amateurishly printed paper forms lay in a plastic tray. "Just read through these. Take your time. Ask me if there's anything you don't understand. Then, just tick anything you don't feel you can perform."

Kevin nodded mutely. The top of the form consisted of an agreement giving their film company the rights to exploit his image. Kevin barely scanned it and appended his signature at the dotted line on the bottom. Then he read the checklist with boxes next to each item. It was like a sleazy version of an application form.

Anal sex. Oral sex. Same sex. Group sex. Threesomes. Toys. Water Sports.

"Water sports?" Kevin turned to the Director who was standing nearby.

"Urinating on each other," came the reply, like an elderly Maths teacher at a secondary school. Kevin nearly dropped the pen. He firmly drew a cross in the box next to it match the one next to "Gay sex". The woman indicated this.

"Not man-on-man. No way!"

The corners of those voluptuous lips creased with a mocking amusement. "Not even bi-curious?"

"Not even just plain curious."

"Pity," remarked the woman, only half-seriously. "There's a big market for it. Still, you won't be forced to do anything you don't want to."

Kevin handed her the forms. "Like applying for any normal job."

The ordeal was over. Kevin felt curiously taller than he had when he'd entered the room. The woman ushered him politely towards the door, filling him in on further details on the way.

"So I just need a written all-clear from a clinic." replied Kevin.

"That's right. They do it all the time for insurance. Tell 'em it's for that, if you're nervous. You'll appreciate it'll be unprotected sex if we use you. We'll call you on your mobile sometime next week to let you know."

"My mobile! Right." Kevin was silently grateful he hadn't given her his home number.

"And don't forget your birth certificate. We'll need to prove you're eighteen."

Kevin's heart fell. It really had been too good to be true. "Alright, then." The flatness of his voice betrayed his despair. He would not be eighteen for another six months. He half-turned to go when he finally plucked up the courage to ask the question.

"By the way, I didn't catch you name."

"I didn't throw it." Her sea green eyes sparkled with mockery. "Rosemary."

Chapter Eight

Rosemary. The three syllables danced like motes of silver in the evening air. They alleviated Kevin's torpor over the next few days as he realised he would have to come clean about being underage. He would linger on them as he filled in the names for the team sheet to be pinned up on the village notice board for the opening league match of the season. He would lie awake at night running them over in his head. He tried to recall every detail about the woman – her thick tan, luxuriant mane of auburn hair, those obscene lips, the self-inflating arse, the dancers grace and the way she elegantly stood on the balls of her toes. Most of all, he recalled the direct way she had of staring straight and unblinkingly into his eyes as if he was the only person in the room. No girl had done that before.

He had posed naked before her and wanked off at her request. She had studied him intently as he did so. As sordid as it sounded in the cold light of day, he felt proud of the fact. It would be a secret he would keep between the two of them. It would be the source of much inner confidence and self-assurance in future weeks. It would sustain him until the brutal reality of the league game against Colstone Celtic, this coming Saturday.

"Bugger about Ken Oliver, wasn't it." Kevin and Tom Fenwick were both propped up against a creosoted wooden fence securing a herd of twenty cattle munching contentedly on the lush grass and chewing their cuds. Recently-born calves gambolled aimlessly around on unsteady legs.

"I was walking the dog up them' fields when I heard the shot," Tom was saying.

Kenneth Oliver was a fifty-three year old beef and arable farmer who owned around one hundred and sixty acres adjoining the Fenwicks. Kevin had been greeted at the breakfast table by the news of his suicide. Apparently, Ken Oliver had finished his usual early morning rounds – breakfast, checking his herd – then casually strolled to a discreet spot on his land, placed a 12-bore shotgun inside his mouth, and pulled the trigger.

"Why do you think he did it?" Kevin had an adolescent's indifference to anyone outside his immediate age-group but feigned a concerned interest out of politeness.

"Same reason they all are, Kev," rumbled Tom, gazing into some vague middle distance. "They're selling their stock for the same price they paid for 'em!" Kevin vaguely recalled a news report in the local Gazette about a farmer in his sixties hanging himself somewhere near Wellthorpe four months ago.

Kevin recalled the few times he'd spoken to Ken in the Spotted Cow, usually on darts night. "He always seemed so cheerful whenever I saw him."

"Aye," replied Tom. "Still, you never know what's going on in some people's minds."

A green John Deere tractor lurched around the corner of Tom's cattle shed and up the rough drive towards them. Kevin brightened upon seeing who the driver was.

Colin Adkins leaned out of the cab and yelled over the roar of the engine. "My dad said we could borrow your sub-soiler, Tom."

"Aye. It's just 'round the back o' the corn shed."

"You missed training, Col'. Not like you," Said Kevin. "Where've you been? Got a woman somewhere?"

Colin avoided Kevin's eye. "Er, I won't be playing for Thormanton next season, Kev."

"Why not?"

"I'll be playing for Norbury. That's why." Colin's confession sounded bitten back.

"I'll give you a hand gettin' it on, Col. It's an awkward bugger to handle on your own," Tom butted in.

Kevin felt the ground beneath him crumble. "When wor' this? You've kept this fucking quiet, haven't you?"

"My cousin Barry's gonna be their Captain next season. He says he can get me a game wi' them."

Kevin knew Barry Reid quite well. He had been the midfield playmaker of his school year – a tall, gangling yet strangely hollow youth it was difficult to strike up a casual conversation with. He had always given the impression of being focussed on something else than the present.

"Never mind fuckin' Norbury!" Kevin ranted. "They could field two teams. What about us?"

Colin impatiently returned to his tractor seat. "Sorry, Kev. But I'm sick an' tired o' getting thrashed every Saturday."

"Christ! Do you think I fucking enjoy it? You're the only one who looks like scoring in front o' goal. Fuckin' Steven Cooke's too busy posing! Don't leave us alone wi' him. I'll slash my fuckin' wrists!"

Colin slammed the tractor door shut and drove off.

"Fuck off to sodding Norbury then! Fucking loser! We don't need you!" Kevin bawled impotently at the tractor's receding wake. He became aware that Tom was gazing at him open-mouthed, as much as the passion on display as the language.

★ ★ ★

Colstone was too large to be a village though not quite a fully-fledged town. It possessed two traditional country pubs, a village hall, a primary school, a garage, and a grocers on narrow High Street on the road to Scarborough. It also had an enviably large playing field that hosted both a football and a cricket pitch.

The changing room block was capacious enough to have a decent-sized shower and toilet cubicle – the yardstick by which some members of Thormanton measured sophistication at this level. The cricket season ensured that the senior Colstone Celtic team would play their opening four fixtures away from home, but the under eighteen side could fit their games in on a smaller pitch running parallel to the cricket field.

Colstone Celtic had been formed after the Second World War by an emigrant Scot as a tribute to one half of that dubious paean to religious bigotry for fun and profit. They played in the familiar green and white hoops, and fading monochrome photographs of past committee members and players stiffly shaking hands with the likes of Jock Stein and several long-forgotten star footballers hung ostentatiously along the walls of their Social Club. The signatures of the 1967 European Cup winners were on display in a glass case behind the bar.

Kevin nervously tugged at his Captain's armband and scanned the tense cluster of faces assembled for his premier pre-match team talk. They were at full strength – for what it was worth. Sammy Patterson looked a size too small for his green goalkeeper's jersey and gloves. Sister Emma looked disconcertingly boyish in her shopworn number seven shirt.

Steven Cooke was inevitably posing in his number nine. Robert Swales and his three younger brothers – Simon, Richard, and John – looked so alike, even their hair styles – as to be generational variations on the same theme. Kevin thought of them as resembling simian version of the Midwich Cuckoos. Peter Russell hung uncertainly on the sidelines. Overweight Nick Cammack looked barely able to tuck his shirt in over his paunch. Paul Myers – ginger-haired and freckled on a heroic scale – fiddled with his testicles. He barely qualified for inclusion as his family – newcomers to the region – had been renting a farmhouse for four years on the boundary between Thormanton and Salton. His family were spoken about in low whispers as possibly bankrupt – hence the reason they hadn't bought a property in the area – and were starting over again. Paul did not exactly socialise with the locals but was moderately keen on football and had been an avid supporter of his former hometown club Stevenage Borough. Christopher Manby pulled the underpants from out of his arse crack through his shorts. The Bash Street Kids, Kevin reflected wryly.

Kevin gave a lengthy preamble about Colstone Celtic's strengths, but he knew they would be more than familiar with the players from past seasons. But, like a seasoned classical actor giving a well-worn Shakespearean soliloquy, he was building himself up to the climax.

"Alright, Colin's gone. I've complained to the League Committee and they've promised to look into it, but don't hold your breath. Seems Norbury have done this sort o' thing in the past. They poached someone from Wellthorpe an' got away wi' it. We'll just have to grin and bear it! Still, we don't need Colin. If we play to a pattern and give it that extra ten per cent, there's no reason we can't sneak a result here and there and make it a season to remember."

Some of the younger lads seemed to take his words to heart. Kevin felt self-loathing at this. It was like a hardened General sending raw young conscripts over the top to certain death in the First World War. Colstone hardly numbered among the local elite – being mostly comfortably mid-table every season – but they always seemed to have plenty of local big lads to swamp Thormanton's best efforts. Still, his charges cantered onto the field with a notable spring in their step and a clear gaze on the horizons ahead. The opening few minutes saw the players contest every ball as if their lives depended upon it. They hustled the opposition in midfield, they cleared their lines efficiently at the back and, once or twice, threatened to break forward to imperil the Colstone goal. The illusion of parity lasted until a disputed throw-in, and, with the inevitably of night following day, a high cross was cleanly met by the forehead of a gangling Colstone forward to nestle in the back of the Thormanton net – and the floodgates duly swung wide open.

Kevin could see everyone's shoulders visibly slump. For the remaining seventy one minutes, Colstone Celtic played at a mocking canter and effortlessly ran in six more goals – giving the intimidating impression they could score six more if they ever got out of second gear.

Afterwards, Kevin sat on the changing room toilet – head bowed – for a long time. The coming season stretched endlessly before him like some unendurable penance. Since his appointment in the hotel, he noticed a certain impatience with the usual humdrum delays he had to endure. He eye fastened upon a half-dressed Sammy across the room and beckoned him across.

"Sammy, about what Colin suggested. You know Andy Blackburn, don't you?

"You mean..?" Sammy's dispirited face lifted with a conspiratorial glee.

"Aye, him, Garry Smith and Alan Hubbard if you can. Fuck the committee! If they want a game, we'll be happy to oblige!"

Sammy grinned. "I'll have a word."

★ ★ ★

Only one thought sustained Kevin throughout the coming week – the phone call. The dark thought that he was underage and be found out blighted it. Regardless, he decided to plough ahead with the HIV test in case. If nothing else, it would ensure a day off at work. He had scoured the internet and located a clinic attached to the University in York that gave free tests. Booking a day off with Tom Fenwick, he caught the Trans-Pennine Express at the local station into the city and then a taxi to the campus.

Kevin's previous hospital visits had been noisily unsettling affairs – but mercifully few. His own infant tears and the bewilderingly chaotic environment of staff running about amidst disconcertingly crippled patients conspired to virtually traumatise him at the time.

The moment he stepped into the clinic's reception area, the cloistered calm reassured him. Only the odd staccato tattoo of a nurse's heels added their own metronomic backbeat to the monastic limbo. The plump, middle-aged receptionist checked the PC for his details and handed him a paper badge to safety pin to his lapels after he'd signed in. Kevin had barely read the copy of the Daily Express in the foyer when the security doors to the centre of the clinic slid open and a white-coated Indian woman in her 30's briskly marched across the threshold to greet him with a professional warmth.

After a few self-conscious words of greeting, she ushered him inside to a small room off the main corridor. She asked him a few questions and Kevin delivered the little white lie about his sex life as neatly as a well-rehearsed actor. The woman seemed satisfied and bade him to lie down on a low bunk bed behind a plastic curtain and roll up his sleeve. Following a routine blood pressure test with a sphygmomanometer, the Nurse left the room and returned after a few minutes with a syringe and took a small sample of blood. Guzzling down the cup of tea and plate of digestive biscuits, Kevin learnt that it would take two or three weeks before he received a reply. He knew it was a foregone conclusion but somehow found the will to lie. "Er, do you think I could have a certificate saying that.... just for work. You understand."

"We'll post one to you," smiled the Nurse. "We'll have your address."

Kevin grinned goofily and limply returned her handshake, suspecting how much of a wet fish it must be. Gathering his belongings, he almost stumbled out of the room.

Gulping down a lungful of the brisk afternoon air, he decided on impulse to take a stroll across the University Campus. Kevin looked near enough a student to pass muster. Getting a feel for the place, his stride relaxed and became more confident as he took in the haphazard mixture of old grey stone and modern redbrick buildings dotted about. An ample-breasted girl of 19 – attractive in tight sweater and jeans in spite of her greasy blonde hair – caught his eye and exchanged a pleasant smile.

Kevin cast approving glances at her receding back all the way to the security barrier – lingering long on the assortment of students sauntering about the Campus in no particular rhyme or reason. They fell into easily classifiable groups – the unshaven nerds, the hearty rugger-buggers, the long-haired, high-cheek boned aesthetes, the girls.

Despite a few boiler-suited, shaven-headed brutes, there was no mistaking the sexual confidence and experience in their laughing eyes and sprightly body language. Kevin's fertile imagination concocted a sexual history for each of them. The large-breasted ginger-haired one hurrying to class with a folder clutched under her armpits was late due to a last-minute bout of anal sex up her ample buttocks. The flat-chested one with greasy brown hair and acne who looked oddly reminiscent of Emma was indulging in a lesbian affair behind her boyfriend's back. The large-boned brunette whose snooty accent Kevin dimly caught had a fondness for being beaten up and ravished by lorry drivers. And the slender, vivacious one with the tight cap of black curls and laughing saucer eyes in the tight jeans and leather boots was being irregularly gang-banged by the rugby team who filled her in like an application form and left her lying naked in the dirt afterwards, aching for more.

Kevin spared the University a last glance as he boarded the bendy bus for the rail station. It might have been a General surveying the field before a battle he expected to win.

Chapter Nine

Kevin was refuelling one of Tom's tractors – the green John Deere still missing a side door after a bullock had rubbed against it in the shed, shattering the safety glass – when his mobile buzzed unobtrusively in his jeans' pocket. Fishing it out, Kevin pressed the "reply", seeing that the incoming number was anonymous and half-guessing who it might be.

"Hi! Is that Kevin?" Rosemary's heart-warmingly familiar American twang came over professionally loud and clear.

"Er, yes. Is this about the, er, filming?"

"Well, just to let you know. We'll be very happy to use you as a performer in one of our productions. How do you feel?"

Kevin closed his eyes and counted mentally to three. It had to be said. "Er, just one problem. I've got a certificate giving me the all-clear, like you asked. But I won't be eighteen until next February. Sorry."

A pause. It lasted scant seconds but seemed an eternity to Kevin. The weight of the world slumped his shoulders.

"Not to worry." The woman's voice sounded as though it had already considered this eventuality long and hard. "I've got a proposition for you. Are you still interested in performing?"

"Aye. Definitely!"

"What about this Tuesday?" Kevin gave it two seconds thought before volunteering he was available. Rosemary gave him the details for a covert pick-up by car that sounded like something out of a spy movie. "I may have something. However, keep quiet about it, though. Can I trust you on this, Kevin?"

"No worries. My lips are sealed."

"Hope not. I need 'em wide open." Kevin felt giddy at the laughter in the cadences of her voice. "See you Sunday, then. Bye!"

She rang off. The diesel had filled the tractor's tank and was threatening to overflow. Kevin took a crafty whiff of its invigorating fumes and felt restored.

★ ★ ★

Kevin astonished his Mother with his early start the following morning. He had rung Tom to request the day off (which Tom, grateful for his presence at other times had granted) and set off for a brisk twenty minute hike to the allotted rendezvous.

Barugh-le-Street was less a village than a suburban side street that seemed to have misplaced the rest of the town. Somehow, it boasted a modest typical country pub (that Kevin rarely patronised) but little else. Fortunately, it at least possessed a park seat erected in a fit of rare extravagance by the local council. It was this that Kevin had agreed to wait upon at eight a.m for his ride.

Eight ticked by on his watch. Kevin fretted impatiently. Every second's delay heightened his fears. Was this some despicable practical joke at his expence – some grotesque prank to illustrate was a truly sad, desperate little virgin he was? Surely not.

At this ungodly hour, there was precious few cars sailing by. But he knew that some local farmers were notoriously early risers and the embarrassment he would be seen loitering here gnawed at him. He was contemplating turning back home and formulating some feeble excuse when a gleaming Vauxhall Astra creep like a whisper round the corner of the road. The thick hedge of the field had concealed it from view.

It drew up to an uncertain halt alongside him. Everything about it denoted a stranger to the area. Kevin had already stirred from the seat.

The driver's side of the car seemed barely able to accommodate the bulk of the well—muscled black man at the wheel. The window was automatically lowered. "Kevin?"

"That's me." The query of his name squashed Kevin's nerves in relief. If the statuesque guy driving did not scream potential porn actor, the two girls in the back certainly did. Even at this early hour, they were impressively made up with their lustrous hair washed and conditioned.

"Hi there, handsome." It was all Kevin could do to stop curling up in embarrassment.

"Watch these bitches, they'll eat you alive." The man's West Riding accent marred the American-ghetto speak. Kevin unhurriedly clambered into the front spare seat with as much dignity as he could muster.

The Astra cautiously moved off and was soon lost from view amid the winding country roads.

★ ★ ★

It looked a nondescript semi-detached with a small back garden in a tidy cul-de-sac. It had to be in the suburbs, of course. How often had their uniquely characterless nature proven a perverse hothouse environment congenial to the growth of aberrant forces – artistic, musical, or criminal? The aim of the original suburbs had been a metaphorical wiping clean of a slate for their incumbents so they could begin anew – preferably a further rung up the social ladder. Instead, in a void sterilised of heritage, new mutated forms bred and multiplied in secret. Isolated from their roots, their children sought fertilisation in more convivial alien ground – foreign music, archaic practises, sexual quirks.

These clean box-like houses were perfect clinical test beds to synthetically breed new forms of life without the danger of contamination from outside. Their discreet barriers erected against any fear of community interaction also furnished the perfect maximum security barrier against prying eyes. All manner of debaucheries could flourish here unobserved. The chill anonymity encouraged it.

Kevin affected an awkwardly-jaunty, unconcerned air as he followed the 2 girls and the driver across the drive. The driver pressed the buzzer.

There was a flurry of voices inside then a blur of movement through the frost glass panes. The handle turned and the door swung as far as the security chain permitted it. Rosemary's face seemed thinner than he remembered but the tan was as walnut-brown as before, the lipstick blood-red, and the oval eyes bright and interrogative. The smile on her face was as professionally reassuring as the Nurse at the clinic.

"Oh, hi! You made it. Come in." She slipped the chain off the door and ushered him inside. Kevin noted she replaced the chain behind him. "You believe in punctuality, don't you, Kevin, isn't it? Can I get you a drink?"

Kevin nodded mutely. As he lingered in the spotlessly white kitchen, he was aware of the muffled thuds of movement upstairs. Rosemary's melting smile lightened her business-like demeanour as she handed him a mug of pineapple juice.

"Cool! Knew you were a guy I could trust." Kevin's spirits were lifted. He felt a momentary closeness with this fabulous woman. Dare he entertain the fantasy of intimacy?

Crushingly, she turned her back on him to have a word with the ominous figure of the intimidating man he had seen her with at the audition – standing in the doorway like a sinister portent. Kevin was somewhat alarmed to see a plump, over-made-up woman in her mid thirties beckon him towards her. The prospect of a sex scene with her deflated him like a punctured balloon.

★ ★ ★

Kevin sat back in his chair and luxuriated at the tender dabs fluttering around his relaxed brow. He felt as lost without Rosemary around him as a child would bereft of its mother. In the background he heard the piping voices new to him.

"Is there enough cereal for the week?"

"Do we need more bread?"

"How are we for milk?"

Kevin would later realise these were production assistants. That such a shoestring production would have such people seemed impressive to him. Kevin was mightily relieved that the overweight woman was a make up artist and was patting him with powder to "reduce the glare from the lighting" as she put it.

The production assistants were nondescript girls and youths drably dressed in jeans and t-shirts. One of the girls' head was shaved to the scalp and her teeth were discoloured. They scurried around like the hunchbacked assistants to a charismatic mad scientist in a gothic horror movie.

The black guy strode past as imperious as a Greek god among mortals in his dressing gown. Kevin had already changed into his (startling) costume and, make-up completed, the woman removed the towel draped around his shoulders and expertly advised him to to disturb it for now.

One of the girls he had travelled with sat beside him, offering to join her in a mug of coffee. The unflattering brown overcoat she had worn had concealed her physical attributes. Kevin had a curious instinct this had been deliberate. The girl had looked ample enough before but her unveiling hinted at the glories barely constrained by the starchy white shirt necessary for her role.

They small-talked for a while. Her name was Sasha. Kevin could have got lost in those wide, saucer-like eyes. Discreet make-up accentuated their cat-like nature but what struck Kevin was their laser-like level of concentration as he stumbled and stuttered awkwardly trying to engage her in conversation about what he knew was the drab minutiae of his own life. Not once did those animated, cat-like eyes glaze over nor did her replies fade to a monotonous, auto-pilot "yes". He particularly sensed genuine animation and interest when the conversation turned to the football team. Kevin got the impression she was asking genuinely curious questions about it.

It turned out that she had once dated a future England international footballer while she was 18. Kevin was amazed when he heard who it was. He was ready to bombard her with questions concerning him but one of the production assistants chimed in. "Okay. Let's make a movie!"

Kevin drained the dregs of his mug and followed in Sasha's precisely graceful wake up the narrow staircase to the attic bedroom. The assistant ushered them into a blandly furnished room where the lone single bed had been pushed up into one corner. The filming set-up resembled a budget-price version of the hotel room audition. A cheaper digital video camera was mounted on a tripod and aimed at the bed flanked by two umbrella reflectors with light bulbs at the centre. To one side was an old-fashioned wooden school desk disfigured by several generations' graffiti and a wire frame chair.

"Say "hello" to your co-stars! Sasha, you already know. This is Linda."

"Busman's holiday for me," Linda giggled in a strong Home Counties accent with a barely perceptible lisp. She was dressed in a stereo-typed schoolgirl's uniform with stockings and suspenders. She was the same height as Sasha but slimmer and with promisingly bulging breasts for her size. Linda smiled sweetly if a little woodenly.

"Right. We'll just give you your lines, you can get changed, and go for a take." Kevin remembered the Director from his audition – still resembling a sleazier, low-rent version of a stereotyped Hollywood version.

Kevin felt the ill-fitting schoolboy's uniform hung baggily on him. He feebly excused himself to visit the bathroom. Pausing to examine himself in a full-length mirror and take a last-minute piss, he took a deep, shuddering breath and strode out to meet his destiny.

"Frankly, I'm very disappointed with your Biology essays. You seem to have trouble understanding sexual reproduction. So, I'm here to give you your practical homework, you bad boy."

Sasha's Lancastrian accent and stiff acting militated against her head-masterly authority as she delivered her lines by rote. She stood over Kevin, hands on hips, a cane in one fist as he sat apprehensively on the bed. The Director looked as unresponsive as a slaughterhouse worker

"Yes, Miss." Kevin had no problem maintaining an erection. It was stiffening involuntarily like some alien cancer possessed of a will of its own. He silently prayed he could maintain it long enough. Unfortunately, the scenario – horny, virginal schoolboy seduced by attractive lady teacher – reminded him of Double Geography on a Tuesday afternoon with Miss Turner. Late 20's, fair-haired, and ample-proportioned – stifling hot afternoons baking in that stuffy classroom while she droned on about igneous rock formations had seen reality fade away as Kevin had fantasised her undoing those buttons on her crisp white shirt to unveil the black lace bra underneath (although it looked drably white and utilitarian from the peek he'd sneaked), little wonder his marks in Geography had been so lamentable.

"Now, we'll start with you telling me how you sexually arouse a woman."

"Er," Kevin stammered all-too convincingly. There was something oddly therapeutic in acting such a nervous, obviously inexperienced character.

"You start with a kiss." She sat astride his legs and locked his lips with hers in a savage vacuum. Her wet tongue expertly roamed his dry mouth like a flapping fish on dry land. It lasted nearly thirty seconds before she teasingly withdrew with a kiss.

"Now, what else?" Linda indicated her breasts.

"Fondle the breasts, miss?" he volunteered.

"Top of the class. Well, go ahead." The prim authority and the stern look affected in her eyes were proving a turn-on in themselves.

Kevin brought his hands up and clumsily stroked Sasha's tits. Sasha rolled her eyes, mock swooned, and arched her back in a convincing simulation of arousal. Gaining in confidence, he kneaded them like dough and plunged his hand down her shirt front.

Kevin had always wondered what silicone breats felt like. The nipples stood perpetually to attention but the rest was like a balloon that could never burst. The soft mounds of flesh yielded to his touch – it was unusual for Kevin to do this without a forced withdrawal from the girl a few seconds later.

"Undo my shirt, you bad boy." Kevin somehow unfastened the buttons with his free hand to allow her repressed physicality to topple free. The bra was purple and lacy and half cup. Several veins patterned the bosom's fading whiteness like spiderwork. His hand expertly snaked around her back to unfasten her clasp. At first, he thought he was mistaken. Kevin's fingers ran panic-stricken along the unbroken material.

With a heavy sigh, Sasha brought her hands up and undid the clasp between her tits at the front of the bra. Kevin forced an embarrassed grin. But the magnificence of those unfettered breasts took his breath away – although grossly out of proportion with her body. He was only vaguely aware of her asking him what else he could do with them.

Without further prompting, he fastened his dry mouth around those rock-hard nipples and sucked as if on a life-preserver, toying with them between his lips and mouth.

Closing his eyes, he heard Sasha's orgasmic moans and sighs in synchronised unison to the manipulations of his tongue. Whether they were faked or not, the sense of power it gave Kevin was overwhelming, like virtuoso mastery of a musical instrument.

"And what else, naughty boy?" As Sasha wriggled out of her gown and shirt, Kevin took the hint and ran his hand up her soft thighs. She parted her legs to permit easy access.

Kevin was in a paroxysm of guilty ecstasy. This was the point girls normally clamped them unassailably shut. This mature, sexy woman wanted him to continue! Kevin's hands fumbled across the flimsy barrier of her panties. Fingers delicately snaked around the annoying garment and got lost in the moist bush behind it.

Kevin was now firmly on alien territory. He penetrated deeper into the fetid undergrowth before his sensitive tips located the gash between her thighs. Delicately, he ran his fingers up and down – her sighs and moans genuine now. He tried to probe further – but found an impenetrable wall of flesh.

"Further down," came the hissed response. Kevin thought better than pretending he was acting in character. Cursing his inexperience, his hands glided easily into her wetness. Her labia parted, Kevin massaged her clitoris. Sasha's breath came in anguished exhalations. Kevin felt lightheaded at his newfound power – how this gorgeous woman could become a mere puppet in his hands.

Sasha's mobile had been set to make a sound like an old-fashioned phone ring in an American movie of the fifties. It broke into the erotic tenseness like a mugger lying in wait.

"Cut!" The Director all but cursed as he called a halt. The cameraman switched off and the pale, acne-ridden lad gratefully lowered the boom-microphone longer than him.

"Oh, hi, Tim!" Sasha flashed her most heartfelt apologetic smile as she fished out her mobile from her dressing gown and answered it.

Everyone pretended to be preoccupied elsewhere as she spoke brightly into the mobile. "No. Not in the office today. Training course. Computer studies. Boss thinks I need to brush up a bit." Kevin visualised the unfortunate boyfriend on the other end. "Look, I'm on my coffee break. I have to get back to my class. Catch you later!" She hung up on the caller and ensured the mobile was entirely switched off before swiftly putting it back into her dressing gown pocket, flashing a nervously-apologetic smile. "Sorry 'bout that. Fiance."

With a theatrically heavy sigh, the Director exchanged a relieved nod with his crew. "Alright, from the top. And action."

* * *

Kevin lay flat on his back staring at an incipient crack in the white plaster of the bedroom ceiling. He had been plundered of his virginity in the most spectacular manner possible by a sexy, well-breasted older woman and it had been captured live on digital video for all eternity. He felt the momentousness of it all sweep over him. It was like being a fragile kite caught up in a hurricane-force wind. The Director and Cameraman were checking the playback facility on the camera while Sasha was in the bathroom.

"Work's okay for me," the Director was saying. "Okay, Kevin, your turn on the boom mike. Sasha and Linda – we'll do the Headmistress, and the Naughty Schoolgirl."

Strangely, Kevin later thought that what followed as his induction to full adulthood. Sasha – fully redressed as the Head Mistress – replayed her prior scene with Kevin but now with a distinct lesbian theme. Linda gave a passable impersonation of a coyly innocent schoolgirl. Sasha gave her advice on what to watch for from "bad boys" and smoothly fondled the woman's breasts and thighs. Their kiss was long and lingering. They undid each other's buttons and helped peel one another's clothes off. Kevin felt his rampant erection constricted almost painfully between his thigh and the fabric of his tight jeans.

To a chorus of breathy, if woodenly-recited, lines about "always been curious" and "the first time", Sasha and Linda were soon down to their matching purple underwear. Sasha took the lead and slowly peeled Linda's bra up from her round, bulging breasts, before teasing the nipples with her lips and tongue. Linda lay back languorously on the bed and obligingly parted her thighs. They French-kissed each other long and hard before discarding their remaining clothes like the skin of overripe fruit.

Kevin gulped audibly as he realised there was nothing faked or mechanical about this. The foreskin was pulling to tightly back from his helmet as to be painful. Although still making concessions for camera angles, Sascha and Linda's lovemaking was too urgent to be a performance. There was a cruel set to Sasha's features as she pinioned Linda's arms by her wrists above her head with one hand. With her other one, she delved deeply between Linda's thighs. Her massages of the younger woman's clitoris were firm and rhythmic and her fingers were easing further inwards with each stroke. Inch by inch, she plunged further into Linda's moist depths, finding her G-spot and massaging it with a steady rhythm.

"Fuck! No!" Linda's gasps were too abrupt and anguished to be acting. She was uttering every foul oath she knew – which startled Kevin who thought her relatively upmarket – and her vacuous face was a tightly clenched mask with a world of ecstatic pain in her voice. Up to her wrist, Sasha held on for grim death as Linda's slighter body bucked underneath her.

"Shhiiitt! Nooooo!" Sasha had the intense concentration of a concert pianist giving a virtuous recital. Linda's cries indicated the bravura passage was nearing its peak.

With a final cry that seemed torn from her innermost being, that vibrated the wax in Kevin's ears, Linda climaxed and, utterly spent, flopped back onto the bed. Sasha withdrew her sopping wet hand and felt into the other's limp embrace. Linda kissed her with genuine affection on the forehead. Kevin couldn't catch the sotto voice intimacies they whispered to one another but they had the authenticity of a long-standing acquaintance. They seemed conjoined like some amorphous mutant – at rest, but potentially hostile and unwise to disturb.

"Oh, I've been doing this three years now. Trying to get my student debt down." Linda could have been chatting about voluntary work as opposed to porn.

"What do you do, exactly?"

"Teaching assistant."

"Does anyone know about...?"

"All this." Linda smiled. "I hope not. Another year and I reckon I'll be knocking it on the head. If the butt and boobs hold out."

What would have been an awkward lull in the conversation gave way to Rosemary's piteous voice from an adjoining room. It was the first time he had heard her vulnerable. "But, Ray..."

"Yeah, well we need some ass-fucking for this scene, and Louise didn't show up." The man's voice was so flat as to be lazily contemptuous. One felt he did not need to raise it as he was accustomed to having his orders carried out.

"Can't Victoria..." began Rosemary, but Ray cut her short.

"Victoria's got a scene later with Vince, and she ain't

contracted for it. You're supposed to be the fuckin' star attraction. Are you gonna' gimme grief over this?"

"You know I hate doing anal…"

The harsh crack of what could only be a slap made Kevin start in alarm and, for a moment, he feared they had overheard him. But he regained his composure. It wasn't so much the actual slap as the fact there had practically been no build-up of fury from the man leading up to it. The scary part was that he did not appear to lose his temper but had acted as automatically as switching on a light. Kevin's mind reeled.

He had encountered violent men before – staring eyed, overdressed yobbos at dances asking sharply who he was staring at, red-faced, shaven-headed men in their 30's with beer bellies and dulled expressions – but their threats had been an elaborate foreplay before the act itself, a means of screwing up their courage. But this guy had lashed out without a second thought or any preamble. Readiness for violence was his natural state.

What made it worse for Kevin were the horrible tones of intimacy that followed – the man imploring Rosemary that he always cared for her and knew what was best, and the woman, his goddess, apologising through incipient tears that she wouldn't do it again.

"Best look the other way in this business," Sasha's voice behind him nearly made Kevin jump out of his skin. "You turn deaf to it after a while." She tenderly laid a hand on his shoulder. "And just be grateful you're not contracted to him."

At length, Kevin was been tape-measured to the camera by an assistant when the man breezed onto the set, his face a rictus grin that somehow never reached his dead eyes. "She'll be ready in a minute, boys and girls," he announced to nobody in particular. "Just powdering her nose."

The Director and his underlings made a show of unconcernedly going about their business as if oblivious to the drama. It was clearly a ritual they were accustomed to.

"You've been a fucking revelation, son. I think we've found a star!"

"Oh, that's okay."

"You won't believe the losers we have to put up with. They talk the talk but can't walk the walk, if you catch my drift." He mimed a limp dick with his little finger. Such was his overwhelming, bullying presence that Kevin felt sympathy for them. "You don't mind a bit of fatherly-advice from one who knows his way around this business, do ya?"

Kevin nodded mutely.

"When you're inside her, don't be afraid to be a bit rough. Grab her by the throat and hold her down. Looks better on screen. Ah, here she is. Elvis has entered the building."

Rosemary had almost pottered into the set like an old woman. No amount of make up could camouflage she had been crying – or a livid weal on her cheek – but she managed a wintry smile and bit back the tears. He made a nauseating show of embracing her face like a favourite daughter in a gesture of welcome. "Let's knock 'em dead, kid."

Kevin later thought the next few hours were the strangest of his life. He wondered where he found the fortitude to manage it. It was like been disassociated from his physical body.

The scenario had been about a haughty office SEO treating a crew of workers snootily and then getting her comeuppance by being gang banged. It had required the level of organisation and choreography of a military tattoo as Kevin, the man and the other two male participants moved around Rosemary's unresisting body filling in every available orifice.

Anally entering the woman while the man took the front as the black guy received oral pleasure and the other guy was relieved by hand, Kevin somehow forced himself through the motions. Rosemary rested her sweating head back against his chest while the man jack-hammered her into submission. "You like that, don't ya'. Bitch!" he gasped through gritted teeth, face contorted in a feral snarl.

But this was something else. Kevin went through the motions of bending her over the bed and, penis glistening like a newly-landed fish under a liberal coating of lube, thrust into her obligingly opened arse.

At the sound of her pained whimpers, Kevin's resolve nearly deserted him. His eyes momentarily locked with Ray's.

For a micro-second, he felt a queasy, conspiratorial air. Now he was the literal tool of this sleazy bully crushing his beautiful demi-goddess. He was just following orders.

The click of the ubiquitous Stills Photographer yanked him back to the present. Communing with himself, Kevin gathered up his thoughts and resumed his jackhammer assault.

Soon, he felt a new sensation. Kevin was strangely gratified by the anguished exhalations he drew from her. For the majority of their association, Rosemary had been the one in control. He had been subject to her whims. Now the sight of her tousled hair and her forehead wrinkled in pain grew oddly exhilarating. This was no furtive, secretive coupling in some anonymous room. Gathered around him attentively like courtiers were the Director and his crew. He controlled the tempo. They would only speak if he willed it. They bore witness to his brutal subjugation of this sophisticated woman. Stripped of all her expensive finery, Rosemary crouched on all fours like the lowliest beast. Her languidly superior tones were beaten down to the sobbing moans Kevin drew from her like a skilled musician in total mastery of his instrument.

Somehow, he remembered he had lines to say.

"You like that!" he spat out, viciously. "Don't you, bitch!"

"Yeah," Rosemary gasped out through gritted teeth.

"Don't stop! You're the man!"

"Who's the daddy, whore?"

"You are! You're my number one guy. You're the daddy, stud! Fucking give it to me."

It took Kevin a few second to grasp what was happening. Rosemary's anal muscles tautened like twine around his rock hard penis. Like some giant alien hand jerking him off, the woman's buttocks were moving in rhythm with his thrusts, chafing his raw helmet against her walls, pushing herself through the pain barrier to a state beyond human endurance. Her pain sounded agonising. His own cries blended into hers as he climaxed. Kevin pulled his cock out in time and gasped as he daubed her sore buttocks with his sticky semen.

Kevin held the pose long enough for the Stills Photographer to rush off a few shots, then he collapsed on top of the limp Rosemary. Sweat, semen, and hot breath commingled. In the blissful stillness that ensued, Kevin became aware of the steady pulse of her breathing as they snuggled up against each other. Memories were stirred of an affectionate cat he had owned as a child that he was prone to cuddling – how it would envelop itself in the warmth of his body and stretch, luxuriating in the touch of another's body. In the moment, he felt closer to Rosemary than he ever had. The remainder of the room melted into an indistinct blue on their periphery.

Kevin and Rosemary's eyes locked momentarily. There was a look of such utter desolation in them, Kevin had to turn away culpably. The man had his hand around her throat and was pressing her back against Kevin's torso. "Yes. You fucking want it!"

Rosemary's body was like a broken bird for the finale. One by one, the other three ejaculated into her gaping mouth, her feelings numbed, her spirit fragmented.

"And cut. That's a wrap!" The cry of the Director seemed a bleakly-appropriate punctuation to the whole sordid business. The others broke character and nonchalantly ambled away from the set to get dressed. Kevin remaining stood over Rosemary's crumbled body. He felt he should offer some words of consolation to her, but it all seemed paltry in the circumstances. The woman's head remained bowed, her eyes bleak and unfathomable. Kevin felt any gesture on his part would be redundant and turned slowly away to the changing room.

A kettle of freshly-mashed tea was awaiting in the kitchen and, although one of the production assistants poured him a cup, Kevin sat staring into the cup until it had gone long tepid. He had only been dimly aware of the black performer speaking to him.

"I'll give you a lift back, mate. Are you wanted any more this week?"

Kevin pushed the teacup to one side and stood up slowly. "No, I don't think I'll be back."

Chapter Ten

Kevin revved up his motorbike and gunned it down the serpentine country lane. An errant fly met a violent bespattered end on his helmet's visor. After all the weirdness of the past week, it was reassuring to feel the metal throbbing between his legs.

He had paid the garage for the repairs in cash and had only just resisted the temptation to say "keep the change." Stir-crazy from weeks of inaction, he had occupied all his spare hours that week zooming down the back lane feeling the exhilaration of speed and that the world was his oyster.

He could have easily strolled the short distance from his house to Thormanton's football ground, but the temptation to pull up on his newly-restored steed proved too tempting. Sammy and Robert were chatting outside the dressing rooms as he drew up to a halt.

"Now then," Robert greeted him. "Bike's alright, I see."

Always the Master of the Bloody Obvious, thought Kevin behind a shit-eating grin. He had expected the mythical time after he had lost his virginity would feel different, but not like this. There was a strange sense of, if not anti-climax, but a sense of being diverted on an unfamiliar new route. The forced gang bang with Rosemary afterwards had cast a distinct pall over his memories. It was as if he had glimpsed the price it really entailed.

"How much did it rush ya?" asked Sammy.

"Not much change out of a hundred quid," replied Kevin.

"You'll be about cleaned out, then," added Robert.

Kevin looked like the cat that had been locked in the cream factory all weekend. "Not necessarily."

Sammy indicated the changing block. "They're here, by the way, Kev."

With a new bounce in his step, Kevin followed Sammy inside their changing room.

Two hundred pounds in cash, on the day. Rosemary estimated that residuals and royalties from this production alone could approach a thousand. Mentally, he had already spent most of it. But that occupied little of his mind right now.

How he had earned it – and what he had witnessed and partaken in – had been compartmentalised away. It had shaken him and motivated Kevin to decide that this would be his sole excursion into the world of hard-core porn. It had served its purpose. He could count himself lucky he had emerged relatively unscathed, enjoyed a top quality fuck with a goddess, and been able to pay his repairs. He would probably be able to spin a few amusing anecdotes from it in his old age. Right now, it unsettled him.

"Here they are, Kev. Andy Blackburn, Garry Smith, and this one's Alan Hubbard."

"Good to have you on board, gentlemen." Kevin exchanged stilted hand shakes with the trio. They looked like Greek gods among the ill-assorted physical specimens who normally populated this room. They even looked like professional footballers. All stood six feet or over.

The regular players had accepted being dropped or being shunted off into unfamiliar positions for the sake of the newcomers – grudgingly at least. Some – notably

Robert's kid brothers – accepted they were too physically immature to compete anyway. Against Denbymoorside, this would be crucial.

Denbymoorside was a market town of three thousand souls on the tip of a rural triangle with Norbury and Salton occupying the other points. Not as large as those other towns, they nonetheless had an enviable pool of playing talent to call upon – invariably based around players a good head taller than Thormanton's. Playing on an energy sapping adult pitch used by their senior side aided the impression that the villagers were out of their depth.

Kevin's block tackle sent one such Denbymoorsider flying. Having brutally won the ball, he was disappointed to see his pinpoint accurate pass go astray as Steven stumbled over his own feet.

Kevin's dispassionate gaze swept across the Denbymoorsiders. A poor lot, he thought. He regarded the player he had just tackled with something approaching pity. Kevin reckoned he had never had his cock sucked by a gorgeous, large-breasted goddess as he had by Sasha the previous Sunday. He could picture her even now, her scarlet lips engulfing his granite-hard stalk, sucking on it slowly and wetly as if on a gourmet meal. He could still see her sea green eyes gazing impishly up at him under those heavy lids.

Kevin dived recklessly into tackles, fifty-fifty balls, and dangerous headers against opposing players a foot taller and far more beefier than him. One thought occupied his mind.

None of them had ever experienced what he had gone through last weekend. None of them had been sandwiched between two hot women in their twenties – his resurgent cock neatly slotted into Sascha's moist cunt while Linda licked the nape of his neck and probed his arse with her fingers.

Kevin had always felt apprehensive in the company of the swaggering Robert and some of the others. Now, he could only regard them with an amused tolerance. None of them had had women like Linda and Sasha simultaneously sit on his lips and cock and wriggle expertly to bring themselves to orgasm.

In spite of Kevin's steely resolve, Denbymoorside ran out easy seven-three victors without ever getting out of second gear. They still found the energy to trot off the field as if the match had been a temporary distraction on the route to a more pressing appointment.

Kevin felt apart from the normal joshing and byplay in the changing room afterwards. The usual rows with Steven about playing deeper in midfield – countered with the usual sulky "you want me to play, don't you!" – seemed trivial.

Strange power coursed through his body. The whole world now made sense. If only the rest of the team could see with his eyes.

"What got into you, today?" asked Robert. "Charging about like you had a fire cracker up your arse. Not that I'm complaining."

Their three consolation goals had all resulted from the new boys. Alan had proven to be a wickedly accurate taker of corners and one goal had resulted from the opposition goalie fumbling one inswinging ball over the net. Garry had headed in another of his corners and laid on a cross for Andy Blackburn to chest down and slot home.

But for the most part, their contrast with the dross around them had been so pronounced as to be comical. At one point, Garry had been hemmed in by three Denbymoorside defenders. Adroitly side-stepping them, he had played a perfectly-weighted cross-field ball that was practically served on a platter for Steven Cooke, only for the latter to stumble over his feet and let it go out for a throw-in.

Scoring three goals had at least lightened the post-match mood in the changing room. Unfortunately, none of the jubiliant Thormanton players had paid much heed to the three new players. Behind their backs, Garry had turned to Alan and Andy. He pinched his nose and mimed flushing a toilet, while nodding at the remainder of the team. Words were superfluous. His mime was eloquence enough.

★ ★ ★

Feeling more than unusually bored at the dismal prospect of the local pubs, Kevin caught a coach into the city. After a desultory pint or two in some city centre bars, Kevin elected to try the Karaoke night club he'd seen advertised in a newspaper.

Despite being about ten on a Saturday night, the credit crunch ensured only about a dozen clubbers were scattered around a bar designed for fifty. The walls were painted an lurid black to render an intimate atmosphere, with a small stage mounted to one side of the Main Bar with a balding, middle-aged Disk Jockey penned in behind his console with two coffin sized speakers flanking him. A beefy minder, whose dapper evening dress was marred by a plastic ID badge, stood sentinel to one side to deter anyone mounting the area without permission.

Currently, two semi-pissed slappers in their mid-twenties, black roots already visible through their blonde hair, were tunelessly bellowing out a shrill, off-key rendition of "I Will Survive", that traditional lament of girl clubbers who realise they're not going to awaken on a

Sunday morning wrapped around a hot, throbbing twelve inches with a six figure bank balance attached.

Having ordered a lager, Kevin thumbed through the comprehensive list of song titles and artists left on each table. He had jotted down his choice on a photocopied ticket and had handed it to the DJ when he turned to visit the Gents.

To access the toilets meant venturing down a steep flight of narrow stairs and, through a pair of swinging doors, into a small anteroom where the "Ladies" and the "Gents" could be found. Kevin strode through the doors where the sight of a striking brunette woman adjusting her tights forestalled him. He froze as she straightened up and he recognised her.

"Oh, hi!" Kevin's greeting died on his lips as Rosemary beckoned to him to keep quiet. Hurt, he was about to protest when the man he had seen with her at the audition swaggered out of the Gents.

"Well, if it isn't Ron Jeremy Junior!" He virtually grabbed Kevin's hand and vigorously shook it in a crushing grip. "How ya doin'?"

"Not too bad, thank you. I didn't expect to see you again."

"Tell ya' what, son" boomed the man. "What're ya drinking?"

"A pint of Fosters!"

"Well, while you're aiming Archie at the Armitage, we'll get ya' one in. Join us upstairs, when you're ready!"

The man draped a proprietorial arm around Rosemary and led her upstairs. Once Kevin had finished, a full, foaming glass of lager sat awaiting his return at their table in a dimly lit corner. Ray was sprawled back on the plastic couch with one hand ostentatiously stroking Rosemary's thigh. Kevin blundered across the dance floor to sit opposite them.

"Tough shit, you don't wanna' carry on, son" said the man. "Believe me, the credit crunch has had no effect on the sad wanker market."

"Sorry," said Kevin. "What is it you do again?"

"I'm Rosemary's manager, among other things."

"Kevin's going to University," Rosemary chipped in. "Training to be a teacher, aren't you, Kevin?"

"Them that can't, teach! And them that can't teach, teach gym!" Ray guffawed. "I heard that somewhere. No offense, son. Never had no' time for school." He abruptly extended his right arm across the table, nearly dislodging Kevin's pint. "Name's Ray, by the way."

"Na' then, Ray." Kevin had learned to brace his fingers against the crushing vice of Ray's grip.

"Failed all my GCSE's, when I was your age, Kevin. You'd've thought I'd thrown a dead pig into a Synagogue. Suddenly mates I'd known for years wouldn't give me the time o' day. Like I was beneath them all of a sudden! Stuck up little cunts!" He spat the last four words out like venom.

"Aw, don't get him started," moaned Rosemary. Ray's momentary glance cowed her.

"Not just mates! Even cousins started looking down their fuckin' noses like I was beneath 'em. Spent months wondering what the fuck I'd done!"

"How'd you get into this business?" Kevin felt impelled to change the subject.

"I saved up and me an' one o' my few remaining mates went to Amsterdam that summer. While they were gettin' ready for University, I paid to get laid for the first time over there." Ray's harsh, nasal voice grew almost wistful. "Never forgotten her. Hair dyed red – I mean really red – like that carpet. Silicone tits out here." He indicated with his hands. "You could still see the scars. Well, one thing led to another, and here I am!"

Ray elaborated by saying that he, and his mate, had got acquainted with an English couple over there. They had met up again back in England, where he and his friend had been paid to fuck the man's wife while her husband filmed it. "There was me an' Frank without a stitch on, this guy wor' crouched behind his camera yelling, "Hit the bitch! Hurt the fuckin' whore!" And she was just lying there, saying "Go ahead! I don't mind." From then on, he had soon made the necessary contacts.

Throughout Ray's tale, Kevin had maintained a poker face that did not give away, for one moment, that Rosemary had slipped off her shoe and was playing footsie with his inner thigh.

"Now, I've more fucking money than I know what to do with. Every stuck-up little cunt, who used to sneer down their fucking nose at me, is breaking their balls paying off their fuckin' mortgage, or their student loans, and jerking off to my DVD's, instead of slipping their fat wives a length twice a week."

Rosemary's toes were as dextrous as fingers as they delicately fondled his inner thigh. Like a good soldier, his penis automatically sprang to attention.

"There's one cunt, who got straight A's, and read History, I think it was, at Cambridge. Last I heard, he was still living at home with his parents. Hasn't worked for years. Sad twat!"

"Well, I'll be eighteen this February," Kevin lamely offered.

"So you've got something to look forward to, haven't you, Kevin." The corners of Rosemary's sensual lips were creased upwards in a mocking smile.

A beer-bellied, shaven-headed singer in his mid twenties had concluded barely croaking his way through "Wonderwall". He exited the stage to an indifferent smattering of applause, and a chorus of derisive cheers from his mates.

"Next up, we've got Kevin, whose gonna give up his version of the Kinks' "All Day And All The Night," the DJ announced. Kevin stood up, though not before Rosemary gave his erect penis a final, mocking rub with her toe. She could have been typing a letter for all the emotion she betrayed.

"I'll be back in a tick," his reply visibly wavered across his vocal range as he regained his composure.

Kevin managed a passable, three minute bellowing that occasionally threatened to strike the correct notes before receiving a lackadaisical modicum of clapping. Kevin was pleased to note several girl clubbers tottering on their stiletto heels in their regulation issue little black dresses with ample cleavages were among those applauding.

Ray was at the bar getting the next round of drinks in and Kevin joined him. The girls were stood a few feet away. Ray discreetly nudged Kevin. "Fancy making the beast with two backs with them?"

"Er, well, I..."

"You wouldn't kick 'em out of bed for farting, would you!" Ray saw one of the girls, brunette and overweight enough to be appealingly voluptuous, texting on her phone. "If he doesn't call you back, I should dump the loser," he said to her.

The girl hesitated a fraction, spellbound at his brazenness. "I don't have a boyfriend."

"What a waste."

"And I'm not looking for another." Kevin would have quailed at her response. Ray looked as amused as a parent at a bratty little girl.

"I get that a lot. Trouble is, the girls that say it usually end up on top o' me in bed so I never learn."

Kevin could read the shock and awe in her face. He could almost feel the tectonic plates shifting underneath her feet. Ray let the tension build long enough like a seasoned professional then broke it by proferring his hand. "My name's Ray. This is Kevin."

Kevin didn't keep track of all Ray said but was dumfounded by the man's audacity and total lack of self-consciousness as he took control of the group. They vampishly played up to his teasing. "You look like the masterful one who takes charge in bed," said Ray to the bottle-blonde.

The brunette laughed and interjected. "No, that's me!"

Ray ignored her – Kevin later suspected an element of calculation in this, because she was the sexiest one there. "And this is the shy, quiet one who turns into a demon in the bedroom and gets out the whips and chains." The girl he addressed blushed under her fake tan but remained captivated by him.

"And what do you do?" asked the blonde.

"I'm a sort of film star."

"Sort of? Have I seen you in anything?"

"That depends. Have you ever seen Hot and Throbbing volumes two to five?"

A second's mulling over, then "that's a porno, isn't it?"

"Oooohhh, you've seen them. Bad girl!" Ray's ribbing caused the brunette to blush an even deeper shade of red.

"You're a porn star?." The blonde's eyes were like saucers.

"Do I have to strip off so you recognise me," was again, aimed at the brunette girl whom Kevin could sense was Ray's ultimate target.

The third girl indicated Kevin with the air of someone having undergone a Damascene conversion. "Is he a porn actor too?"

"Him? He's out with me on Doctor's orders. He suffers a rare complaint called boobphobia!"

"Boob what?" giggled the blonde.

"Boobphobia. It's a rare psychological complaint where the patient has a fear of a large pair of breasts."

Kevin wished he could shrink to an inch high. "Like mine," said the brunette, playfully waggling her own pair close to Kevin's sweating face.

"Exactly like them. He's out tonight to see if he's conquered his fears." Ray's eye was caught by an impatient gesticulation from Rosemary with an empty glass from her table. "Got to get back, ladies. Catch you later."

It was only when they got back to the table that Kevin finally found his voice. "I could hardly believe what you wor' saying to them. I wor' half-expecting one of 'em to slap your face."

Rosemary smiled. "Been teaching you bad habits, has he, Kevin?"

Ray shrugged indifferently. "What was I supposed to say? The usual barrage o' fucking bore? "What do you do for a living?" "Hairdresser, that must be interesting!"" He mock-yawned theatrically. "They've heard all that shit before from every other dull fucker. They know you're only coming onto them to get inside their knickers. Challenge them. Show 'em you're not impressed by them." He took a swig of his drink. "Give me a few more minutes, I'd've had 'em walking out of here like ducklings in a line."

Ray's conversation seldom strayed far from work. "Tell you what, cos' I like you, son, I'll reserve you a slot with Rosemary. I'll even throw in another girl for a threesome."

Leering disfigured Ray's face and voice. Kevin was reminded of a rat he had come across eating stray mounds of rolled barley in Fenwick's farm yard.

"Oh, ta!"

"Get you match fit for all those horny girl students. You'll have so much experience you'll be beating them off with a shitty stick."

"You reckon so?"

"Course I do. Women can smell losers a mile off. They can smell 'em like a pig smells truffles". He ruffled Rosemary's hair in an aggressively-familiar manner that the woman could scarcely bother to hide her dislike. "Ain't that right, my little sugarpot? You'll have more pussy than a shithouse seat while every other guy'll be beating their meat like it's going out of fashion."

An overweight girl in the group at the bar had concluded her version of Amy Winehouse's "Valerie" to a vociferous round of cheers from her circle of friends.

"Thank you, Louise. Next up, we've got a duet," boomed the DJ over his speakers. He consulted the ticket. "It's Ray and Rosemary singing "I've Got You, Babe" by Sonny and Cher."

It was obvious from the face Ray pulled that this was unexpected, and unwanted. Rosemary tugged at his sleeve. "Shit! No fucking way, woman! I've told you before."

"Aw, c'mon! Just this once," she pleaded.

"Fuck this! Ask young Kevin, instead." Before Kevin could react, Rosemary was up from her seat in a swift, fluid motion and pulling him, only half-resisting, across the dance floor to the stage.

Unfamiliar with this sixties oldie, Kevin stumbled uncertainly over Sonny's lines for nearly a verse before he got into the hang of it and was able to pitch his voice to harmonise with the woman. Their voices overlapped and interweaved as the song drew to a climax – strangely complimenting one another – Rosemary's was deep and breathy, Kevin's cracked and nasal – as they harmonised, they pulled towards the middle so that their intermingled tones became a new entity.

The big hand they earned sounded as heartfelt as the boozy, cynical atmosphere of the club would permit. Kevin managed a dazed grin – this was becoming addictive. Rosemary imperiously acknowledged the cheers like an aloof Roman empress confronted by a plebeian horde. She drew Kevin up to her and kissed him savagely full on the lips. Kevin might have enjoyed it more had he not been aware of Ray's ominously still form out of the corner of his eye. He was also aware that Rosemary had surreptitiously slipped him something down his trouser pocket.

The Town Hall clock was chiming midnight as Kevin, Ray, and Rosemary staggered out of the club. Ray had his right arm around Rosemary in a way that was too physical to be protective. Kevin noticed he seemed to be more "possessive" of her since the duet.

"See you in February, son," was Ray's parting shot. He fumbled inside his jacket. "One moment." He pulled out a thick wedge of rumpled bank notes and almost brusquely handed most of it to Kevin. "Change your tailor, son."

"Oh, ta!"

Ray and Rosemary sauntered off with a dissipated grace to the nearby taxi rank. The woman shot him a long, lingering look over Ray's shoulder and tipped him the wink. It was a sly, sensual gesture that hinted at mischief, and untold pleasures to come.

Chapter Eleven

"Tests have confirmed a new case of foot-and-mouth disease in Surrey. It is the sixth case in the county since the initial outbreak at the start of August – and the fourth case in the Ryedale area. Around 50 cows on the farm – which is within the 3km protection zone set up after the latest cases emerged – were slaughtered as a precaution."

Kevin strained one ear to catch the news report on the local radio network as he gulped down his breakfast cereal. The smell of burning toast assailed his nostrils and he hurried over the save the blackening bread.

"The crisis has restricted movement within a 3km protection zone. Tests were carried out after the animals displayed clinical signs of the disease. A spokeswoman from the Department for Environment, Food and Rural Affairs said last night: "Positive test results for foot-and-mouth disease have now been confirmed at the site where it was decided that cattle should be slaughtered on suspicion. The affected animals are within the existing Protection Zone and this now becomes the sixth Infected Premises since March the third this year."

Kevin popped the toaster and grimaced at the coal black toast. The strident chimes of the telephone in the reception added to his irritation. Kevin discarded the unappetizing slices of charcoal and darted into the adjoining room to scoop up the receiver. "Hello? Can I help you?"

"Now, Kev," began Tom Fenwick. "How you doing? Alright?" To Kevin, this awkward preamble of small talk from the normally taciturn farmer indicated something troubling.

"I was just about to set off," said Kevin, wiping a few stray crumbs of breakfast from his mouth.

"Good thing I caught you in time," said Tom. "DEFRA's been onto me an' Harry." He was referring to the Department of the Environment, Food, and Rural Affairs. "You've heard on r'radio that there's been a case o' foot-and-mouth up near Wellthorpe?"

"Aye. Just caught it on Radio York."

"Well, farm's gonna' have to be placed in isolation. They say nobody can come in or out." An ominous pause. "Including you, Kevin."

Kevin's mind reeled. "Christ! That's a bit of a bugger."

"Me an' Harry can manage for a while without you. But there's nowt' we can do about it. It's not our decision. I'm afraid we can't pay you for the time off-work. Sorry about this, Kev."

Kevin tried to keep a firm grasp of his eroding sanity. "Well, I suppose it's better to be safe than sorry. I don't blame you, Tom. Can't have me infecting your cattle. Don't worry yourself, Tom. I'll find summat' else."

"Well, keep in touch, Kev, an' I'll let you know when it's okay to come back. Take care o' yoursen'." The receiver been hung up on the other end of the call echoed hollowly down the line. Kevin slammed the phone down with a mounting anger. The fabric of his life was collapsing like a flimsy pack of cards.

My Award Winning Financial Services client is looking for a Trainee computer Operator to provide first line problem solving for issues associated with a wide range of mainframe computer facilities, communications, network equipment and management diagnostic tools, You will have the following skills/experience:

- *Proven team player, able to work effectively and closely with others.*

- *Proven to be able to work weekends and nights on a shift rota that covers a 24x7x365 operation.*

- *Proven ability to learn and follow processes but also able to identify and suggest improvements to work processes.*

- *Problem solving skills.*

- *Able to deal with urgent issues in a calm but timely manner.*

- *Must be self motivated and reliable. The current team works on a 4 x 12 hour shift basis – 4 days on, 4 days off. To find out more please send an up to date CV. Vulcan Technology is acting as an Employment Business in relation to this vacancy. Vulcan Technology plc is an Equal Opportunities employer; we welcome applicants from all backgrounds.*

Kevin folded the long sheet of white paper as it spewed forth from the slot in the computer in the Salton Job Centre. Compared to some he'd scanned that afternoon, this had potential. He adroitly manoeuvred the touch screen so that it came back on the next job in the list.

Customer Service Advisor- East Leeds / near Junction 46 M1 – Basic from £12,000 OTE £2,000

Our client is an award company. The company has been established for over 20 years, has over 400 employees UK wide with a turnover of £100 million plus. With an impressive portfolio of world class products the company continues to enjoy year on year growth and success. There is now a new vacancy for a Customer Service Advisor to join the team. This is an office based position initially based from their Leeds office (near Junction 46 of the M1 / East Leeds area). This is a mixed and varied Customer Service, Administration and Sales Support role. The successful candidate must have proven experience of Customer Service in a business to business environment. You will have an excellent telephone manner, clear communication skills, be positive and professional. You will also need to be IT literate. The company offers a competitive salary, eligibility to company pension scheme after one year's service, 20 days holiday (plus statutory days) increasing to a maximum of 25 days with each full year of service . Also the company has an excellent track record on training its staff and promoting from within. This is a fantastic opportunity to join a leading company in an exciting role. Benefits: Basic salary £12K + £2K.

Kevin had heard sufficient horror stories concerning the oppressive sweat shop conditions of the average call centre from an older female cousin who worked in one. Sales certainly did not appeal to him in the slightest. Having to rely on cold-calling harassed strangers and forcing them to part with their money, and being similarly reliant on this for your own income, seemed desperate beyond words. But it was one of the few jobs on offer for which he felt qualified. He pocketed the sheet of printed paper and consulted the next one.

Static Security Guard – Various sites, North Yorshire Must be willing to train for SIA licence. Duties will involve acting as a deterrent, patrolling site and other security duties as required.

Must have own transport and hold a full license, as you will be required to travel to various sites within 20 mile radius of Scarborough.

Duties include: *Dealing with customer queries/complaints, providing a visual deterrent, customer care: signing-in visitors, keeping accurate records & writing short reports, which may be used by the police or courts. The role is that of a static nature.*

The employer has claimed an exception under the Equality Act 2010. 60 hours per week incl night shifts.

Kevin relished the prospect of security work even less. He had often called at the house of a school friend whose Father worked as a security officer for some government building. The man mostly laboured on the night shifts and seemed in some dreadful limbo state between slumbers and wakefulness. These thoughts niggled Kevin as he patiently sat in the waiting area for an advisor to become available.

Kevin's eyes listlessly roamed the strangely soiled sterility of the job centre. Could there be a more depressing place, he wondered? Posters blared out the benefits of remaining upbeat and positive about your current situation with an almost Orwellian flair. Beaten-down men, in their drabbest clothing, milled listlessly about about as aimless as the cattle in the Fenwick's sheds, neutered by the almost surgical removal of the ritual, routine amd status of regular employment in their lives.

At length, an advisor became free and summoned him over to sit awkwardly on a steel frame chair opposite her desk. She was a frumpy, middle-aged woman in shapeless clothing whom it was impossible to imagine ever being young. She took Kevin's print-outs and entered them one by one into her PC.

"You're aware that your first two applications are from employment agencies?" she inquired, cold eyes scouring him over rimless spectacles.

"Er, yes. Why?" stumbled Kevin.

"It's just that there is a possibility that neither of these jobs even exist."

Kevin felt the earth give way under his feet. "Then why advertise them?"

"So that they can take your details to add to their database." It was as if she was patronisingly explaining the facts of life. "But you didn't hear that from me."

At the end of a heartbreaking few minutes listening to the woman outline a few home truths about job hunting, Kevin felt more demoralised than when he first came in. Out of a bundle of potential job details, that left only the security post. He thanked the woman and strode outside, making a vague promise he would get in touch with the company himself. Once he was a discreet distance from the office, he screwed the print-out into a contemptuous ball and tossed it carelessly into a plastic bin.

★ ★ ★

The job centre was sited alongside the British Rail station near a right-angled bend in the main road. Kevin paused on the corner to cross the road and catch his bus home. A juggernaut lorry thundered past him – temporarily obscuring his view of the street. Once it had passed, Kevin was nonplussed to see Sasha on the pavement on the other side of the street. Her bright-as-button eyes impudently regarded him with a gently mocking air. She was clad in a sleek black trouser-suit and leather jacket – both items new to Kevin. He had thought her drab overcoat at the porn shoot reflected her taste, but now he saw it was a deliberate act of camouflage to deter predatory males.

"New in town, stranger?" Her teasing tones drifted over the dreary hubbub of the traffic.

★ ★ ★

Sasha squinted down the wooden cue and sent the white ball careering lazily down the green baize. The glancing blow it struck the red ball sent the latter spinning into the nearest pocket. Kevin noted she had simultaneously set up the white cue ball neatly aligned to pot one of her remaining reds. It was becoming obvious that Sascha was hardly a novice at this game.

Apart from a solitary, unshaven middle-aged man propping up the bar, gazing emptily into the dregs of his pint, and the beer-bellied landlord engrossed in his Sporting Life, they had the pub to themselves. Kevin unburdened himself of the day's anti-climatic events.

"Security work?" echoed Sasha. "That sounds exciting." The corners of her mouth were buckling into an amused grimace all-too reminiscent of Rosemary.

"Beggars can't be choosers," conceded Kevin. "It's a pay cheque. I should be used to whoring myself for money by now," he added under his breath. Kevin's cheeks burned, but he realised it was innocently meant. As much as he was pleased to talk to Sasha again, she brought with her a lot of baggage he would rather not relive.

"I think Rosemary misses you, in her own way," Sasha gaily chattered. She expertly sunk the penultimate red ball and sized up the options to pot the last one.

Kevin tried to steer the conversation away from this. He brought up the subject of his forthcoming University course.

"Don't know why you're putting so much faith in getting a degree," snorted Sasha. "They're hundreds of students can't get a job with this credit crunch. An' they're still saddled with debts they'll spend the next few years paying off." A pause for effect. "I've worked with some."

She was not telling him anything he hadn't already considered. "My cousin Glenn did Business Studies at

Bristol. He said it was a good place to get your horizon's broadened, your mind expanded, and your cock sucked." He had almost hurt his ribs upon collapsing with laughter as his louche relative had casually dropped that into the conversation two years ago. Kevin had claimed it for his own and had been dying to use it on somebody since. Sascha's fit of giggles gratified him.

"One-track mind!" she tut-tutted. "Can't you think of anything else, for once."

Kevin was starting to see just how sexuality motivated most people's actions were. Their desires were cloaked in other goals such as status, power, and wealth, but, at heart, matters of the flesh was the impelling force. Many sublimated their passions so much they were no longer aware of them. No wonder so many sexless nerds at school subsumed their physicality to shut themselves away and devote themselves to passing exams that might confer the status they needed.

"Who knows," replied Kevin. "The economy may have picked up in three years time. Can't get any worse."

Kevin saw her glass was empty and offered to buy her the next round. "Just a tonic water, thanks, Kev. It flushes out the system" Kevin clambered up from his seat and ordered her drink, and a half a lager for himself, for which he carefully counted out the loose change jangling in his trouser pockets. He was still compelled to watch the pennies. The money from one of those non-existent jobs would have come in handy.

"Vanessa told me she got a First in History at Birmingham," said Sasha, once Kevin returned to his seat and plonked the drinks down on their respective beer mats. "Nowadays, all she can get is work in a call centre."

"Vanessa?" Kevin could not place the name.

"Fellow performer. I'll introduce you." She made short work of the remaining ball with a trick shot that curved the cue ball around an obstructing yellow of Kevin's. One of the watching barflies visibly double-taked.

"How did you find me?" asked Kevin.

"You gave us your home address, remember? Rang your Mother. She told me you'd be here."

"Job hunting."

Sasha potted the last balls with calculated insouciance. "Too bad we didn't bet something on this."

"I have to watch my pennies."

Sasha led Kevin to a secluded seat away from the snooker table as the two pot-bellied men who had put their money on the table after them took their turn. Kevin thought it a pity that his being in the company of such a strikingly sexy woman was only being witnessed by these losers, and not by anyone he knew.

After further small talk, Sasha addressed the elephant in the room. "Sure you don't want a repeat performance. You went down well last time." She laughed at the unintentional double-entendre.

"Doing it with you was okay. More than okay. But afterwards..."

"The gang bang!" Kevin looked around anxiously in case anyone overheard Sasha. "I prefer them to conventional one-on-one's to be honest."

"It's odd. If you'd asked me before, I couldn't have got my clothes off fast enough. But seeing what's-his-name..."

"Ray?" Kevin could hardly bring himself to say the name. "It happens to most girls in my business," said Sasha with authority. "We're vulnerable at that age, meeting a guy who says he knows it all. He says, "I'll take care of you," and then slowly manipulates you."

"He's her manager as well as her boyfriend?" queried Kevin.

"She earns the big cheques and he spends them!" Sasha drained her drink in one gulp. "At least, he did".

Her tones were significantly in the past tense. Kevin recalled what he meant to ask her. "She slipped me this note a few days ago. Not sure what she meant." He handed it to Sasha.

The woman nodded. "That sorta' brings me to the reason I'm here. Fancy a day out somewhere?"

★ ★ ★

Kevin eased himself into the comfortable depths of the passenger seat of Sasha's Porsche. As smooth as a whisper, the car sped down the motorway to the city, only keeping one ear open for Sasha's monologue.

"In a worst-case scenario, a gonzo director will take a girl to a hotel room and have their friends shoot a cheap scene in which she's humiliated in every orifice possible. She walks home with a thousand pound, bowed legs, and a terrible impression of the industry. It will most likely be her first – and last – shoot, and she'll regret it to her dying day."

Kevin was mulling this over in his mind in relation to what the woman had already told him at the start if their journey. "So Rosemary's gonna' form her own company and mekk' her own films?"

"There's legitimate films being shot on digital video. Amateurs are selling porn shot on their own mobiles. Compared to some of those no-talents, Rosemary will be Orson Welles." She snorted. "The Orson Welles of hard ons."

Kevin hesitated before broaching the inevitable. "What about..."

"Prince Charmless? As of a week ago, he's history!" Sasha flicked on the indicator to take a side road into the city centre. "She dumped him."

Her route took her through the bustling city centre to the calmer environs of the outer suburbs. Kevin judged the destination to be one of the drably anonymous hinterlands between the prosperous and the poverty-stricken. Sasha spun the car around on what seemed a sixpence and, barely decelerating, pulled up to a halt alongside Rosemary's barely-less extravagant sports car.

Kevin followed in her resplendent wake as she strode across the paved walk up to the front door. An expensively-manicured index finger, (whose long nails Kevin estimated probably still had some of the skin off his back caked underneath them) pressed the doorbell. No response. Sasha was about the press a second time when he noted the door was not closed. She eased it open.

"Hello? Only me!"

Kevin sensed a portentous gloom in the hallway even before he and Sasha heard Rosemary's muted sobs drift out of the kitchen. Abandoning caution, Sasha flung herself around the corner to take in the older woman's figure hunched in a bundle on the floor.

"Christ! Rosemary? What's wrong?" she said as she rushed to her side and gave her a long hug. Kevin had already absorbed the shattered crockery and "BITCH" and "DYKE" crudely scrawled on the walls in crayon. "Was it Ray? Has he..."

Rosemary shook her head. "No. I was out shopping when he called." She smiled wanly. "Nice of him to let me know he was here."

Sasha tenderly picked the woman up from the floor and led her over to a chair before boiling the kettle and making a cup of coffee. Kevin loitered purposelessly on the fringes feeling utterly redundant and way out of his depth emotionally. Finally, for wont of anything to do, he gathered up a duster and pan and cleaned up fragments of broken glass from the kitchen floor.

He perversely prided himself on a job well done as he dumped the last of the junk in the plastic bin. Sasha and Rosemary had taken themselves off to the living room for a heart-to-heart that Kevin elected to distance himself from. He was vaguely aware of somebody making a mobile phone call.

"Thanks, Amanda," said Sasha. "We won't forget it." She craned her neck around the door to indicate Kevin that he could join them.

Rosemary's tears had evaporated. Some of her old spirit had returned. "Sasha said she told you about my plans for the future?" Kevin grunted assent. "I'll be in the market for people I can rely on. I hope we didn't put you off last time."

"Beats patrolling some warehouse for twelve hours at a time," teased Sasha.

"I'll think it over." The smell of her perfume brought back golden memories. "You'll be alright?"

"I've been on the phone to two friends of mine. Amanda and Louise. They'll put her up for a while," said Sasha.

"Just to tide me over. I can't stay here," said Rosemary. "I'll be needing studio space as well."

Sasha gave him a lift home and Kevin pondered upon the offer for much of the remaining week. It impinged on his thoughts during the weekend match as well at Nunthorpe Athletic.

A dormitory village two miles from Norbury, that could boast a post office cum shop, it's club tended to be a spill over team for those unable to get into the town side. They still tended to be too good for Thormanton, with a resounding five-nil victory that flattered Kevin and his team.

The absence of Andy, Garry, and Alan soured the prematch atmosphere in the changing room. Sammy, naturally a glass half-full man, had bubbled with nervous anticipation at their expected return and vaguely promised they would be along soon, but the others were too resigned to their fatalism and knew better.

Still, Kevin had played with a notable spring in his step and was starting to see the opposition as little more than obstacles in his path to demolish. The separateness his ancillary activity gave him enabled him to approach each match coldly and ruthlessly, taking his time to evaluate what needed to be done and where to effectively play each pass. Everyone else on his team ran about like headless chickens. Kevin had even indulged himself in the odd dribble and crafty feint, but the effect had been spoiled by nobody on the end to challenge for his crosses.

Emma had displayed her customary perky enthusiasm, and made the occasional darting run down the right flank, but Steven, ploughing his usual lone furrow up front, had neither the guile nor the physical bravery to escape the man marking of the burly Nunthorpe centre back who had effectively smothered him out of the game.

As they spiritlessly trooped off the pitch at the end, Robert sought out Sammy. "Where wor' the three wise men today?" he demanded.

Sammy shrugged helplessly. "Well," muttered Steven, "We won't be seeing them again. Whadya' think, Kev?"

"Kev" did not respond, but not from rudeness. He had already made his mind up about continuing with Rosemary. But now, the germ of a new idea had begun to take root. It was so startling that Kevin felt everything around him was diminished to a background hum. If it succeeded, the unavailability of the three newcomers would be reduced to a mere footnote.

★ ★ ★

Kevin surprised his Mother by foregoing his usual practise of spending Saturday night drinking at the local pubs or braving the few Karaoke bars scattered about. Another evening around the pubs seemed pointless.

Kevin occupied his idle hours by cleaning up some old books of his in the bottom of a drawer and taking them into the upstairs attic to be forgotten about for an eternity.

One such volume, its hardback covers long torn off and lost, caught his attention. He forgot the exact title but it was an amazing stories collection of true events throughout history. One chapter – illustrated by lurid cartoon drawings – held more than a passing fascination for him.

"Marco Polo (1254-1324 AD) went on a journey from Venice to China that lasted 25 years. In his "Travels of Marco Polo" he records the danger of "assassins", who would attack Westerners, in suicide missions. The suicide assassins were organized by a chief known as "the old man of the mountains" who maintained a fortress that was painted with the imagery of Paradise. He would teach his followers that the quickest way to Paradise — where you would be served by seven virgins — was through suicide, while killing infidels"

Engrossed, Kevin read on. The assassins would be so hyped up with various narcotics and the promise of an eternal afterlife of sensual pleasure that they could easily slaughter countless desert-hardened warriors before eventually succumbing to greater numbers. These assassins would attain a virtual fugue state where they would be so "pumped up", that normal pain would scarcely register. In such a state, they could accomplish terrifyingly high casualty rates.

Kevin stacked the books awkwardly into a cardboard box and carried it up the stairs to the attic.

Chapter Twelve

The scenario, for the shoot, at Rosemary's temporary new address had been a young plumber arriving at a house to assist two young, bored housewives, who had been reading a sex manual with predictable results.

Kevin had been rifling through Rosemary's fridge for a carton of the inevitable pineapple juice when something struck him. "You've got a lot of celery in this fridge, Rosemary," he called up to her. "Eggs too!"

"I know," the answer boomed down. "Trade secret. Supposed to increase the amount of semen you produce."

Kevin realised how matter-of-fact he was getting about the whole business when he realised he was paying more attention on positioning the boom mike correctly than the girl-on-girl action taking place on the bed.

Their names were Kath, and Joanna. The latter was a well-spoken (verging on posh) brunette in his mid-twenties from Solihull. For a girl of her age, Joanna's breasts were disappointing sagging and her naturally big-boned stature ensured she was constantly fighting a losing battle with weight. However, she made a genuine attempt to deliver an honest acting performance – something she later attributed to having studied Drama at a northern University. Joanna had needed very little motivation to convey pain when Kevin had fucked her up her ample arse – that broad posterior threatening to dwarf his erect prick.

Rosemary had been on hand to liberally smear the lube on. Despite the pain in her voice, not entirely fabricated, Joanna was still enough in control to grind her buttocks in synch with his pumping – keeping him hard but never enough to prematurely ejaculate. For all that, Joanna's size still possessed an almost maternal quality that Kevin found comforting to cuddle up against once they had shot their mutual loads.

Kath, by contrast, was lithe and in her late thirties. Stretch marks betrayed she was a Mother of two and employed as a Customer Service Advisor in a Call Centre when not looking after her household. Her skin, compared to the fresh pinkness of Joanna, looked used and dirty and she had mounted his cock and ridden with something approaching contempt. Long, lank brown hair was deliberately whipped into Kevin's face as she bent down and shook her head around. For all that, Kevin preferred Joanna and selected her for the blow job shot. Having someone of her obvious breeding and sophistication on her knees sucking gluttonously on his knob was true power.

Kevin was amused to see both women had tattoos prominently etched into their flesh. Kath had the twelve signs of the Zodiac running down her spine, with larger versions of Scorpio and Leo in symmetry on her shoulder blades. Joanna, by contrast, had a naked woman sporting a pair of oversize butterfly wings, in flight, on her lower back. He vaguely recalled Sasha and Linda had tattoos as well. Was it some kind of compulsory option for a porn actress? Kevin wondered.

The clock on the wall said it was nearly six pm when Rosemary called it a day. Outside, a light shower was drumming a tattoo against the window pane, seeping into their brains like static Kevin, sandwiched between Joanna and Kath, glanced down at his flaccid penis. "If I keep up at this rate, it'll drop off."

Rosemary laughed breathily. "It'll make a helluva' noise when it does!"

"I can't believe there aren't loads of guys begging for their turn at stardom," said Kevin.

"None that are suitable," replied Rosemary.

"Believe it or not, acting ability isn't high on their list of priorities," chipped in Joanna.

Joanna yawned and clambered to her feet. Wrapped together in their embrace, the three of them could have been newly-born baby animals secure in their nest against the bleak outside world. "I'd better be getting back."

"You can stay the night, if you want, Joanna," Rosemary offered, but the younger woman blearily shook her head as she retrieved her neatly stacked clothes.

"Those essays won't mark themselves." Once fully dressed, Joanna kissed Rosemary, very long and carnally for a casual farewell, before trooping off downstairs. A few short seconds later, Kevin heard her car drive away.

"What's so funny?" Kath had been nuzzling the nape of his neck when she broke off to ask. Kevin had been so engrossed in his thoughts, he hadn't realised he had been chuckling softly.

"This non-league side beat a Premiership team. The following Saturday, they lost a league game four-nil against a team ten places below them, and they were lucky to get nil!"

Kevin, fully-dressed, sipped his herbal tea as Rosemary sat opposite him, patiently listening to a litany of lower league sides' giant-killing exploits against glamorous Goliaths.

"The point being," she sighed. Kath was still napping upstairs.

"The three M's. Motivation, motivation, and motivation. They were playing Premiership footballers in front of a big crowd – and it was rumoured their Chairman had slipped them a few quid under the table an' all."

Kevin outlined his plan. Rosemary needed a few horny young men in reasonable physical shape to perform. She had explained there was a thriving market for this age-group and – for reasons of confidentiality – was unable to use the usual stable of recognised male porn stars. Kevin had been seeking something to bind his players together in a common cause but had been repelled by sullen indifference bordering on outright hostility. Money could grease the grittiest of cogs, but Kevin suspected there was a greater lubricant for a horde of heterosexual teenage lads with enough sperm in their loins to fertilise the world but none of the social opportunities or skills to enhance their chances. He had often heard them moaning about the slim pickings locally – their unabashed lechery at the semi-naked girls hanging out at bars and clubs in town – the obvious inference that, for all their obnoxious swagger, they were still, that hated word, virgins.

Rosemary mulled it over at length. Kath, clad in an Oriental dressing-gown, had come down for a drink.

"Gang bangs always sell well," pondered Kath between sips of herbal tea, as matter-of-factly as discussing a new extension to her patio.

"One problem, Kevin," mused Rosemary. "I'll need to rent some place locally. Something as complex as this needs to be out of the way."

"Ray certainly can't know about this," added Kath.

Kevin volunteered to mail her the latest issue of the Gazette, which advertised local accommodation. There would be a training session this Thursday, and he could bump into the rest of the team, prior to Saturday's game, at dart's night in the Spotted Cow, on Friday.

"You'll have to organise them, as normal." Rosemary was visibly warming to the subject. "It's important that nobody outside the team must know, Kevin."

"We have a girl player, Emma..." Kevin began.

"H'mmmm. Not for now. Start with a small number at first — just to see how it goes. We'll break them in slowly."

Kevin glanced at his watch. "I'd better be getting back. I'll put the word around. Discreetly."

Rosemary arose from her armchair. Her face was unusually animated, as if by the stimulus of the idea. Her eyes danced and her professional smile looked uncharacteristically spontaneous.

"People only respect power and success in this world, Kevin. And they don't care too deeply how you come about it. We'll have to work very closely on this, Kevin." Her face was less than three inches away. "You're gonna have to be my number one guy, Kevin, the one I know I can trust. Together, we'll accomplish great things, you and I, Kevin. Great things!"

There was a buoyancy in Kevin's step as he mounted his motorbike parked in Rosemary's drive. As he kick started the engine into spluttering life, Kevin realised the rain had eased off and the Sun was peering out from behind a cloud, brightening the drab suburban street like a portent of redemption.

Chapter Thirteen

Kevin carefully clipped the square out of the inside back page of the Gazette. It contained little more than a paragraph, but – like many initially innocuous events in history – he was all too aware of the momentous story it fronted.

"THORMANTON SPRING LATE SHOCK AGAINST WELLTHORPE!" blared the modest headline. Below was the concisely-edited match report. There was something patronising about giving the typecast duffers, of the Salton and District Under 18 League, top billing, for such a modest accomplishment.

Kevin smiled at the thoughts he anticipated going through the sports editor's head. Let's give these losers their time in the Sun before normal service is resumed as soon as possible.

"Thormanton, for so long the eternal wooden-spoonists of the Salton and District Under 18 League, sprung the surprise of the weekend by gaining a late 1-0 victory over rivals Wellthorpe."

Robert Swales and Nick Cammack had been earmarked for the great experiment. Kevin had formulated a theory of having two defenders stick closely to Wellthorpe's star midfielder Duncan Rothwell to man-mark him out of the game. Robert would apply his bulky physique to being Rothwell's shadow, sitting tight on him and giving him no room to manoeuvre. Nick would operate as a sweeper ready to nip in and tackle should Rothwell elude Robert's tender mercies.

"From the start, the villagers played a disciplined game plan to man mark Wellthorpe maestro Duncan Rothwell. The tactic worked a treat as, without his midfield prompting, the Wellthorpe attack made little headway against a solid Thormanton defence."

Kevin had decided to start the great project in a modest way with Nick and Robert. He had broached it in an oblique way by inviting them around to his home one night during the week whilst his Mother was out researching at York University Library.

"Seen anything like this before, lads?" Kevin felt oddly like some disgusting, middle-aged pederast in a grubby raincoat seducing two innocent schoolboys. He knew they both devoured printed porn and would be more than eager to view a hardcore DVD.

"Nicholas Cammack and Robert Swales played out of their skins to nullify Rothwell."

They sat impatiently expectant through the opening sequences shot on location on a separate day. Nick and Robert fidgeted through the leaden acting as Sasha and another actress exchanged stilted lines in the grounds outside an obviously deserted comprehensive school. Then, a badly-edited cut flashed up the classroom set in Rosemary's house.

Shocked guffaws erupted involuntarily from Nick and Robert's gaping mouths at the spectacle of Kevin in his schoolboy outfit. They both sat forward in their chairs in rapt attention as the scene played out.

Although flatly lit and slackly directed, it succeeded in its modest aims and Robert provided a mock round of applause at the conclusion. They paid the remainder of its sixty minutes scant heed as, bursting with curiosity, they pumped him with questions.

"Sell the sizzle, not the steak," Kevin recalled reading in a sales leaflet once. Having played his trump card, Kevin told him that Rosemary was in the market for more young studs.

It was left vague enough for them to insinuate anything. There was a chance that insecurity, shock, or macho bravado would impel them to refuse outright. He breathed a mental sigh of relief as their body language perked up at being told there was an opening next Sunday. Kevin coerced them by saying that, if they played to order on Saturday against Wellthorpe, he would furnish them with the details.

A hundred negative scenarios played themselves out in Kevin's boiling brain in the few days leading up to Saturday. Would they think he was bluffing? Would they get cold feet? Would they talk about it to someone and the scandal would break prematurely – with the very real danger of eradicating his sex life whilst it was still budding? He'd performed the hard sell on the consequence-free sex and the two hundred pounds almost as an afterthought. He'd impressed on them the urgent need to be discreet about it in front of the rest of the team – not to mention everyone else locally. He neglected to mention that Rosemary felt both these lads were either virgins or inexperienced enough to forego the HIV testing.

* * *

Keith Black, the Manager of Wellthorpe, was a nasty, belligerent sod. His stocky figure resembled an agglomeration of boxed-off corners from his extreme, buzz cut hairstyle, that made his head look like it was chiselled out of granite, to his unnaturally right-angled shoulders. He cultivated the manner and appearance of a psychotic ex-member of the SAS. Only his short stature humiliatingly betrayed the truth. He had spent practically all his working life in some undefined sales capacity and was currently engaged in buying up barley and wheat from local farmers for a biscuit factory. He often hinted at some unspecified link to a Northern Counties East League team in the past, and would dredge up some laborious anecdote about his time there, but it had probably been a fleeting association.

At the annual league committee meetings, his obnoxious interjections left a bad taste in everybody's mouth and he liked to boast how he ruled his Wellthorpe players with a rod of iron. When one of his players had attempted a move to play for Norbury, Black had bragged he could blacklist him so utterly he would be lucky to get a game for Thormanton. Kevin still squirmed at the memory of that remark when Eric Skilbeck relayed it to him afterwards. He had been assured it hadn't been meant as an insult, in much the same way as a laddish joshing of nerds is laughed off with the supremely patronising "He knows we don't mean it! It's just a joke!"

But it stuck in Kevin's craw and he had added Black's name to his ever-expanding shit-list.

Now, Kevin almost felt sorry for him. They were confronted head on with something utterly alien with a brutish disregard for the etiquette that dictated their lives and left them bruised, battered and bleeding in their triumphal wake.

Wellthorpe never numbered among the elite of the league. They invariably ended their campaigns mid-table but their stock had risen in recent years due to the presence of one Duncan Rothwell.

Rothwell's face wore the self-absorbed thousand-yard stare of the addicted sportsman. A natural at cricket, he was invariably first of the school team sheets and had impressed local scouts enough to be given a trial at nearby Middlesbrough. It appeared to have come to naught, but his presence alone – he towered above his fellow teammates both literally and metaphorically, a Gulliver among a stocky collection of Lilliputians – had elevated Wellthorpe over their fellow mid-table mediocrities.

Even in the pre-match kick about, there was an unhurried precision to everything Rothwell did. For someone so tall and gangling, he was astonishingly graceful with no wasted movements, and when he completed a pass or a shot, he remained frozen, as if posing for a photo. Whereas Steven's on field posturing looked as forced and unconvincing as a histrionic actor, with Rothwell it had become so ingrained that the face had grown into the mask, it looked entirely natural. In the previous season, he had torn Thormanton apart like some narcissistic action hero disposing of anonymous extras, securing two goals in a five-nil rout.

The match began on a note of deceptive familiarity. "Ready, Emma?" called Kevin from outside as the girl changed in the Thormanton changing rooms.

"Just a sec!" came the upbeat reply. Kevin paused midstride to take in the squalid spectacle of Steven Cooke and John Swales taking furtive turns at squinting through a hole in the wooden wall at the unsuspecting girl within. Both were grinning broadly and Kevin could chart the progress of Emma's disrobing and dressing in the expressions of their faces. Both withdrew guiltily as she finally drew her crisp white shorts up over her taut, white buttocks.

The portly, middle-aged Referee ensured his "Bobby Charlton" comb over was in place before blowing hard on his whistle for Wellthorpe to kick off.

Kevin had learned to appreciate the early minutes of a game. They often constituted an illusion of parity with the opposition. Then, the first goal would fly in, and the floodgates burst open. But, not this time.

Rothwell received a sideways pass deep in midfield and looked set to embark upfield on one of his patented surging runs where opposition defences parted like the Red Sea. On this occasion, he ran straight into an uncompromising block tackle from Robert Swales. It had the disquieting comedy of an unstoppable behemoth malfunctioning and the impression was that the earth shuddered under the impact.

Kevin smiled approvingly. He also noted the sight of Nick standing poised a few feet away providing cover. Rothwell clambered uneasily to his feet. His expression was that of a discomfited actor thrown completely by an unscripted ad lib. He seemed to mentally dismiss it as an aberration. It would prove a fatal error of judgement.

Intercepting a mislaid cross field pass, Rothwell again looked set fair to dictate the pattern of play only for a sliding tackle, straight out of the text book, from Robert to put paid to such plans.

The paradigm for the match was set in stone. Throughout the first half, every time Rothwell picked up the ball, he barely had time to settle before Robert Swales would come flying in with all the fourteen stone bulk at his disposal to ruthlessly rob him and leave his pretentions of sporting aesthetics lying mugged in the dirt. On the few occasions Rothwell was able to ghost past Robert, Nick Cammack was strategically placed as cover to get in a tackle and sweep up any incipient danger.

Like a stand-up comedian before an unreasonably hostile audience, Rothwell and the rest of his hitherto complacent Wellthorpe players were dumbfounded.

Uncertainty infected them like virulent flu. They were a beat slower in the tackle and pass. Thormanton scented this. Previously cowed footballers like the younger Swales' brothers and Paul Myers seemed to grow an extra inch as, discerning glory, they put themselves about with more assertion and vigour. In spite of the odd flap, Sammy Patterson dealt competently, if colourlessly, with the few long range shot and desperate high crosses that the blunted Wellthorpe attack was reduced to. His defence was in no real danger of being breached. What, to an onlooker, resembled a scruffy midfield tussle was an epic triumph to Thormanton. They reached the half time whistle in the unaccustomed achievement of a goal-less draw.

As reality set in, Keith Black's imploring on the touchline grew more comically abusive. "Gerrup, bloody Rothwell!" He was of the generation to who "bloody" was still a shocking word. "I've seen better organisation from an epileptics' squitters!"

Kevin idly wondered about the unexpected literary inventiveness and a surreal imagery Salvador Dali would envy that obnoxious little turds like Keith Black could summon up from the dark recesses of their limited minds. He recalled reading somewhere that anger provoked unusual bouts of superhuman strength. Could the brain benefit too?

Several of the middle-aged women watching nearby registered outrage. "Sorry 'bout the language, love," Black offered to one of them. "Won't happen again!" Then, he winced as Robert virtually took the ball off Rothwell's toes. "Fuckin' Rothwell! Tha's playing about as well as my arse chews gum!"

Another revelation. This was truly a day for them. Male anger in the great unwashed produced endless involuntary genital references. In the end, it literally all came down to orifices. The magic of sex and reproduction was negated to the level of a good shit.

The contrast between the two changing rooms for the fifteen minute interval at half time could not have been more pronounced. The sullenly mute Wellthorpe team sat, shoulders hunched and cowed, in a ragged semi circle around Keith Black as, purple-faced with wrath, he vented his fury. Rothwell and his colleagues wore the exhausted thousand-yard stare of those who had lived through some terrible natural disaster.

"Can't you do summat' 'bout those fuckin' sheepshaggers? They don't deserve to be on the same fuckin' pitch as you!"

"What the fuck can we do?" Rothwell could restrain himself no further. "They just keep on coming – like they're on fucking drugs or summat'"

Black's words penetrated the plaster wall between the home and away dressing rooms but, apart from provoking the odd mocking snigger, it barely encroached on their consciousness.

"Nil-nil! Christ!" exclaimed Steven to nobody in particular. "When wor' the last time we wor' nil-nil at half time?"

"You can tell they're not enjoying it," Emma gabbled excitedly. All personal snubs and slights were forgotten in the excited tumult. Exclusive personal cliques were ignored.

Kevin crossed the room to where Nick and Robert were standing strangely apart from the rest. Their excitement was different too. Inner.

"You two have been a fucking revelation!" said Kevin. "I've told you before. Stop Rothwell playing and you stop Wellthorpe."

"Aye," Sammy chipped in. "I've barely had owt' to save."

As Kevin wheeled away, Robert discreetly tapped him on the shoulder – a comically-uncharacteristic gesture from one so normally boorish and assertive. "'Bout tomorrow. Is it still on?"

Kevin nodded almost imperceptibly in reply and raised a warning finger to his lips.

The second half picked up almost exactly where the first left off. Robert and Nick carried out their man marking of Rothwell with an almost-militaristic inflexibility. If Robert's unbridled brutality was niftily evaded, Nick's intelligent cover play more than compensated.

Bogged down in midfield, Wellthorpe lacked shape and purpose. Heavily reliant on Rothwell's guile and delicate skills to unpick stubborn defences, they were forced to heap responsibility onto the shoulders of their lesser journeymen. Their abilities in this sphere were only comparable to Thormanton's, and the stimulus of glory had given Kevin and his players an extra yard of pace.

A long clearance from John Swales ballooned out for a throw-in. One of the watching relatives of the players made a start to retrieve it, but Keith Black forestalled her.

"Alright, luv! I'll get it." Having scooped up the ball, he made a point of summoning Rothwell over to take the throw.

Only Kevin noticed that the older man leaned across to whisper something in the youth's ear. Rothwell nodded in acknowledgement before taking the throw.

It took a few minutes for Kevin to latch onto what had gone on. Slowly, surreptitiously, Rothwell drifted out wide to the left wing. Playing robotically to order, Nick and Robert trailed after him, leaving a gaping hole in the heart of the Thormanton defence.

With three minutes left, Kevin grasped its significance. A carefully weighted cross field pass by a Wellthorpe midfielder saw Barrie Allenson – an otherwise unexceptional centre forward – in acres of space run onto it.

Like a guided missile, he set off directly for the Thormanton goal with no defenders to impede him. Full backs John Swales and Peter Russell each did a double take and ran infield to intercept him, but were sluggishly off the pace.

Sammy Patterson – energised by having to work for once in this match – irresolutely came out of his area to narrow the angle but the gesture had token resistance written all over it. As Kevin sprinted back for all he was worth, he sensed, rather than saw, Allenson pause and chip the ball over Sammy's head. It was weighted perfectly to bounce once over the line.

Kevin nearly twisted his back as he launched himself into the air. In a flurry of uncoordinated limbs, he exploded into a spectacularly inelegant bicycle kick to get himself under the descending ball and volley it back in a perfect arc in the direction it had come from. The palpable sense of relief at having cleared certain danger anaesthetised Kevin against the jarring thud as he clattered the turf.

Their spirits invigorated by this escape, Thormanton rallied with a vengeance. The loose ball was played on by Peter Russell to Emma. Gathering up the pass, she barely broke her stride to sprint down the wing, virtually hugging the touch line. With a slight feint of the shoulders, Emma dodged a clumsy two-footed tackle by a Neanderthal Wellthorpe full back and astutely played the ball into Steven Cooke's path.

Goal hanging as per usual, Steven barged his way onto the loose ball with all the crude determination of an obsessive school swot chasing a career. Wellthorpe's first choice goalkeeper had been rested for what Keith Black regarded as a non-event match. The substitute was a portly sixteen year old who tended to tag along with the others more in enthusiasm and a social life than any sporting ambitions. Heavily committed to attack, Wellthorpe had left a yawning gap a mile wide.

The face of their goalkeeper could not have been a greater personification of comic horror than if he suddenly been catapulted into a heavyweight boxing match. Miscast as an authoritarian custodian between the sticks, the lad dithered uncertainly in the limbo between the goal line and the penalty box – and was hopelessly lost.

As if his whole life had been leading up to this moment, Steven drew his right foot back and unleashed a venomous low shot underneath's the keeper's diving body to nestle snugly in the back of the rippling net.

A cousin of Kevin's once said that he understood what people had meant by remembering where they were when they had heard of Kennedy's assassination. In 1998 he had been fumbling for his socks whilst still in bed and wondering why his radio was tuned to some saccharine musical wallpaper instead of Radio One, until an announcer's voice came on. Kevin would recall every inch of his posture as he scrambled to his feet – his peripheral vision taking in Steven's breakaway goal occur like some pre-ordained practical joke. As the net billowed, time seemed to stand still.

Thormanton and Wellthorpe players froze like flies in amber. Kevin could read the thoughts going through Steven's mind in every inch of his broad back – incomprehension, relief, and, ultimately, elation. Swinging on his heels, he went apeshit – surging back to the centre spot with his right arm triumphantly aloft.

He halted in the centre circle as if staking his territory. One by one, the other Thormanton footballers converged on Steven and piled on top of him, bringing him down. Steven disappeared under a human mountain that failed to hear the Referee blow the final whistle. Wellthorpe's players, by contrast, looked as punch drunk as a boxer on his last legs.

The mood had not abated by the time Thormanton had chaired Steven back to the changing rooms like an African potentate. Anecdotes were breathily exchanged and relived, re-polished and gaining much in the retelling. Robert struck up a desultory refrain of Queen's "We Are The Champions" as he basked naked in the showers. Such was the euphoria that nobody bothered that Emma was still among them. She blushed and giggled at the sight of Robert's engorged wedding tackle waggling under a fine spray of water but took it in her stride.

"Well played, Emma." The girl had barely noticed Kevin's eerie calm amid the jubilation. "I must admit I had my doubts about you, but you've certainly pulled your weight."

The girl glowed with pride – and maybe something more. "Thank's, Kev'. Going to the pub tonight?"

"Not tonight. Helping someone move house."

The door to the Wellthorpe changing room remained closed for a very long time.

Chapter Fourteen

Hobbs Farm House lay a good three miles, to the west of Thormanton, off a side road, on the main route to Salton. It had been purchased, along with eighty acres of prime arable land by a farmer living on the far side of Thornton Westborough. The farm had ultimately proven too small to support the elderly bachelor who previously owned it and he had sold it at auction to retire on the proceeds by the sea. It had brought up its buyer's total acreage to just over four hundred and the sprawling hectares of harvested stubble had been converted to grass and hosted a herd of grazing store cattle.

The grey stone farm house was rented out via a letting agency for an additional source of income. Its relative isolation had led Kevin to suggest it to Rosemary as an ideal venue for what they had in mind. The rent would be automatically debited from her account monthly and visits from a potentially inquisitive landlord would be minimal.

Kevin's normal impulse to rev up his motorcycle was inhibited by the metaphorical proximity of his two diverse worlds – the public and the private, the mundane and the profane – so close to home. It was as embarrassing as strolling down a bustling street with his flies open. He cast covert glances over his shoulder as he swung the bike into the front drive. A red Porsche was parked awkwardly in front of the house with its boot open. In the even green terrain surrounding it, it stood out like a pustular sore on healthy skin. Boxes of personal effects were strewn haphazardly about the cinder path drive.

Rosemary marched out of the front door, shirt sleeves rolled up. "May I give you a hand, Madam?" Kevin greeted her in his best mock-jobsworth voice.

Rosemary's melon slice smile revealed perfect, even teeth. "Just in time. We need a strong pair of arms."

"We?" echoed Kevin.

A slight giggling announced the appearance of two figures emerging from the shadows in the doorway behind Rosemary. Kevin took in the fake tans and tightly-cropped T shirts that seemed to be the uniform of the professional porn performer. "They'll be upstairs ready when you've finished unloading."

Kevin hefted in the packing cases with a strength and speed he did not know he possessed. The two girls sat sipping iced tea in the cool of the living room amid a chaos of unpacked boxes. Rosemary assured him they would both be ready once everything was unpacked. The woman's stark modernism soon imposed her personality on the homely farm house like some technological virus. Once it was over, Kevin gulped down a mug of steaming coffee and mounted the stairs two at a time.

The American woman had already set up a home-made studio in an upstairs bedrooms. The DVD camera, lights, and reflectors had been erected to showcase the plain bed. It felt like been reunited with old comrades.

Rosemary called it "gonzo porn." There was no elaborate storyline or pretentions to "artistic" camerawork – just wall-to-wall fucking. This suited Kevin down to the ground, as he was starting to count down the moments between each session as he once had football games.

He was also finding that the names and backgrounds of the girls were starting to merge into one amorphous mass of faked tans, purple lipstick, and bottle blonde. But Anna was destined to linger in the memories long than most. A short bell of auburn hair offset an unremarkably pleasant face with little of the tightly enclosed qualities of the other girls. Her stocky peasants body was forgiven by the largest pair of natural breasts Kevin had ever seen outside the pages of a men's magazine. They were barely restrained, like two idle Zeppelins, in the scant confines of her purple bra and skimpy T-shirt.

Her blonde partner had a slender, willowy figure and pert breasts, and could be considered more conventionally pretty, but Kevin was never to recall her name afterwards.

Up until today, the act of shooting your load between a girl's tits had struck Kevin as a supremely pointless exercise – an elevated form of masturbation rendered ridiculous by the presence of the woman at close quarters. But once Anna had unhooked her bra and released those glorious mammaries, the impulse nearly overcame him like some ingrained Pavlovian reflex. Rosemary's eyes betrayed a teasing twinkle as she asked him which actress he wanted to try first.

Anna's tits were grotesquely out of proportion to the rest of her body. It was difficult to discern much of her midriff under their pendulous magnificence. None of which mattered much to Kevin as he brutally "rogered" her in a manner he would not have thought himself capable of a few months ago. Their mouths locked into a savage vacuum as their tongues rummaged about in each others palates like primal beats scouring for food.

Kevin finally disengaged himself and descended upon those relentless breasts like a hawk. Somehow, he was able to fasten his lips around the full circumference of her areola, teasing the nipple with his tongue. He could not resist a bout of "motorboating" (as he later realised it was called) – secure in the knowledge it looked good on camera.

Engrossed in his suckling, he was vaguely aware of the woman spreading her thighs invitingly open. An image of Rothwell sent sprawling by a block tackle from Robert strangely flickered across his mind as his rock-hard penis punched its way into her moist grotto.

Anna exclaimed an inarticulate cry of what could have been both pain and pleasure. Fingernails like talons raked his back. There was no denying him. Kevin felt a sensation of power oddly similar to beating her up and exalting in her agonies. Her face, so placid and provocatively cool minutes before was disfigured with emotion.

"You like that, don't ya! Fuckin' whore!" Kevin needed no prompting for his lines Lost in the moment, they came naturally to him. His rhythm increased and became harder.

This buxom goddess was his to do what he wanted. Kevin's well-muscled arms pinioned her down onto the bed like a rapist. She was an impersonal sex toy to slake his dark pleasures. The violent wobbling of her enormous breasts were as stimulating as the slapping of his scrotum against her body. He felt the skin around his knob was a mere membrane that would split to reveal the throbbing power within like a cocoon around a butterfly.

The familiar tingle at the base of his penis sparked into life, slowly snaking its way ever upwards. Long practise was rendering the act like a routine at the gym. By maintaining a certain pace and rhythm, Kevin could keep himself hard without shooting his load. He could feel the faint irregularity in the roof of her vaginal walls that, past porn partners had advised him, was the mythic G-spot.

He could just about attain enough length and hardness to clumsily rub it. It chafed against his tender helmet.

Anna responded by tightening her thick thighs around his midriff, nearly squeezing the air out of his body. For someone accustomed to holding down fractious calves, Anna's bucking body presented few problems. She was picking up the pace of his frantically increasing thrusts, her cries more anguished. The telltale sting was poised atop the glans. Kevin maintained the moment for a long as possible as Anna came like a balloon deflating.

Sated by pleasure, she could barely bring any life into her final cry that sounded more torn, as opposed to exhaled, from her throat. He felt a viscous fluid stream over his thighs from her sore cunt.

Like the true pro he prided himself on being, Kevin swiftly withdrew his cock and pointed it over Anna's tits. She gasped at the warmth of the sticky white substance spattered over her nipples. She seemed to be having trouble catching her breath. Denuded of all energy and emotion, Kevin crumpled gently down and buried his face in her waist and felt his eyelids flicker shut.

"Cut!" Rosemary's voice rang out like a pistol shot. The rest of the evening smacked of severe anti climax. Anna somehow managed to recoup her stamina and assume the dominant role in the obligatory girl-on-girl episode. Their acting came across as unconvincing it comparison to what had just happened. But Kevin appreciated the rest, sitting back in a canvass chair. He held the boom mike unobtrusively over the bed out of camera shot. It cast a visible shadow over the scene, but Kevin had long learnt technical excellence was low on Rosemary's list of priorities.

Having smeared his cock with KY jelly, Kevin roused himself to join in the regulation threesome. The other girl was as well-muscled as a dancer and she gyrated her buttocks enticingly as she lay prone before him. Kevin bounded on top of her and forced her legs apart. The woman authentically mimed mortal terror as Kevin held her down and rammed his erect manhood between her arse cheeks.

Kevin knew from rote what was required from anal sex scenes. The man took violent pleasure and the woman pain. His mouth contorted in a feral smile. The afternoon's triumph over Wellthorpe infected him with a savage resolve. Had returning soldiers fresh from a day's bloodletting in the front felt the same? The woman's howls were abruptly muffled by Kevin ramming her face down into the pillow. Her tensed muscles gripped his cock like a vice but Kevin ignored the pain – his helmet was growing progressively sore – and rammed it further inside the woman.

It had been like wrestling a recalcitrant calf for ear-tagging or castration, but his superior weight and determination prevailed, and he commenced pumping forcefully.

The pain from his cock galvanised him as much as her agonies or the feel of her flesh. Yet, Kevin could sense her cries were partly acting for the camera for her tight arse was rhythmically jerking his rigid penis as securely as a broad right hand masturbating. His semen spurted forth to dilute the scarlet of her bleeding arse.

Then there was only silence, save for their shallow breathing as he flopped down onto her slender back. He looked as if he had just bested her in some wrestling contest. Would the bleeding be patched up before Robert and Nick arrived for their stint before Rosemary's camera tomorrow, he idly pondered.

Chapter Fifteen

It had been a week since Wellthorpe. Nick and Robert had reported for duty to have their every grubby whim catered for by Anna and the other girl. They had followed Kevin's lead by relating their sleazy adventures back to the rest of the team – except Emma. Kevin felt a strangely protective urge to keep the girl remote from this. But Steven, Sammy, and the others had been informed in no uncertain terms of the physical rewards on offer for playing above themselves, and to Kevin's tactics, in the upcoming matches.

Robert was particularly graphic in his recollections. "I wor' up her front porch, and Nick up her tradesman's entrance, an' she didn't mind a bit. Water off a duck's back. She all but rolled over over and asked for more. The other one wor' shaved down below. Looked like my Grandad's gob before he popped his dentures in!"

The financial aspect would be merely the icing on the cake. Were they in any doubt, Robert and Nick's wide-eyed recollections were backed up with physical evidence on the complimentary DVD's they'd been given. Kevin could see he had them hooked. Even the professionally blasé Steven looked uncharacteristically awestruck.

Thornton Westborough away were next on the fixture list. Their neatly trimmed ground was sited alongside a single-lane road, scarcely more than a track, out of the village. A derelict Portakabin served as changing rooms. Thornton Westborough tended to blunder in the lower half of the league, never troubling the likes of Salton or Norbury but regularly putting Thormanton to the sword with something to spare. They enjoyed the good fortune to play some of the table leavings of nearby Salton to bolster their motley collection of farm labourers and apprentice bricklayers and plumbers, often resulting in them playing like two teams who were total strangers to one another. Fresh from a four-nil hammering at Norbury the previous Saturday, they relished the prospect on taking their frustrations of eternal cannon fodder Thormanton. Every over-confident, unruffled move they made as they half-heartedly went through their pre match warm up routines betrayed this. It continued several minutes after the portly, greying referee blew his whistle to signal the commencement of hostilities. Thornton Westborough started strolling about the park attempting mazy dribbles and stringing neat passing moves together – only to hit the granite wall of the sex-motivated Thormanton tackling. From that point on, their delusions of a walkover melted into the ether as they realised they were to be the hapless bit-part players on this occasion – the Eintracht Frankfurt to Thormanton's Real Madrid.

The prospect of a fuck with a tanned voluptuous goddess had impelled Richard Swales to forego his natural impulse to selfishly dribble and, either, concede possession or get bogged down in an isolated corner of the pitch. Instead, he flighted over a high ball that hung tantalisingly in the air before his elder brother Robert met it perfectly on his forehead. Robert's eyes remained open, as opposed to being screwed up in an involuntary reaction, and they rewarded his due diligence by the sight of the ball flying past Thornton Westborough's comically flapping keeper to bulge the back of the net.

It was like a pin going into a balloon. Thornton Westborough were a pallid shadow of their early assurance. A long goal kick from Sammy Patterson bisected the centre of he opposition defence to bounce into the path of the goal hanging Steven. He leapt for it like a fish for a worm on a baited hook. Unable to be offside from a goal kick, he angled his body to gain minimal contact with the ball in the penalty area to steer it past the goalkeeper to trickle over the line. Steven hadn't so much fired the ball as helped convey it on its way.

Half time came with Thornton Westborough in a state approximating shellshock. Thormanton maintained their pressure in the second period with Kevin cutting through the opposition half to unleash a showy cannonball shot that left the goalkeeper rooted to the spot and the crossbar vibrating like an overused telegraph wire. Emma, her slender back to goal, gracefully erupted into a bicycle kick that drew a full stretch save from the galvanised goalie. Paul Myers stooped low to get a header in from the loose ball that smacked the side post. After three spectacular efforts in quick succession, it was anti-climatically disappointing that Steven ultimately got his chest to the ball to clumsily scramble it over the line.

Three-nil up with a little under thirty minutes to go, Thormanton eased off the accelerator and toyed with Thornton Westborough. Apart from a desperate long range shot that harmlessly thudded straight into Sammy's stomach, there was little danger of Thormanton's defence being breached.

With less than a quarter of an hour on the clock, Kevin felt it only fair to give young Chris Manby a run-out for the closing minutes as substitute for Paul Myers. He could afford to be generous. The lad got little enough match practise as it was. It would also be easier to justify his presence tomorrow at Rosemary's. For he had decided that the entire male team would participate. It would do to get them blooded – to bait the hook, to give them a glimpse of paradise and even a brief taste of its joys. They needed to be convinced that the offer was genuine. Kevin couldn't complain if one or two still found it hard to believe, even after listening to Nick and Rob raving nonstop about their lewd experiences for most of the week.

★ ★ ★

Jenna's dyed-blonde tresses showed only the scantest glimmers of black roots as she mimed being forced down onto her knees by Kevin and the other lads in Rosemary's studio. The purity of its colour and her creamy skin made the woman look unsettlingly wholesome among these depravities. She resembled a mature Alice lost in a fleshy Wonderland as the lads' erect pricks converged on her from all angles like beggars homing onto an unwary tourist. It suited the scenario of an innocent housewife being gangbanged by a troupe of rough painters and decorators renovating her house.

The prior establishing scene of the workers turning up at the house and being put to work by the "housewife" had been shot almost as a conventional film with memorised dialogue and short takes. Some of the lads were barely passable as actors and audibly stumbled over their lines as well as occasionally marring Rosemary's intricately-designed visual compositions.

This scene-setting continued until Jenna's character was summoned on a pretext inside the bedroom by the labourers. As she curiously peered around the door,

Robert's hairy arm shot out and yanked her roughly inside, slamming the door behind her.

From this point on, cinematic artistry was trampled underfoot. What transpired next was painstakingly choreographed and rehearsed and just about passed muster on the screen. This was mostly so it could be filmed on one, long take. Short, sharp takes could not be accommodated alongside the sexual performance of the cast. Besides, it would be distracting.

Robert and Steven pinioned Jenna by each arm and brought her before Kevin and others – all stark naked. She could have been some miscreant about to be punished by an autocratic ruler. "What are you doing?" pleaded Jenna in character. "I'm not that sort of girl. I've got a husband."

With their free hands, Steven and Robert each grasped half her shirt and tore it apart to unveil her breasts held in abeyance by a purple underwired push up brassiere. Steven undid that bra with a practised hand and her breasts wriggled free. Although they drooped noticeably, as if ashamed of something, they were still impressive for a woman Kevin estimated to be in her late twenties or early thirties. It was all he could do to curb himself suckling at her hardening nipples as he gently eased her short skirt and scanty undies down around her ankles to reveal her shaven vagina.

Steven pulled her hair back from the nape of her neck, tilting her head back. Hemmed in from all sides by the lads' hardened cocks, Jenna gave a convincing impersonation of confused terror and vulnerability commingled with incipient arousal.

Robert had pride of place, going first, and he brutally rammed his manhood into Jenna's gaping mouth. It slid smoothly between her red lips and caught the back of her throat with a gargling choke. A novice might have pulled up there and then for fear of asphyxiating her, but Robert was adept and experienced enough to continue unabated with a steady pummelling rhythm that slapped his dangling scrotum hard against her delicate chin.

Jenna uttered an inarticulate whine of pained pleasure that hiccoughed in time with Robert's plunges. His cries grew more urgent and insistent. The woman was trained enough to know what this signified so she relinquished her moist hold on his engorged member and fastened hungrily onto Steven's instead, with barely sufficient time to draw breath. There had hardly been a pause as she resumed the same unceasing suction with a desperation identical to latching onto an oxygen tube.

The woman was an old hand at this game. That much was obvious. She was skilled enough to keep seven horny teenagers erect for minutes at a time and varied the rate at which she attacked each penis. Jenna's previous pose of terrified subjugation had surrendered to lusty eagerness mixed with a professional calm. From time to time, she cast conspiratorial glances and winks up at whatever lad she was servicing. It was difficult to tell whether she was still in character.

Kevin could only guess at the emotions of whichever punter would view this. How many cold, unattainable, bitchy women would she be a substitute for? What perceived slights would the innumerable, frustrated, disappointed men who purchased this be exacting a proxy humiliating revenge for?

Incredibly, five minutes had elapsed without a single ejaculation. Kevin could only marvel at how easily they had attained the necessary stamina as a by-product. Prior to this, it would probably have been over in a matter of seconds like a damp squib.

"And, cut!" It had been easy to forget Rosemary crouching behind her High Definition camcorder mounted atop its tripod. "Okay. Change position. Onto the sofa."

Like a trained military unit, the cast assumed new poses for the continuing scene. A universal lighting system had been set up to accommodate this. The lads fluffed their own pricks as Jenna pulled herself off her knees and, with the practised grace and ease of a dancer, lay spread-eagled out on a strategically placed sofa with her long legs hooked over the back rest. "Fuck me! Harder! Harder! Fucking harder! I fucking need it! I need it so badly!" There was something both stimulating and repellent about her cut glass accent enunciating such obscenities. With Herculean effort, Kevin willed himself to hold back the volcano fermenting in his balls. Nearing the end of a penultimate take, a new problem occurred.

"Shit!" he cried, out of character.

"What is it?" snapped the Director testily.

"Fucking cramp! Sorry."

"Cut!"

Kevin hastily massaged a leg encumbered with shooting pains by it being held rigid in the same position for several minutes. Eventually, he nodded to indicate that he was ready to continue and impatiently waved the attendant Fluffer away.

"Right," sighed Rosemary with a heavy patience. "Once more, from the top!"

Kevin reflected that an advantage of this new position, uncomfortable as it must be for Jenna, was that it enabled him to knead her breasts while been simultaneously sucked off. Of course, he had to watch his blocking and ensure he didn't obscure the camera's viewpoint of the woman's upside down head hungrily feasting on his manhood as he unrelentingly pumped at her mouth. His muttered oaths of "You like that, don't you bitch," and other obscene entreaties fell from his lips as easily as the lyric of a popular nursery rhyme. No such lines had been scripted. The performers were expected to improvise them on the spot. Kevin felt the emotional coarseness and vulgarity of the seasoned porn actor was growing ingrained into his DNA. It was coming as naturally to him as breathing.

Jenna serviced all the lads in this manner for a good few minutes more before, at a pre-arranged signal, they disengaged and all, save for Robert and Kevin, expended their semen by splashing it almost contemptuously over Jenna's face. Kevin noted she barely flinched. Instead, she writhed in a mock rhapsody of sensual elation. She could have been some bizarre half-sentient plant replenishing itself on rain and sunlight.

After a brief rub down with a wet flannel, Jenna was ready for the grand finale. The other lads retired from the studio to get washed and dressed while Jenna, having gained second wind, cleaned the cum off her glistening body.

Jenna was a versatile woman. Robert entered her by the front standing upright, while she clung onto him with her arms and legs curled around his body. Robert had very little to do in the way of movement, and − for all his body strength − would have found it difficult anyway − so Jenna latched on onto his hard cock and pumped against it like a woman demented. Kevin enabled her generous body to support itself by propping her up from behind while simultaneously thrusting his own manhood up her anal channel. Smeared liberally with K Y Jelly, it lid in as though manufactured with it in mind.

Locked together, the three of them somehow succeeded in maintaining a complimentary rhythm. They paid little heed to Rosemary as he unclipped the camera from its tripod and moved smoothly on foot for a more intimate angle. Kevin, through a haze of ecstasy, was dimly aware of the woman discreetly scrabbling around on the floor underneath them.

Afterwards, Kevin would view the near-surgically detailed view of his and Robert's cocks thrusting back and forth into Jenna's two orifices as unnervingly similar to a startling close up of some bizarre alien creature attempting to ingest its prey. He would have decidedly mixed feelings as it would haunt his darkest nightmares for years afterwards. All sensuality and any pretentions at love were obliterated. There seemed something dehumanising about it – a glimpse of the demon lurking under the skin.

Kevin's penis was growing sorer with the concentrated activity of the past half hour and he prayed it would soon be over. A familiar, faintly-pleasurable stinging sensation began to inexorably climb up from the base of his flapping scrotum. He no longer cared if Rosemary felt it would be too soon. Judging from the rictus contorting Robert's face in unison with his ascending moans, he would not be the only one cumming.

Their final cries blended in a discordant harmony of violent pleasure. Robert and Kevin's bodies nearly crushed Jenna between them. They clung together for a few seconds before awkwardly disengaging. Their movements were ungainly and Kevin almost limped out of shot to gather up his clothes.

It was as if leaving the realm of sexuality had robbed the trio of all their previous grace and physical certainty.

They dressed quickly and lumbered downstairs to grab a drink and a bite to eat. Ironically, after all they had gone through together in such intimacy, their conversation with Jenna was stilted and inconsequential. Kevin would struggle to recall it later. They could have easily been mundane office workers after a numbing shift. One by one, except for Robert and his brothers, they exited Rosemary's house back to their banal everyday worlds. They never saw Jenna ever again.

Almost, never again. The story had a sequel that caused Kevin in particular to reassess the afternoon. It had been Nick Cammack who had happened to be in York on some errand on a Saturday afternoon. Strolling down a main street just off the Main Shopping Centre, he had chanced to espy Jenna, unfamiliarly clad in a heavy woollen pullover, jacket, and medium length skirt – looking unassailably buttoned up and respectable. She looked no different to the myriad women shoppers and pedestrians milling around.

She was unlocking the door to a spacious four by four Estate car parked by the side of the street when their eyes met. They briefly acknowledged each other's presence with tight, nervous smiles. Then Jenna ushered her two infant children into the back of the car before driving off.

Chapter Sixteen

"Thormanton, the eternal wooden-spoonists of the Salton & District Under 18 League, have surpassed all expectations by notching up their fourth consecutive victory this season. A three-one home triumph over Colstone Celtic ensured they are handily placed one point behind unbeaten leaders Norbury." When Kevin read the match report in the Gazette, Thormanton's improvement in form had ceased to merit pride of place and was the third paragraph down in the section devoted to the Salton and District Under 18 League.

"Goals from Steven Cooke(2), and Simon Swales had sewn up the game by half-time for the villagers, who started the game like an express train. After the interval, they toyed with their opponents and a late strike from Vasey was too little, too late."

Kevin could still recall the shocked expression on Sammy's face as Colstone netted a late snapshot out of nowhere with two minutes to go. The horror of what it might mean to the lad was etched into every line on his face at not keeping a clean sheet for the first time in weeks. Kevin made a point of retrieving the ball and whispering reassurance to him. He knew Sammy was too valuable to them all to be risk being demoralised.

"It's alright, Sammy!" said Kevin. "Our fault! We fell asleep. Didn't close the bugger down! You're not to blame. An' you're still on for tomorrow!"

Sammy's slumped shoulders visibly straightened out and his posture improved. It was for the same reason that Kevin brought on Chris Manby as a substitute for John Swales for the last ten minutes, as he had for all the preceding games (even though there were no injuries) and taking turns at choosing the man to be replaced – reassuring them it was nothing to do concerning their performance but to ensure that everyone was given a fair crack of the whip.

"What makes this turnaround in form to amazing is that, with the sole exception of girl winger Emma Patterson – they are fielding virtually the same team as last season."

Nunthorpe Athletic – not quite a town, too large for a village – were next. It boasted a shop (a rarity these days when so many local amenities were being closed down) and a garage that still did repairs but no longer bothered to sell fuel. In truth, it was little more than a single one-street satellite of Salton with its own primary school and suburban side-streets attached. In Premier League terms, the team was strictly Aston Villa – bobbing along underneath the giants of Norbury and Salton against whom they measured their standards by losing to by narrower margins than Thormanton.

Thormanton's visits were eagerly anticipated as a chance to ratchet up their own goals for tally. But, this year, their hopes floundered like a well-rehearsed joke before an unsympathetic audience.

Robert and John Swales were operating an effective, disciplined zonal marking system that completely nullified the complacent Nunthorpe strikers. Previously idle Thormanton midfielders funnelled back to help out in defence. Free kick routines functioned with a clockwork efficiency. Instead of languidly goal-hanging, Steven Cooke worked tirelessly up front, getting into free space, unselfishly dragging the Nunthorpe players marking him out of position, and generally forcing them to work overtime. The midfield behind him harried mercilessly and always had a free man to pass to. The entire unit performed as a cohesive, well-marshalled unit against which, Nunthorpe were crushed.

Robert Swales used his bulk to maximum, intimidating effect by disrupting to Nunthorpe goalkeeper at a corner, swept in by Emma, into punching the ball into his own net on seventeen minutes. Steven raced through onto a defence-splitting pass by Kevin to dribble around the keeper and virtually stroll the ball in for the second, with less than three minutes of the first half remaining. His newfound assurance gave birth to a supreme moment of mocking arrogance as he paused on the goal line with his foot on the ball. He almost dared the Nunthorpe players to take the ball off him, then, as they roused themselves, he cheekily backheeled the ball over the line. The Nunthorpe footballers glared daggers at this, but it was water off a duck's back to Steven as he nonchalantly jogged back to his own half with a bumptious spring in his stride.

When both teams re-emerged for the second half, Nunthorpe cut a sorry sight as, reluctantly stumbling outside the club house, they despondently gazed at the turf, heads slumped.

Thormanton buzzed animatedly around them like hyperactive fawns. A close range volley from Steven following a goalmouth mix-up and a glancing header by Paul Myers, from a free kick by Emma, completed the rout. The dazed, disbelieving faces of the opposition after such thrashings was developing into an agreeable end-of-match ritual for Thormanton.

The upcoming porn session at Rosemary's was the elephant in the Thormanton dressing room afterwards. Partly this was due to Emma's unsuspecting presence, but, mostly, it was a strange superstition as if it was some shared hysteria fantasy. Apart from the odd, sly glance, and mutual nod of agreement, it received barely a mention except in a matter-of-fact way referencing times and dates.

★ ★ ★

As his Captain read out the report at their training session at a five-a-side pitch adjoining the main playing field at Norbury Town F.C., Colin Adkins gazed blankly as if he was the victim of some cosmic practical joke. He saw his new team mates regarding it as little more than some quirky comedy sketch unfolding in an obscure foreign country that scarcely concerned them. "....it has already proven to be a memorable season for the villagers."

Richard Swales, underage – like a third of the occupants in the Main Bar of the Spotted Cow in Thormanton – stumbled to the end of the paragraph. He, Sammy, Steven, Paul Myers, and Chris Manby were clustered around a table reading the Gazette's sport section. Elder brother Robert and Peter Russell were playing darts a few feet away.

Landlord Allan Talbot pottered away behind the bar, beer gut barely held in check by an over-ornate leather belt sporting a macho bull's head for a buckle to remind him of a holiday in Spain four years ago. Ex-RAF, in some menial capacity, he betrayed a fidgety impatience to receive payment while customers counted out their loose change. Only two things commanded his undivided attention – ex RAF officers and the very rich. The only drawback was that everybody else tended to be ignored at such times and his wife Christine and their two daughters had to cover for him.

Thursday night tended to be a highlight of the week for the locals lads, with the prospect of only one dreary day standing between them and the weekend. Apart from several middle-aged barflies propping up the bar, the only older habitués were Harry Fenwick holding an ostentatiously loud conversation with neighbouring farmer Jack Slingsby. As Richard came to his end, he obnoxiously butted in.

"Been' playin' their reserves, have you?" Harry's too loud voice almost echoed off the four walls of the bar.

"Why not come along an' see for yourself?" retorted Paul.

"Got better things to do on a Saturday afternoon," said Harry.

"So I've heard," muttered Robert under his breath to Peter Russell, making a surreptitious "wanker" gesture, out of Harry's sight, to emphasise the point. Peter stifled a guffaw.

"Well, you've had a good innings, lads," boomed Harry in that upbeat tone he assumed to sound patronising. He ambled forward and placed aggressively friendly meaty hands on Chris and Richard's shoulders. "I'll give ya' that. But it's Norbury this weekend, I've heard. They're fuckin' big twats, an' they can play a bit, too! Come this Saturday. ya' won't know what's hit ya'!"

Something in the strange smile on Robert's face perturbed Harry.

A large market town like Norbury had an unfair advantage over a village like Thormanton in its bottomless pool of talent. The local comprehensive school boasted an impressive annual haul of trophies to its name, so each year's Norbury side had a strong vein of already-fostered team spirit pulsing through it. Prior encounters with Thormanton were so embarrassingly one-sided that many confessed to losing count of their goals scored. Despite Thormanton's recent form, it was obvious from the studied nonchalance of their pre-match warm up that Norbury viewed this as little more than a formality.

Colin studied his old team mates closely as they went through the motions of limbering up pre match. A newcomer would have perceived nothing. But Colin noted the cocky confidence in their new prouder demeanour and the visible eagerness to commence playing. Previously, as one of their number, Colin had been all too aware that they viewed a game against Norbury – even on their own turf – with all the enthusiasm of a condemned prisoner marching to the electric chair. This newfound arrogance was disconcerting. A few of them were noticeably "peacocking" with ostentatious new hair styles and wardrobe. Some of it verged on the tackiness often condescendingly ascribed to previously lower class lottery winners.

With hindsight, one isolated incident stands out, epitomising when an individual or unit has progressed from one state to a higher one. It was not the crunching tackles that felled the Norbury players like so much timber. It was not the sight of Sammy Patterson – last week's aberration still fresh in his mind – flinging himself about the box, like a frenzied acrobat, with scant heed for his personal safety as he dived at the oncoming feet of brutish thick-thighed Norbury forwards. It wasn't even the two goals they scored – Emma ghosting past the opposing full back far too easily. Her cross was cut back and Steven reacted half a yard ahead of everyone else to sidefoot in the second midway after the interval. The officials proved not to be of the highest standards and, with the luck that often characterises the successful, Paul Myers gathered a forward kick by Robert on his chest and controlled it with his arm before blasting it into the roof of the net for the third. Norbury's pleas fell on deaf ears and the Referee allowed it, and for the remainder of the game, they staggered about like confused actors improvising in an unfamiliar role.

No, none of these priceless moments stuck in Kevin's mind as being significant. The precise moment was seventy three minutes into the match when he confidently trapped the ball near the touchline and looked up to see Colin steaming in towards him, eyes gleaming with frustrated rage, for a tackle. Kevin remained stock still on the ball, deliberately making himself an easy target, as his old school comrade drew closer. Then, with a deft timing and grace that would have done justice to an old time silent screen comedian, Kevin adeptly backheeled the ball and turned smartly on his axis to nimbly evade the tackle. Colin connected with thin air, but, unable to arrest his momentum, continued hurtling ever forward until he tripped over his own feet. Emma saw what was coming with all the horrified fascination of witnessing a car accident.

Colin pitched forward flat onto his face into a steaming cow pat recently deposited there by the few cattle grazing nearby. Dazed, as much by the impudence of Kevin's skill as the impact, it took Colin several moments to grasp what he had plunged into. Aghast, he spat the excrement out of his mouth and rubbed his face clean with an almost epileptic fury.

Tears streaming down his ruddy face, Robert Swales brayed with laughter several hours later. "Christ! Now he really is full o' shit!"

"Fuckin' Colin certainly knows how to pick a winner, don't he!" sneered Steven.

"Serves the twassock right!" snarled Sammy.

"Twassock?" echoed Steven. "Don't tha' mean "wassock"

"No," added Sammy. "Twassock! Same as a "twanker"!"

More guffaws ensued. "Well," conceded Robert. "He's a cunt o' some sort!"

"When's t'return game at their place?" piped up Steven.

"Last match, innit?" replied Sammy. Kevin nodded. "The climax of the season!"

"Tha' know's what a climax is, don't ya' Steven?" Robert's eyes sparkled with malicious amusement. Once the shock of their initiation into Rosemary's world subsided, old rivilaries and cliques had soon resumed. "It's that bit just after she yawns an' looks at her watch."

In spite of the chorus of mocking laughter, Steven was cocksure enough after recent events to preen. "Fuck off! I've had no complaints."

Rosemary's voice was as slow and sensual as syrup – slow and sensual as the baby oil Kevin rubbed into her inner thighs. Her magnificent body glistened like that of some fabulous exotic goddess. He looked up at Robert Swales and could see that he was engrossed in the sight as much as he.

The woman lay on her front on a towel on her bed. Her eyelids were closed and her face was relaxed and dreamy, but she was still awake. Rosemary was entirely naked, as indeed were the four lads. Long familiarity with each other's bodies had robbed them of any hesitancy or sheepishness. Fucking the same woman, frequently at the same time, had had a curious bonding process on the lads.

Steven and Robert were stood at one side of her, Kevin and Sammy at the other. Generous portions of baby oil were squirted onto their rough hands and liberally smeared onto Rosemary's body. At her urgings, their rubbed the viscous liquid into the very pores of her skin. The muscles and sinews of her honed body stood out in arousing relief.

Fumbling and clumsy at first, the boys gradually got the hang of it and began to slowly knead her soft flesh in elaborate patterns. A covert glance at his colleagues showed Kevin that they were sporting erections as prominent as his.

"We'll make a Yorkshire woman of ya' yet, Rosemary," chipped in Robert.

"I think I've had quite enough Yorkshire in me for a while," Rosemary responded, smiling sweetly.

Kevin's hands lingered longer than they needed to kneading Rosemary's buttocks. A tremor of illicit excitement shivered through his body. The memory of him buggering her remained unusually vivid, considering all that had happened since. "I'll be altering our formation for next week's match. Steven, I want you to drop back deep into midfield."

Steven's smile froze. "Will I fuck!"

"What?"

"I'm up front or I don't play," Steven bristled. "Who's scoring all our goals?"

"Big fucking deal," Sammy shot back. "I must have let only one goal in during three hundred and sixty minutes!"

"No offense, Sammy, but a blind, crippled hunchback could keep goal behind our defence. And I'm slogging my guts out up front!"

Kevin stood his ground and coldly folded his arms across his broad chest. "The answer's very simple, Steven. My way or the highway! And you know what that means. Kiss goodbye to your film career!" His coldly glabrous expression swept the room as he saw he had everyone's attention. "The same goes for all of you! One man rocks the boat, no more trips around the bay."

A shock of fear. He meant it. The unthinkable had been spoken.

"I thought we were sloppy at defending corners today. If Sammy hadn't been on his toes, we'd've paid for it! So we'll be practising new routines for defending set pieces this Tuesday and Thursday," said Kevin.

A discreet cough from Rosemary alerted the four lads that they were neglecting their attentions to her body. There was a brief embarassed silence. The low rumble of some vehicle – larger than a car but not a tractor – slowly drawing up on the road outside, then slowly pulling away barely registered.

"All finished are we, ladies?" Rosemary's imperious tones rendered their bickering like a nanny with a group of fractious toddlers. She rolled over onto her back and closed her eyes to forestall further conflict. "Now, do my front."

Chapter Seventeen

"Going my way?"

Emma felt a frission of tension tickle the nape of her neck when her eyes had locked with Rosemary's during the Norbury match. She was all too aware of how red her cheeks were burning and couldn't control the impulse to look away immediately. The girl hadn't felt this way since she caught her first glimpse of secondary school crush Dave in the queue for dinner three years ago.

Emma cast covert glances at the woman throughout the game. She surveyed the on field action with the despotic cool of some fabulous Roman Empress. The younger girl reckoned Rosemary was in her mid thirties and immaculately dressed and coiffed. Her brunette bell of fine soft hair shone in the afternoon sun. The woman's exotic scarlet lipstick made her full mouth plumply sensual and slightly mocking. The long, slender legs of a professional dancer were encased in tight leather trousers and boots while a pair of voluptuous breasts strained against a crisp white business shirt and navy blue jacket.

The woman's expression of interest in the game seemed real. Emma couldn't imagine such a fantastic creature taking a genuine fascination in something as dull and plebeian as a game of amateur football. She hadn't a clue who this exotic being was and was desperately curious to learn about her. Emma had not seen her around before and found it impossible to place her among the drab fashions of a locality that seemed to have gone to seed somewhere around the mid seventies.

On one occasion, in the frenzied aftermath of the second Thormanton goal, Emma sneaked a peek at the woman only to nearly whither in embarrassment on the spot as she realised Rosemary was gazing directly at her. Emma's first impulse was to avert her face, but something in the teasingly upturned corners of her appraising lips halted her. Emma felt almost mesmerised by the woman's heavily lidded eyes. It was as if they were penetrating to the very core of her soul. Although she squirmed slightly, Emma felt unabashed by the experience and even found it giving her a second wind to complete the ninety minutes on a relative high.

Emma was further intrigued to see her team mates chatting animatedly to the stranger as if already well-acquainted with her, to judge from their easy, if somewhat bashful, familiarity. Even Sammy, her own elder brother! How and when had he met her? She seemed utterly remote from his usual social strata. However, she saw the advantage and seized her opportunity. Discreetly edging to her brothers' side as he talked coyly to the woman, she coughed self-deprecatingly and nudged his arm.

"Oh, Rosemary, this is..." began her brother.

"The famous Emma!" came the unexpected reply. Emma felt ten feet tall. The woman was scanning the girl's face in a curiously triangular manner, from left, to right, and finally to her lips.

Something about the woman's eyes and their hooded, interrogative stare seemed to strip Emma bare and hold her innermost secrets for everybody to read. Somehow, she found her voice.

"That's right."

"I've heard so much about you from Sammy and Kevin." The woman regally extended her hand and took Emma's limp fingers in a firm, comforting grip. "We girls must really get together sometime."

She briskly bid them farewell and turned smartly on her heels, leaving an awe-struck Emma in her resplendent wake. A cheery wave, and she sped off in her Porsche.

The memory of her closeness and voice kept Emma going throughout the long, dreary week working behind the counter at a newsagent in Salton. From time to time, she fancied she might have caught a glimpse of the woman strolling down the streets. Lying awake at night, Emma pondered if that deep tan was all-over and how natural it was. She was convinced she had caught a hint of a tattoo below the nape of her neck. Emma tried to emulate the woman's cat-like walk in her full length bedroom mirror.

How did Sammy know her? He had kept suspiciously quiet about where he went to on Sundays, but Emma was not fooled by the nondescript air he cultivated whenever he staggered back home around seven in the evening. Her parents seemed to miss it, but Emma sensed the aura he was giving off like an electric fence.

Saturday saw Thormanton home versus Denbymoorside for the return fixture. Emma gave a decent account of herself on the left wing but was continuously scanning the touchline for the woman.

Denbymoorside gave an indication of how far they had progressed since the start of the season. Kevin was particularly pleased with the final six-nil margin. After the earlier seven-nought thrashing, this was settling old scores with a vengeance. Emma noted the changes in Kevin. There was a cocky confidence as he strode about the pitch with a spring in his step that Emma found attractive. As long as he was in charge, she felt safe and confident that the team would endure. He was the confident leader who guide her down the unknown path to success. Before, he seemed dowdy and hesitant – easy to ignore. Now he radiated self-assurance and Emma felt comfortable in his shadow.

For all that, Emma still felt left out amid the general jubilation and backslapping in the changing room afterwards. Partly it was the fact she had to change and shower separately but mostly it was the sense of not being party to some secret the lads shared. Somewhat forlornly, she set off on the half mile trek back home.

Emma sensed, rather than heard, the Porsche draw up alongside her, as smooth as a whisper. Rosemary wound the automatic window down.

"Going my way?"

Booking Wednesday off work had been blessedly easy – late October was not a time for mass holidays. The weather was surprisingly mild for mid Autumn, even sporadically sunny, and Emma felt overdressed in denim jeans and heavy woollens and somewhat plain and cloddish compared to Rosemary when the woman picked her up on the outskirts of Thormanton. She was clad in a stylish roll neck black sweater that tantalisingly clung over bra-less breasts, and a long blue skirt slit along the leg. She lounged in the driver's seat of her Porsche and beckoned Emma into its mysterious depths with an airily permissive hand. A wicker basket enticingly packed with wine bottles and Tupperware containers crammed with food filled the back seat.

Emma had recommended an area on the moors several miles away from the village as her family had picnicked there many times before. From the ordered, almost suburbanised, green and brown fields around Thormanton, the harsh rattle of a cattle grid vibrating the Porsche's tyres heralded an abrupt change of scenery. Bleak expanses of purple heather stretched monotonously into the shimmering distance, like some alien planetscape. Isolated hamlet villages nestled uneasily amid the steeply rolling hills like leeches on the hide of some vast prehistoric beast.

Rosemary parked the Porsche in a convenient lay-by and she and Emma carried the hamper to a short distance away. Emma laid out the tartan travelling blanket at a point she knew from prior visits afforded them the best view.

They gaily chatted away as they made short work of the sandwiches. Rosemary sprawled out elegantly on the blanket like some fabulous jungle cat while Emma squatted awkwardly on her haunches.

Emma was explaining the significance of some fluted limestone shafts close by. "They're called "the Buttertubs". Some folk say it's because they look like butter tubs farmers used to deliver to grocers. Others say that it's because farmers on their way to market used to hang stuff too heavy to carry over the edge. Then, they'd collect them on the way back."

"You're lucky to live somewhere as idyllic as this, Emma" said Rosemary.

"I suppose so." Emma sighed with a heavy patience.

"But you'd rather have some fun." Rosemary sensually chewed on a plump strawberry.

"In my worst nightmares, I'm stuck here for the rest of my life."

"You must have friends here?"

Emma had been having this conversation with herself for a long time now. "Yes, but all they go on about are lads and their friends' weddings and babies. They can't wait to get married." Secretly, Emma might not have minded so much if the "lads" subjected to their fantasies were not such a motley assortment of rat-faced, chubbily-built yokels.

"As if that'll solve all their problems," said Rosemary, almost wistfully.

Emma leaned forward. "Ever been married, or engaged, Rosemary?"

"Sort of. Close, but no cigar. I've nothing against it as an institution. It's when people use it for reasons it wasn't meant to be for...."

"What do you mean?"

"When people use it as a respectable cover for all kinda' vices. Some people think of domesticity as something boring enough to hide all sort'a dark....." Rosemary's voice tailed off as her attention was caught by a beige sports car racing along the road, snaking away like a grey thread in the distance. "That car?"

Emma squinted into the sunlight. "Oh, that'll be Malcolm Bradshaw. His dad owns a printing business near Whitby."

Rosemary studied the car. "Let me guess. A bit of a poseur?"

Emma giggled. "Forty two inch waist and he wears tight leather trousers at our local."

The two chuckled conspiratorially. After further gossip and bitchy observations on various other locals, they rose to their feet to walk off the stodginess of the meal. Inevitably, their talk turned to the football team.

"I'm glad we're doing well, but I feel so left out," Emma conceded. "I was thinking of dropping out."

"All girls together!"

"Sammy never liked me hanging around him at school. I don't see why they can't let me tag along to these get-togethers they have on Sunday."

Rosemary's right hand tenderly brushed Emma's shoulder. She was growing increasingly tactile with the younger girl, constantly leaning in to emphasise her point. "Keeps you in trim, in nothing else, Emma."

"Tell me about it. I hope I'm in as good a shape as you are when I'm your age, Rosemary."

"My age?" echoed Rosemary, mock offended.

Emma squirmed. "You know what I mean."

"Like everything else, it's something you have to work at. You should see my High school photo, Emma. Geeky's not the word!"

Emma somehow found the courage to ask the question she feared would rend their friendship asunder. But it was a feature of life that constantly bombarded her from all angles in the trashy magazines she devoured, and something about Rosemary suggested a kinship with that world.

"Rosemary, have you ever..you know?" Emma gestured around her own pert breasts.

"Had surgery? Silicone implants?" Rosemary's tones were mock-imperious, as if offended by a mere underling. For a ghastly moment, Emma worried she had crossed a line from which there was no turning back. However, the woman's full sensual lips creased into an elusively mocking smile. "That would be telling." She echoed Emma's gesture over her own magnificent breasts. "However, they are genuine! That's something of a rarity in my business."

Rosemary could see she had Emma hooked and could reel her in at her leisure.

"Your business?"

Chapter Eighteen

The Norbury and District Young Farmers Association was holding a barbecue at a cleaned out cattle shed at Hagg farm. Robert Swales had no idea who owned the farm but it was on the road between Wellthorpe and Denbymoorside. Driving there, it was easy to find due to its unnaturally illuminated state. After a bone-jarring crawl down a rutted farm track, Rob and his brothers pulled up in their car in the grass paddock used as a temporary park, and clambered out.

Rob never cared much for the Young Farmers Association. His Father had coerced him into joining but, on the three occasions he had attended their socials, he had felt marginalised and patronised. Few had taken time to talk to him, and then only from a sense of duty. Repelled by the upper middle class snobbery he felt, he had allowed his membership to lapse, and the experience had faded to less than a memory.

But everyone was welcome to attend the barbecue as long as they paid the ten pound entrance fee. Barbecue was a misleading term. There was no open-air roast. It was merely a disco dance or rave in an farmer's shed. A temporary bar had been set up in one corner while black-suited bouncers stood sentinel on the door. Robert gave them two twenty pound notes that would cover him and his two brothers. As the bouncer fumbled for change, Rob fretted impatiently.

"Hurry up, man! A man could die o' thirst out here!"

"What's yer' hurry?"

Change received, the brothers strolled inside. Settings may change but the *mise-en-scene* of local dances remained depressingly the same. Girls dressed to kill dominated the dance floor while the men hovered on the fringes, drinks in hand, predatory vultures sizing up a warm of peacocks but too scared to pounce.

Rob was relieved to see some other Thormanton lads scattered about. It might come in handy if it came to a fight with a pack of lads from another district – as occasionally occurred at other dances he'd been to. His gaze took in Kevin propping up the bar. Colin Adkins was stood behind him. They greeted each other with a wary formality.

"Now then," rumbled Colin. "Heard you're through to t'semi finals."

Thormanton had indeed waltzed past Thornton Westborough at a canter four–nil in the first round of the league cup the previous Saturday.

"Aye," answered Kevin. "Heard you beat Wellthorpe."

"Aye. Got Salton in our semi."

"Least it's not you dirty fouling twats." A spotty, rat-faced youth at Colin's shoulder butted in sourly. It took Kevin a moment to recognise the Captain of rivals Norbury Town out of his football kit.

"Who's dirty?" retorted Kevin.

"What else do you call it? You dive in for every tackle wi' yer' studs up," moaned the youth. "We can't go up for a header without meeting your elbows on the way down. It's like playing the fuckin' SAS on a suicide mission!"

"I heard Thornton Westborough had trouble raising a team to play you," added Colin. "Suddenly, everyone remembered their long-lost Uncle George and Auntie Shirley from Australia wor' visiting them that weekend."

Kevin strode away from them feeling a good foot taller. "Mebbe you're not as good as you think you are," he left as a parting shot.

Kevin strolled over to where Steven and Nick were standing on the rim of the dance floor eyeing up the talent on offer. Steven sipped at his pint of bitter and sighed at one particularly well-upholstered fake blonde cutting loose around a pile of handbags. "Looks like I'll be walking home tonight with a permanent erection screaming for mercy!" he brooded.

Nick perked up and nudged Kevin's elbow to indicate he should follow his gaze to the entrance. "Not necessarily."

Standing uncertainly in the open doorway was Keeley-Anne in a low cut shirt and short skirt and two girl friends. The latter two might have been specially selected by Keeley-Anne for their relative plainness to set off her own impish attractiveness. Her cats green eyes locked with Kevin's. The tension between them as an almost tangible presence.

It took nearly twenty minutes for the girls to screw up their courage to approach Kevin. Both parties maintained a tight, surface politeness.

"How ya' doin'" ventured Kevin.

"Alright," Keeley-Anne sucked provocatively on her drink straw. "Heard your team's doin' okay." She had never betrayed much interest before when Kevin had tried to drag her along to watch him play.

Kevin smirked enigmatically. If only she knew. "Get you a drink in?" he offered.

"If you want," replied Keeley-Anne. Kevin nodded at the dance floor. Nick and Steven had already paired up with the other two girls.

Keeley-Anne liked Lady Gaga, so Kevin knew there was a more than even chance of her agreeing to dance along with the track as it segued in from the preceding one. They fell into the old routines very quickly and Kevin felt an almost nostalgic pang for old times when they had previously dated. All the same, although they had enacted these rituals many times before, Kevin sensed a subtle difference and he wondered what it was. Then, as she leaned towards him in the lull between tracks, the alienness of this posture in Keeley-Anne alerted him to what it was. His body language was aloof and erect and she was trying to eagerly encroach into his body space. The power balance had shifted on its axis.

"Haven't seen you around for a while, Kev," she asked. "What you been doing?"

"This an' that." Again, that enigmatic smile. He was aware of his newfound power. Keeley-Anne could not possibly suspect what was boiling behind his bland countenance. Let her do all the work.

"How's Peter?" he couldn't help asking.

"Me an' Peter agreed to give each other a bit more room,"

Kevin smiled knowingly. "He's been posted abroad, then."

It was a direct hit. She squirmed slightly under his level gaze. Her lips tightened in irritation. Then, the next track blasted in and they resumed gyrating.

Robert had got a round in drinks in for himself and his brothers when he sensed, rather than saw, Colin and the Norbury Captain talking to Harry Fenwick in the limbo between the bar and the dance floor. Harry, inevitably, was coming to the end of a dirty joke.

"...so he gets his cock out and starts wanking off on her tits. The whore looks up and screams "Oy, you didn't pay to do that. And he says "Don't worry. I'm just browsing!"" and he mimed a jerk-off gesture to stress the punchline.

Robert could not resist it. He had long suspected that Colin regarded himself as a cut above the rest and he despised him for it. "Now, then, Judas!" he boomed.

"Ignore this ignorant twat, Col," said Harry as the trio swung round to acknowledge him. Harry Fenwick was one of those men who contrive to look sleazy and seedy no matter how immaculate his grooming. "Some of us haven't forgotten how to be sociable."

"It's not like you lot have missed me," added Colin.

"Aye!" beamed Rob. "Another win last weekend. I'm starting to lose count. Heard you could only draw at Salton."

"Their second goal wor' miles offside," grumbled the Norbury captain.

"Tough titty," sneered Rob. "That means we've just about caught up wi' you wassocks!"

The Norbury Captain turned his back on Robert. "An' they say cheats never prosper."

"My old man used to watch Leeds United years ago when Don Revie wor' their Manager," said Robert. "Everyone whined and bitched about what a dirty bunch o' cunts they wor'. An' what happens? Nowadays, everyone says they wor' t'best English team there ever was! Better than Man U' an' Liverpool!"

"Your point being?" said Colin.

"Pardon us for not knowing our places," Rob laughed. "It's just we thought we thought we'd like to win summat' other than the Fair Play Trophy this years." Their annual presentation at the League's buffet had become a standing joke in the area.

With that, Rob turned his back on them and sauntered off singing mockingly. "You've either got, or you haven't got, style!"

"Style, me arse!" jeered the Norbury Captain. "Dirty twats kick anything that moves."

A strange, secretive smile disfigured Harry's face. "You don't know how dirty."

Kevin had successfully isolated Keeley-Anne from her two friends – who seemed more engrossed in Nick and Steven anyway – and ushered her towards the door. As the attendant on the front table stamped their hands with a "pass-out" to prevent freeloaders gaining access, Kevin looked up as a familiar slender shadow fell across him and Keeley-Anne.

"Hi, Kevin. She looks pretty!"

Kevin preened under Rosemary's appreciative stare and draped a proprietorial arm around Keeley-Anne's shoulders. The American woman was dressed to kill in tight leather trousers that seemed spray-painted onto her long legs and taut buttocks. The dark blouson looked suspiciously colour co-ordinated to her trousers and the make-up accentuated the cat-like set of her sparkling eyes. The ensemble was so striking that Kevin failed to note an identically-clad figure hovering uncertainly by her side.

"Hullo, Kevin," mumbled Emma. The younger girl had somehow mutated into an embryonic twin of Rosemary. Her mousey bell of brown hair had been cunningly dyed to match the artificial lustre of the American woman. The subtle sheen of make-up had been applied to make Emma a virtual mirror image of her escort. It was only familiarity with Emma's normal complexion that made Kevin realise how much Rosemary normally put on her own face.

Emma's normally drab exterior had been a blank canvas for Rosemary to mould into her own image. Despite differences in build, height and face, the end result was eerily similar.

Gazing rapt at their oddly alien likeness, Kevin felt unusually aroused and felt a fleeting whim to fantasise what they might look liked naked alongside one another. He was vaguely aware of an unusually nervous Keeley-Anne snuggling up into his waist, hardening his already-stiffened penis even further. She virtually pulled him away. "See you later," said Kevin as a parting shot. "I think."

The spectacle of the two females proved a godsend for Kevin in coercing her into the murk of a nearby straw shed. He cupped her face in both his hands in a pose he had learned from his most recent performance for Rosemary, and savagely kissed Keeley-Anne full on the mouth. Awkward at first, she eventually responded and uncertainly followed suit by probing his mouth with her moist tongue. For a few moments, she dared to match him every step of the way in lustful hunger. Kevin's expert hands took their cue to stroke her pert young breast. A shudder of illicit pleasure earthquaked her body to the core of its foundations.

Kevin's relentlessly questing fingers crammed down her open cleavage and fondled with the yielding mound of flesh nestling in her upholstered bra. He trapped the erect nipple between two fingers and ran it between them. Her breath came in increased gasps. Any moment now, she would collapse and tumble head first into the abyss he was coaxing her towards.

The bitch would finally be his. Once, she had held herself aloof and apart from his hesitant persona. Now, she was experiencing something akin to those football sides who had been pummelled into shocked submission by Thormanton F.C. She had complacently agreed to a dance and a half-hearted necking session thinking she would be in control of the situation as before. Now, she was overwhelmed by the tidal wave of dark sensuality threatening to engulf her. Like anyone in way over

their head, Keeley-Anne physically panicked.

"No!" She pulled apart with an angry jerk.

Kevin's face darkened with fury. He wasn't in the mood for this. His voice was ominously calm and level, as if emphasising how much he'd prefer to bawl her out. A confident smile lazily disfigured his features. "Who are you trying to kid?"

Without waiting for permission, he swept her up in his arms and French-kissed her hungrily, his free hand somehow managing to undo her buttons and expose a pale breast. Kevin could almost feel her body on the verge of responding.

With a whimper, Keeley-Anne tugged herself away and backed into a corner. She hastily tucked her breast away and refastened her buttons. "I said no!"

"Your body says summat' else."

Keeley-Anne straightened her clothing. "I'd like to go back inside, please." Before, she would have said it coldly. Now, there was a tremor in her voice.

Kevin's hooded gaze did not flinch. "C'mon! If your nipples wor' any harder, they'd pop!"

"What's gotten' into you? You were never like this before."

Kevin impassively folded his arms. "Just because squaddie's been posted abroad, am I supposed to be grateful for a few crumbs from his table. If he's that fuckin' ace, why don't you stay faithful to him?"

Keeley-Anne's eyes were glistening. "If that's your attitude, I'd rather I never see you again!"

"I'm not in the fuckin' mood for this, bitch!" It had sounded okay when Rosemary had given him the lines to memorise for her shoots, and Kevin had felt curious to see how they would work in real life.

Keeley-Anne opened her mouth to protest but Kevin forestalled her by ramming his squirming tongue down her pallet and virtually devouring her face. His free hand brutally gathered up the shivering mound of flesh that was her right breast and pinched the nipple. He ran his other hand, that was holding her in his grasp, over the gap between her buttocks and was satisfied to see her body quiver in arousal.

Kevin wrenched backwards from Keeley-Anne as if from a physical blow. The girl's eyes were startling white saucers as humiliation gave way to sudden shock. She wriggled free of his trembling hands and slapped him hard across the face. Turning on her heels, she stormed off, the echo of her sobs hanging in the air.

The slap cleared Kevin's head.

Gathering his wits, Kevin waited a couple of minutes before straightening his clothes and lumbering back to the dance hall. Having satisfied the minder on the door with his "pass-out", he apprehensively paused on the threshold and surveyed the inside.

Keeley-Anne and her two friends were nowhere to be seen and the sight of Nick and Steven picking their way across the dance floor to the bar in ill humour told its own story. He ventured half-heartedly to join them at the bar but the snarling response from Steven discouraged him. "Thank's a fuckin' bunch! Whaddya' say to her?"

The two lads stomped off disgustedly to order their drinks. At a loose end, Kevin wandered back to the fringes of the dance floor. Two slender figures artfully clad in black dominated the arena, reducing those around them to lumpen bit-part players. The accelerating beat of the frenzied electro-dance track impelled them into a blur of sweaty limbs flailing about. The music changed to some saccharine boy-band ballad and Emma and Rosemary provocatively snuggled up against each other and elegantly marched off the floor – like prima ballerinas from a stage. The sea of blank-eyed girl dancers around them parted like the Red Sea to let them pass.

On impulse, Kevin's eyes caught Sammy stood alone, eyes pensive under a crude fringe, the expression not happy. He regarded the girls every step of their trek back to the bar. Something was visibly gnawing at him. Disquiet pinched the corner of his disapproving lips.

Oblivious to his feelings, Colin and Harry Fenwick ambled bumptiously over to the lad. "Your Emma look's very sexy tonight, Sammy," boomed Colin. "I hardly recognised her."

Sammy hardly turned to acknowledge him. He grunted under his breath.

"Well," said Harry, an edge to his voice. "She's been taught by a pro."

Sammy glared daggers at him. "What was that?"

Harry's eyes narrowed meaningfully. "Wanna' watch yoursen', Samuel. Looks like your little sister might be picking up some bad habits. An' hanging out with the wrong kind o' people."

"What the fuck's that supposed ta' mean?" Sammy's fury carried clearly over the noise of the music.

For answer, Harry sauntered off laughing to himself. Sammy glared daggers at his retreating back, his insides knotted in turmoil. In the background, Kevin's mind was racing. There could be no mistaking the undertone to the man's mockery. Could he know? He made the link between Emma and Rosemary. Harry was an avid consumer, nay, devourer of hard-core pornography. Harry cared little for the football team but was familiar enough with their previous ineptitude to put two and two together regarding Thormanton's recent run of victories. What happened next confirmed Kevin's worst fears.

A flurry of violent activity at the bar caught Kevin's eye. Two burly Bouncers were barging though the crows to forcibly separate Steven and Harry who were taking wild swings at each other. The drinkers around them cleared the area as errant sprays of spilled lager drenched the floor. Kevin had never seen such naked hatred in Steven's normally bland face.

"You dirty bastard!" spat Steven.

"Alright! Alright!" the first Bouncer interceded. "Pack it in! What's your problem?"

"What's up whi' you?" jeered Harry. "Can't ya' take a joke?"

"Funny fucking joke!" echoed Steven.

"What happened?" asked the Head Bouncer.

"Little twat just set about me," said Harry, arms apart in a gesture of injured innocence.

"Dirty fucker felt up my arse," exclaimed Steven. "Fuckin' turdburglar!"

"Well, whatever," butted in the Bouncer. "Shake hands and there's an end to it, or we'll have to ask you to leave."

Steven deliberately withheld his hand from Harry's mockingly outstretched arm. He sullenly averted his eyes.

"Do as he says, Steve!" Rosemary's clipped tone sliced through the tension like a hot knife.

Steven's eyes momentarily met hers, and, for an instant, there was something in the woman's that utterly defeated him. He morosely offered his right hand with ill grace to Harry who half-heartedly shook it. The lad picked up his pint of lager and moodily trooped off with Nick.

As the crowd around them dispersed in dribs and drabs, Harry returned Rosemary's level gaze. "You've got him well-trained, if you don't mind me saying."

Rosemary's mock-sweet smile was cold enough to chill the blood. A look of mutual understanding crossed between them. Harry was the first to look away and he sloped off to rejoin Colin, and the Norbury Captain at the bar. Rosemary serenely returned to Emma's side. Kevin, like a satellite unmoored from its orbit, stood isolated and adrift in the melee.

Chapter Nineteen

"The twat knows!"

Kevin leaned urgently across the small table while Rosemary sat back elegantly in a comfortable armchair in the coffee bar at a bookshop. It was a suitably incognito venue for what was turning into a crisis meeting. For the moment, her rented house (which she mostly inhabited at weekends) was out of the question. Instead, an email between the two of them had sent Kevin catching a train into the city and following directions to a major book shop in the shopping centre. Many of the shelves in the DVD and CD sections were bare, for within four weeks of their conversation, the shop would be summarily closed down, along with its sister branches in other towns and cities, as the credit crunch claimed yet another victim.

"You're sure of this, Kevin?" Rosemary's languid purr held the mildest of curiosity.

"The cunt's been dropping hints in t'pub all week." Kevin had grown accustomed to Harry Fenwick's lascivious nature and had long regarded it as part of the furniture of working on the farm. In recent weeks, he had developed a critical distance towards it, seeing clearly how much it betrayed the older man's limited outlook on matters of the flesh. He could also feel some sympathy for

Tom's barely perceptible squirming in embarrassment at Harry's more vulgar pronouncements.

But, ever since the fateful barn dance, Harry's smutty jesting had acquired a new, dangerous tone. He was no longer dropping them into the conversation to impress a lad he still thought of as apparently naive to gain a cheap laugh. Now, he was lobbing them calculatedly to test Kevin's responses.

A news article on a suspected celebrity AIDS case had occasioned a telling remark of "Gotta be careful of where you're ramming ol' Percy these days. 'specially if you're sharing her wi' a lot of other blokes!" Another headline on a call–girl scandal involving a senior politician had provoked an enigmatic taunt of "Well, there's whores and there's whores." Harry had fixed Kevin with a challenging glare before returning to his pint.

"Has he told you?" she inquired.

"Not in so many words. But he's bin' dropping not so subtle hints in t'pub."

"Who is this guy again?"

Kevin related a short history of Harry Fenwick. "It's cos' he's always visiting this picture palace for wankers in York that he coulda' found out. The sort of film club that doesn't show Ingmar Bergman seasons. If not, he must've a library full o' DVD's. God knows, he's always braggin' about how he can get his hands on the real hard stuff."

"Might be harmless. Whaddya' think he wants?"

"Fuck knows!" In truth, Kevin was alarmed to the core that an outsider had rumbled their arrangement, and the consequences that might ensue, not least that it could all end.

Rosemary's eyes grew cold and searching. "Married man, you say?"

"Aye," answered Kevin. "Not that it makes much difference. I've heard one or two o' locals say he always cottoned on wi' another woman elsewhere."

"It figures." An enigmatic smile. "They're always the worst."

Panic made Kevin blurt out what he later regarded as superfluous information to fill the nervous silences between their talk. "Mind, I've heard if his Missus' ever found out, she'd divorce him and he'd risk losing his share o' t'farm."

Rosemary thoughtfully sipped her latte, as if savouring the flavour. Kevin hadn't the appetite for his own foamy, tall cappuccino. "So, are we gonna do owt'. Rosemary?"

Rosemary drained her drink before replying. "Just make sure what he knows about us. Then, tell him I'll see him at ten p.m. this Saturday night, at my place. Call around yourself an hour later, Kevin. I should be finished by then."

"Why? What're gonna' do?"

Rosemary gracefully waved a hand to attract the attention of a hovering waitress. "Satisfy his show business ambitions. Up to a point. Fancy a refill?"

★ ★ ★

It was all due, in part, to his fourteen year old son's desire to drop his childish hangovers and make a small profit into the bargain. Wellthorpe village held a car boot sale every Sunday in a grass field rented out behind their village hall. Harry Fenwick's eldest son Michael had noticed his old toy cars and tractors gathering dust in a cardboard box in the attic and, feeling they were serving no useful purpose and wanting to save up to buy a motorcycle like he'd seen Kevin riding, asked if there was any place he could sell them. His Mother had seen a temporary sign on the road near Denbymoorside advertising the monthly sales every Sunday, made inquiries, and had dragooned her reluctant husband to accompany Michael, bristling with the newfound energy of entrepreneurship, while he proudly displayed his modest wares. Harry had sat patiently reading the Farmer's Weekly to while away the long hours spent watching passers-by indifferently inspect the toys only to stroll on with a shrug of their shoulders. He had managed to chat for several minutes with some old acquaintances he had bumped into, but the final day's tally of a little over ten pounds had seen them operating at a loss when the fee paid for hiring space at the sale was taken into consideration. Neither seemed too deflated, however. Michael was moderately satisfied to have earnt anything from something he regarded as an embarrassing reminder of bygone days, and Harry had found his interest piqued by what he had witnessed in passing on the road there and back.

The route to Wellthorpe meant passing Rosemary's rented house. Harry had spotted Kevin's motorcycle in the yard straight away, and recognised Peter Russell and John Swales stood idly outside. The striking, tanned woman in her 20's he did not identify, but something about her tantalised his memory. On the way back, Nick Cammack and Sammy Patterson were in the yard, mounting their bikes and waving goodbye to a stylishly dressed brunette woman who air kissed them by way of farewell.

The identity of the first woman gnawed at his brain for the next three days until he idly consulted his program for the upcoming season at his porn cinema, and her face beamed out at him from one of the film posters. Harry had almost burst out laughing. At first, he'd dismissed it as too wild a theory. Coincidence, surely?

The following Sunday, he had driven his pick-up truck down the same road on a whim. What he saw as he slowed to get a good look at Rosemary's front drive nearly made his eyes pop out of his head on stalks. The girl performer he knew only as Claudia Climax, but Kevin called Theresa, was stood outside the front porch smoking and chatting animatedly to Robert Swales and Chris Manby.

One girl resembling a porn star could be coincidental. Two, however, struck Harry as something else. He accelerated away before anyone spotted him. The night that Kevin, Steven, Sammy and Robert had been massaging Rosemary, he had slowly driven past in his pick-up, noted their bikes in her drive, the upstairs light on, and driven off, a lascivious smile disfiguring his face.

From that point on, one thought dominated him. Some offhand inquiries around the pub made him ascertain that the lads in the football team were congregating for secret meetings at some unspecified location on Sundays, and that Emma had definitely never been invited. He vaguely knew the farmer who owned the rented property and phoned him up on the pretext of inquiring on behalf of someone who wished to live there. From the ensuing conversation, he had learnt all he needed to know. The current resident was a single American businesswoman who mostly stayed there for long weekends. The owner lived out of sight of the property at the other side of a village, and knew little of what went on. The rent was automatically paid out from her bank account to his, and he had very little contact with her otherwise.

Over one Sunday, Harry parked his pick-up down a nearby farm lane, concealed behind a thick hedgerow. The pair of binoculars he sported were normally the province of Michael, but they served Harry well. A steady stream of motorcycles, borrowed parents' cars and bicycles drew into Rosemary's front yard in quick succession around ten p.m.. He smirked in cynical amusement at Robert, Kevin, Sammy, Steven, and the rest being cheerfully ushered into the house by the brunette woman he knew was the renter. His eyes ran over the tight leather trousers and skimpy t-shirt. Nice tits, he thought.

Play his cards right, he might enjoy that body. He'd certainly satisfy her more than those limp-dicked "little boys" she was entertaining. Harry felt a surge of irrational hatred he later realised was jealousy at the easy familiarity the woman displayed with the lads – embracing them, kissing them full on the mouth, playfully slapping their arses.

Harry had brought a Tupperware carton full of sandwiches which he indifferently devoured during the long hours spent observing the house. He couldn't help noticing that the bulk of the lads spent the day sat around in the downstairs kitchen and living room. The American woman tended to be upstairs most of the time, except for the few moments when she strode downstairs to summon up two or three more lads to replace the handful trooping exhaustedly out of the bedroom. Whatever was happening was centred around upstairs, which fed Harry's overworked imagination.

Trouble was, the bedroom curtains were fully drawn. Apart from a teasing rustle, they kept their secrets well concealed. It had been like that for over an hour and Harry had been on the point of conceding defeat, when a flurry of activity at the window attracted his attention. What he saw was to remain seared onto his retinas for the rest of his life.

The woman was slim, toned like a ballet dancer, fully breasted and with an all-over tan. There was some kind of ring running through her belly button, and an exotic snake-like tattoo whose design he could not discern. It was only when he saw her shaven vagina that Harry grasp the fact she was utterly, un-self-consciously naked. Her hair was auburn and she was sweating like a thoroughbred. It must have been the heat that caused her to draw back the curtain briefly to enable her to open the window a smidgen. In the seconds before she drew it closed again, Harry swore he glimpsed Robert Swales, bare-chested at least, seated behind her.

It was enough. He put the binoculars down, and checked his rear-view mirror. The pick-up spluttered into life and Harry reversed down the track like a man possessed. He deliberately avoided driving past the house, choosing a longer route back home, in case he was recognised. He had seen all he needed.

As it turned out, Rosemary did not need to use Kevin to make initial contact with Harry. He had driven past her house during the week, when she was away, and stopped his pick-up just outside her drive. He had laboriously typed out a suitably threatening note on his son's computer and had it printed out. Harry had outlined his suspicions and intentions to tell the boys' parents unless he was involved in their shenanigans somehow. He left little doubt as to how he intended to be involved.

Harry felt it was only fair. Why should a bunch of little boys get to enjoy those magnificent female bodies? They were the nearest he had seen approximating the type of topless models he viewed on page 3 of The Sun or the many porn magazines he devoured. Although married for nearly twenty years, since the age of nineteen, Harry had already enjoyed several extramarital affairs behind what he viewed was his wife's unsuspecting back. The first had occurred less than four years after their marriage. Sheila had been heavily pregnant with their first-born and Harry had carried on for nearly two years with an overweight married woman living in a council house in Denbymoorside. He and a mate had been drinking at a local when they had got into conversation with a mutual friend of the woman. Invited to her house for a party after closing time, and with no greater ambitions than free drinks, Harry and his friend found themselves among a mere eight or so people in a semi-darkened living room with dance music blaring.

After a few conversational banalities, Harry had danced with the woman, vaguely aware she was coming onto him. Though a few stone overweight, she showed little compunction about displaying her more than ample flesh in a tight black dress and, as the music slowed down, they drew together stiltedly.

Harry considered himself fortunate that, apart from his mate (who could be relied upon, being married himself) he knew nobody else there, and was confident they didn't move in his social circles back in Thormanton. A brief, hurriedly-snatched snogging session later, and he was following her upstairs to her bedroom. Harry was mortified to learn he hadn't a condom on him, but she said she was on the Pill and seemed unconcerned about the health issues.

After several weeks enforced abstinence at home, Harry's body exploded into meteors of frustrated lust. Lighting up for a post-coital cigarette, the woman (whose name was Sandra) explained she was married. Her husband was an oil-rig worker in Aberdeen whose work meant long absences from home.

Sandra had been just the first. They had drifted apart more from mutual indifference than anything. Although fat, Sandra had been about the most comely of the handful of flings he had enjoyed. Certainly, none compared to the mysterious American woman or the nude girl he had glimpsed through the binoculars. Yet a snotty little virgin like Kevin and his mates were getting unlimited access to these goddesses. Harry bristled at the implied social slight.

He had hand-delivered the letter through her mailbox on the Monday following the contretemps at the barbecue. Kevin had been instructed by Rosemary to keep an eye on the house during the week while she was away and she had even given him a spare key. Amid all the junk mail accumulating on her front door mat, Harry's unstamped letter stood out like a sore, throbbing thumb.

Kevin had waited until he was alone in his bedroom at home, out of earshot if his Mother, before speed-dialling Rosemary on his mobile. "Er, yeah, can I help you?" Her inquisitive drawl sounded off-puttingly alien and loud in the sedate calm of the Troughton home.

"It's me, Kevin."

"Oh, hi!" He would have to keep this short and anonymous. He briefly outlined the contents of Harry's letter and gave the contact address.

"Yeah, I've got that. Thank you for letting me know." Rosemary's voice was guilelessly bland. "Catch you later. The time we agreed. Take care, now."

Chapter Twenty

It tended to be forgotten that even the most ruthlessly successful football teams have runs of inexplicable loss of form. Don Revie's brutishly efficient Leeds United had started their final season crushing all before them, but had barely limped over the finishing line as champions. Now, Kevin sensed something similar infecting Thormanton F.C.

A disputed penalty, coolly converted by Steven, had secured a late 2-1 victory away at Wellthorpe. Complacency started to take its toll, and Kevin reflected he might have to crack the whip in training this forthcoming week, and start threatening to withdraw places for some of them at Rosemary's the following Sunday.

Sammy had pulled his goalkeepers shirt over his head. "Er, Kev. Alan, Andy and Garry have been in touch wi' me. They wor' wonderin' if we might need 'em?"

A beam of sadistic amusement contorted Kevin's lips. "Aye, Sammy, I've got the perfect role for them." He nodded towards a door off to the right. "That shithouse might be clogged up. We'll need someone to unblock it."

"I think they meant..." began Sammy.

"I know what they meant." The frustrations and problems of the past few weeks had eroded Kevin's normal patience. "They piss off double-quick when we really needed 'em, and come crawlin' back when we start winning. Fuck 'em!"

A derisive laugh and cheer from Robert. "Do we look like we need any help?"

Nick shuffled forward. "Er, Kev? I don't think I'll be able to make Thursday. I've got a cousin's twenty-first party that night and..."

Kevin's clipped reply could have frozen an ocean. "We can't afford to carry passengers, Nick. If you can't make it, I can always draft in someone who can." He nodded at eternal substitute Chris Manby who perked up at the news. "Seven P.M. prompt. I expect you all to be present!"

As he stormed out of the room, Kevin softly closed the door behind him as if emphasising how much he would prefer to slam it.

However, Kevin was conscious of his own level of performance falling short on the day. Tackles were mistimed, passes near their own penalty area too lackadaisical (one had been intercepted by Rothwell, fuming for vengeance, whose subsequent pass resulted in the equalising Wellthorpe goal) and too many of his distributing balls from midfield had gone astray. Showering down afterwards, Kevin knew only too well the reason. From this Saturday evening onwards, after Harry Fenwick paid his visit to Rosemary's rented house, it might all change for them. Lurking at the back of his mind was the truly horrifying thought that it might even be the end. The endless empty months ahead yawned uninvitingly. Preoccupied with his imagined dreads, Kevin barely had the energy to chat to anyone that evening.

Rosemary's house was wreathed in an atmosphere of eerie calm when Kevin pulled into the front yard on the motorcycle. Parked next to Rosemary's gleaming Porsche was the mud-spattered green hulk of Harry's farm pick-up. Its mere presence a hostile alien stain.

Kevin was aware of the hollowness in his chest as he mounted the front steps and pressed the doorbell. He had been familiar with the feeling just before his first porn session. It was ironic that they were affecting him now at what bleakly promised to be the final act.

Rosemary breezily opened the front door to greet him in a suspiciously cheerful manner. She was made-up, with her long hair piled up and severely pulled back from the face, strangely enhancing the cool, semi-aristocratic mien. A long, garishly oriental dressing gown covered her body from neck to knees. Judging by the heavy creaking underneath it whenever she moved, Kevin guessed she wasn't naked for once.

"Ah, Kevin. Just in time. I need a hand." She drew him inside and locked the door behind them. Kevin limply followed her upstairs in her brisk wake. He noted that the high heel shoes she was wearing were clumping a lot louder than they normally did. She even looked taller. This wasn't how he had been expecting her to behave when he called. Somehow, he found his voice, croaking with nervous tension.

"Did Harry....?" he began.

She nodded. The door to her upstairs studio was pushed open and Kevin stood frozen on the threshold at what he saw.

Harry had called earlier that evening. There could be no doubting that. Lolling on the bed, his vacant eyes rolled in their sockets as he cast them around the bedroom, trying vainly to focus on something. They locked with Kevin for a instant, but seemed to look right through him.

From time to time, he tugged at the handcuffs affixing him to the brass bedstead, but without any real effort, as if they just some minor irritant he was vaguely aware of. Even more strangely, he seemed only semi-conscious of the apparel he was clad in. Presumably, Rosemary had dressed him up in it. There was no way on Earth that Harry Fenwick would have normally been seen dead in a pink, frilly dancer's tutu, black lace bra and panties, and fishnet tights and suspenders. A hurried application of a garish rouge lipstick completed the grotesque ensemble.

"Fucking hell?" Kevin ran across the room to crouch by the befuddled farmer. The older man smiled absently, but hardly registered his presence. "Harry! What's happened?"

Rosemary locked the door behind her. "Oh, you two guys know each other. That's sweet!"

Kevin looked up into her coldly mocking face. "What the fuck have ya' done to him?"

Rosemary busied herself setting up the camera and lights for a shoot. "As we agreed, he called around at nine. Just for a chat. For our mutual benefit, as he so charmingly put it. I said I was pouring myself a drink. Would he like one? He did."

Kevin patted Harry's unresponsive face. "You mean, you put summat' in his drink?"

"G.H.B."

"Come again?"

"Georgia Home Boy."

"You've lost me."

"Liquid E. He'll be like that for the next twelve hours. Pity. Waste of a good claret."

"Why?"

"He wanted in. Threatened to tell if I didn't play ball. He got what was coming to him. It'll be a cold day in the Sahara before I let a creep like that inside me." Her briskly dismissive tone put a very definite full stop to the day's events.

"Whaddya' want me to do?" Kevin stammered.

She imperiously indicated he should take his place behind the camera. Kevin squinted down the view finder and saw Harry in hideous focus.

Rosemary rummaged inside a drawer and produced a grim, black leather face mask which she donned. With a theatrical flourish, she flung off her gown to reveal what had been creating the ominous creaking whenever she moved. It was due to the black leather, strapless corset, elaborately studded with vicious metal spikes she was wearing. A matching G-string was attached by a single thong at the rear, neatly bisecting her firm buttocks. Rosemary managed to elegantly sweep across the room on a pair of high heel platform PVC boots that would have reduced most other women to tottering.

Out of the same drawer, Rosemary pulled out a soft leather whip with, at least, nineteen strings – each measuring fourteen inches long.

Kevin felt his penis harden more relentlessly than he had ever known it before. Rosemary proudly strode across the room and held Harry's face up to ensure an excellent view for the camera. She nodded to Kevin to activate it. Stood over Harry's prone form, she yanked his knickers down to his ankles, like a recalcitrant toddler, and cracked the whip across his pale, flabby buttocks.

"Ready for my close-up, Mister DeMille."

★ ★ ★

It was growing foggier. Eerie, amorphous shapes floated wraith-like in the glow of his headlamps. The juddering of the potholed and rutted farm track vibrated the pick-up's suspension and amplified Kevin's trembling a hundredfold.

Kevin had driven the pick-up enough times on the Fenwicks' farm to be familiar with its awkward gear stick and brakes. He had yet to pass his driving test and his four-wheeled excursions had been limited to rough farm tracks and lanes. He was slowly driving down one now. However, to get there, he had driven down over seven miles of country road in pitch black at two a.m. in the morning. He knew that the local police were especially industrious on Saturday night, and the ensuing morning, on the prowl for drunk drivers.

Once or twice, a car had passed him coming the other way. Kevin caught himself sitting unnaturally upright in his seat to give a credible impression of an experienced motorist. Once or twice, he cast anxious glances at the passenger slumped forward, but held upright by a seat belt, beside him. Harry Fenwick was awake but barely conscious. He gazed blankly at the view through the windscreen, and occasionally at Kevin, but was clearly not in this world.

Kevin felt as dazed by the events of the past few hours as Harry did. He had gone through the motions of filming Rosemary as she had gone about her physical chastisement of the older man with a vengeance. He had winced once or twice at some particularly savage blows and could see the red welts vividly standing out against the pale pink of his arse. A pathetic rivulet of blood trickled down his bare leg.

It took ten minutes but seemed to last an eternity. Finally, she straightened up and strode imperiously to check the digital camera. Satisfied with the play-back that everything had been captured perfectly, Rosemary switched it off with a triumphant flourish.

"What now?" asked Kevin.

"Dump this loser somewhere." Kevin had no idea his goddess could be so ruthless. "His vehicle's out the front."

"Well, I can hardly return him home," pondered Kevin. "But he could be left parked down a lane somewhere."

"Whatever!" Rosemary yanked off her leather mask.

"Only one thing..."

"What?"

"I haven't a driving license for ...."

Rosemary sighed with a heavy patience. "Okay! We'll work something out. Wait a few hours. This shithole ain't exactly the Big Apple or LA. Cops have gotta' sleep sometime." She caught Kevin's wary glance at Harry's prone form on the bed – a beached whale dangerously out of its depth. "No sweat. He'll be in lala land for a good few hours yet."

"Well, if I load my motorbike in the back, I can dump him a few miles from here," Kevin ventured. "Coppers won't be about much after closin' time. An' they'll be more interested in a town like Salton. It's just that....."

Rosemary's face softened. She took Kevin's worried face in the palms of both her gloved hands. "Hey, you're really spooked out by this, aren't you, Kevin. My big, brave boy."

"I'm sorry, Rosemary. But I've been shit-scared about this all day an'..." Her practised touch was already energising his cock. A few minutes ago, he feared he would have cum in his underpants for the first time since he was at school. Something about Rosemary's dominatrix persona had both aroused him, and chilled his bones to the marrow.

She stilled his voice with her index finger to his lips and drew him closer to her. Her lips locked his in a savage vacuum as she expertly French-kissed him. Kevin's anxieties and fears melted away in the heat of her body and its overpowering musk. The feel of her naked flesh encased in form–hugging leather restored him and he felt himself responding.

Rosemary's lips moved from his mouth to his ear lobe. She nuzzled it teasingly. "Take me into the other bedroom and fuck me!"

Kevin had heard an erect cock described as "being angry" before, but, until then, had never made the connection. Now, he realised any other simile would be shallow in comparison.

Rosemary had an unsettling, semi–stoned expression on her face as she practically tore off her dominatrix outfit. Her splendid body was tanned and honed, the full breasts showed telltale signs of droop with age but were as appetising as ever with their pert nipples threatening to burst through the surrounding sea of red areola. Kevin stepped out of his boxer shorts and gasped as the cool air hit his genitalia. Both were naked, and, for Kevin, their confrontational stances seemed queasily similar to a pair of professional wrestlers he had recently viewed on satellite tv.

Kevin broke the tense silence hanging in the air by darting across the short distance between them and pounced on the woman, brutally manhandling her onto the bed. His horny hands roughly gathered up her tits and squeezed them to the nipples. Rosemary whimpered in pain. Kevin followed up by fastening his mouth around her left bosom and sucking mercilessly.

Kevin held her down and parted her impressively-muscled thighs with a dexterity borne out of long afternoons wrestling recalcitrant cattle. He felt his aroused penis could have punched a hole through steel, so hard and unyielding it felt, and it needed no guidance to follow the well-trodden path to Rosemary's moist crack. Kevin was not blasé enough to still be excited by the still novel sensation of a beautiful woman willingly parting her legs for him. He was adept enough now to tease the edges of her vagina with the rock–solid helmet, painfully holding the foreskin down, and dispassionately observe the woman writhe and groan as if her body was possessed. Kevin toyed with her mercilessly, cranking up the tension to breaking point, and then ratcheting it up some more. "Fuck me. For fuck's sake! Fuck me!" Her feelings were his to control. Her body was an extension of his impulses. Her words gave way to an incoherent moan, and then he was roughly inside her.

There was nothing gentle or considerate about his lovemaking. Kevin attacked her with a barbaric relish. His thrusts were animalistic and violent. His scrotum slammed hard against her body but he charged headlong through the pain. Pearls of sweat stood out on his red face. His teeth were carnivorously bared as if about to rend her bloodily apart. Rosemary could not have looked more vulnerable and battered had she been beaten up.

And then, it was over. Kevin came inside her with a great surge that he felt sucked the juices from the tips of his toes and the nape of his neck. As his energies dissipated, he held Rosemary down a moment and stared down intently at her perspiring face. There was something in her gaze that utterly defeated him for an instant, then he scooped up her head and violently locked lips. He feasted on her for nearly a minute, then collapsed into those luxuriant breasts.

He could have died for such a moment of supreme ecstasy. It was only then that he realised this was the first time he had fucked anyone without a camera filming him.

They had lain there in silence for nearly an hour, like two animals huddled together in a burrow. All Kevin's fears and tensions had melted away. With this woman by his side, he felt ten feet tall.

Fully dressed, Kevin felt no qualms about what to do next. Dressing Harry Fenwick in his own clothes proved a lengthy and awkward business, but he had prevailed, and the virtually insensible farmer soon presented a less alarming spectacle to the world. Rosemary had insisted on one refinement. Harry would still be wearing the fancy knickers, used for the dominatrix poses, underneath his trousers. His Y-fronts were retained by the woman for as a souvenir, and tangible proof for the next stage of her plot.

Kevin switched the pick-up off and extinguished the lights. The courage his brutal sex with Rosemary had invigorated him with was staring to evaporate. Casting covert glances around him, he made sure Harry was comfortable in his seat and clambered outside.

Kevin heaved his motorcycle down from the rear of the pick-up, gunned the machine into life, and roared off into the early morning. The pick-up, with a sleeping Harry Fenwick sprawled across the seats, looked sad and lost in the purple hue of the coming dawn.

Kevin slept very soundly for what remained of that night. In the pub, the following week, Harry was unusually subdued with none of his habitual braggadocio. He barely met Kevin's eyes when in conversation and his responses were limited to a few perfunctory monosyllables. From the pain-filled grimaces which contorted his face whenever he sat down, and the often deliberate way he moved, he was still feeling the sting of Rosemary's lash. Kevin wasn't to know, but easily suspected, that Harry had received a bubble-wrap envelope by recorded delivery that Tuesday, addressed to him and marked "Private and Personal". It contained a single DVD and a type-written note with no sender's address. Harry had to wait until his wife and children were safely asleep before he dared view it on his own player, but he already knew what it contained.

There, in murky colour was an uninterrupted ten-minute shot of him, garishly dragged-up and buttocks bared, being flayed mercilessly by the masked Rosemary. It would be impossible to discern her identity, but he was all-too recognisable. Harry gazed at it in horrified rapture. He could recall nothing about the night. His last memory was that Yank bitch pouring him a drink, and him settling back into an armchair, gradually becoming more relaxed and slowly drifting off.

That she had drugged him in some way was obvious. He had woken up sprawled across the driving seat, horribly cramped and with his neck aching, to the sound of birds singing and plaintive peeling of church bells. It had been easy for him to dismiss it as the outcome of "being on the piss" except that he felt none of the headaches or usual after-effects of a night's carousing. On the contrary, he felt quite perky, save for the soreness on his buttocks that chafed every time he sat back in the driver's seat, and the unfamiliar silky feel of whatever underpants he wore.

Upon returning home, he had bluffed it out with his wife that he had returned earlier when she was asleep, and had woken up before her. Harry was more than relieved that she was downstairs when he had dropped his trousers to change his underwear, only to start at the frilly pink lady's knickers hanging under his beer belly instead.

The note was impersonal and business-like, promising him that another copy would be sent to his wife, and possibly to a local newspaper, it he tried to muscle into Rosemary and Kevin's activities again. Harry paled visibly. He knew his wife would not hesitate to divorce him, and take the kids, if confronted with incontrovertible proof of his unfaithfulness.

There had been one or two narrow escapes before. Like many in his profession, for all the patronising contempt he displayed for those in other jobs, he secretly feared being forced to become the unspeakable, a working stiff in a factory or some similarly demeaning environment.

Let them carry on fucking the bitch! They deserved each other. It was only later that he wondered what she had drugged him with.

Chapter Twenty One

The race for the league title was tightly balanced. With just two games each to play, Thormanton and Norbury Town were ahead of the rest of the pack by a considerable margin. The villagers were level on points with Norbury, with a superior goal difference. By a supreme irony, the two teams last game of the season would be against each other. When the fixture list had been initially drawn up, Norbury had expected little more than a leisurely triumphal parade. Now they were to be fighting for their lives like some elegant thoroughbred hound trying to dislodge a mongrel terrier that had fastened onto its jugular.

Kevin knew he was going through the motions. His positional sense and ability to plan ahead and pass to a free colleague compensated for a multitude of deficiencies. When he launched himself into a flying tackle, he knew he was doing so more out of frustrated anger than to rob an opponent of the ball. In doing so, he had received a timely ticking off from the bald, middle-aged referee.

Thornton Westborough, at home, should have been middling opposition, but Thormanton were making heavy weather of it. Up front, Emma darted about with her elfin mobility, but Steven was labouring to shrug off the attentions of the burly Thornton centre half. Already, the referee had spoken to him about the injudicious use of elbows while waiting for a corner.

Thormanton remained upbeat throughout the interval as they downed their orange slices. "We can beat these useless twats!" implored Robert, pounding his chest in some primeval gesture. "They're crap! We've thrashed 'em once already. Just a bit o' bad luck, that's all!"

Thormanton resumed their assault on the Thornton Westborough penalty area, but their sluggishness denounced their confidence. Sure enough, Thornton Westborough won a corner after a hopeful long-range punt by one of their forwards was deflected out off Chris Manby's shin. The ball was floated into the Thormanton penalty area, and a lofty opposition centre forward beat Richard Swales to the ball to head it past Sammy Patterson goalwards. Robert Swales was stood sentinel on the goal line. He craned his neck as the ball struck the underside of the bar and rebounded downwards. The football bounced halfway on the goal line and Robert swung a relieved boot out blindly to clear it.

The referee blew for a goal. Robert was dumbstruck. "What? Never!"

The referee ignored his protestations and waved airily the game to restart with a kick off. Robert charged towards him to remonstrate with the referee like a man possessed. "No! The whole ball has to be over the line, ref! It wor' never over!"

"Sorry, son. It's my decision." The middle-aged man turned his back on Robert.

This only incensed the lad and he tried to dash around the front to confront him. "Don't turn your fucin' back on me! That ball wor' never completely over the line. Are ya' blind as well as fuckin' stupid?"

The other twenty one players froze in horror. A line had been crossed and there could be no going back. The referee composed himself and, with a cold deliberation, reached into his breast pocket to flourish a red card right in Robert's face.

"That's it. I'm not putting up with a foul-mouthed little pillock like you! Get off this bloody pitch!"

Almost in tears, Robert turned on his heel and trudged dejectedly off the field. Thormanton never awoke from the ensuing torpor and left the pitch in a similar dispirited demeanour once the final whistle had been blown.

"The whole of the ball has to be across the line. Every cunt knows that! Was he fucking blind? Even fuckin' Thornton Westborough knew it wor' never over the line!" Robert sat slumped on the benches in the changing room, barely audible through sobs, as Emma consoled him with a tender arm around his shoulders.

"Couldn't ha' come at a worst time, Rob." said a half-dressed Sammy. "They'll ban thee' for this. Chuck' the book at ya'."

"And you'll miss the semi finals," added Emma.

Nick perked up. "What about the three amigos? They might still be willing."

"Fuck them!" Kevin's face brooked no dissension. "They buggered off at the first sign of work. And I'd rather not bring in outsiders, if you catch my drift." He clapped Emma on her slender shoulders. "Emma, I'd like to play you outta' position next weekend."

The girl glowed behind her uncertain smile. "Ya' can't expect her to tackle some hulking great twat of a centre forward."

Kevin smiled – exulting in the moment. "I'm glad you take that attitude, Steven. She's taking your place up front at centre-forward. You'll be dropping back to defence."

Everyone else laughed but Steven went puce.

Alone with his thoughts, Kevin trudged back home. There were only a few short weeks until the end of the season. Once it was over, the woman would leave the area with all she wanted and the whole affair would fade away to nothing more than a memory. Although on the surface, he had gone along with this, part of him felt desolate at the sensual void that would leave in his life.

"Thought you'd be dancing a jig all the way home." Emma's cheerful voice sliced into his glum thoughts as she playfully leapt onto his back without warning.

"Why's that?" he grunted.

"Our Sammy's worked out that we're level on points with Norbury, if they beat Colstone, which they should," she beamed.

Kevin shrugged. "It's only a game, Emma."

Emma came as close to doing a double-take as Kevin had ever seen her. "Never thought I'd hear you say that!" Her eyes gleamed with mischief. "Or have you suddenly more adult things to think about?"

"Such as?"

"You know. Very *adult* things."

Kevin halted in his weary tracks. Alarm bells were ringing stridently in his head. He expected the girl would discover the truth sometime, but now, of all times. "How did you find out? Who told you? Sammy?"

"Few weeks back. Rosemary told me. That day she took me out for a picnic on the Moors."

It made sense. "About the same time you changed your hair style to match hers?" How could he have failed to suspect. Sammy's attitude had been bitter and resentful to his sister in recent weeks.

Emma spun on her heels in a model-like circle as if showing off. "Sammy thinks I don't know. Mind, he has been walking around with a face like a bag o' spanners recently. It feels funny having a sex-god in the family. One day I might get to watch one of your films."

Kevin felt her innocence was a dagger in the bowels. He turned his back on her abruptly. This was a complication he could well do without. "Just as long as you don't go spreading it about. You know what your parents are like."

Kevin failed to catch the crestfallen expression on the girl's face. "Look, Kevin, I admit I was shocked at first. But, as long as we're winning. Christ, the look on those Salton players when they realise we're gonna' give 'em a game! And we can all do with the money."

"What? You haven't....."

Emma giggled. "If you could only see yourself, Kev! It's okay for a bloke to do it, but you're a selfish prude when it comes to a girl." She teased him by holding the ensuing pause as long as she dared. "If you must know, the answer's no. I haven't gone into the film business. I don't think I'd have the nerve. You ought to have a key in your back, Kev, you're that easy to wind up."

"But you said summat' about money?"

"Just hush money. I didn't earn it the hard way, if you know what I mean."

"As long as that's all it is. Just be bloody careful, Emma."

Their walk brought them to a fork junction in the road and they branched off from each other on their separate routes. Emma paused in mid-stride and turned to call out to the sullen lad one last time. "See you later, stud. I'm out on the town tonight. Special occasion."

The significance of the date had evaded Kevin's preoccupied thoughts. "Oh, sorry Emma. Many happy returns."

★ ★ ★

The flat of a strong pair of hands raked her spine down to the small of her back. Emma closed her eyes behind the blindfold she wore and arched her spine in a state of rapture. Her masseur had taken the professional tactic of applying the oil to his hands instead of applying it directly to Emma's body. His expert touch seemed to stimulate thousands of nerve endings in his wake. No less stimulated were Emma's nostrils by the heady, intoxicating scent of the aromatherapy oil whose warmth alone eased the tension she felt after this afternoon's match.

"Enjoying your birthday present, Emma?" Rosemary's voice sounded as if she was to the left of Emma. The woman had insisted she enjoy this massage blindfolded, the better to appreciate the sensuality of the touch and smell.

Initially apprehensive, Emma had gradually succumbed. She felt it a pity she could not enjoy the sight of her masseur's toned, bronzed body, stripped to the waist, as he went about his work.

Keeping his fingers stiff, the young man spread them out and raked them down Emma's back from her shoulders to buttocks. Deep, underlying tissue tensions were released. Emma felt greatly daring at the top of her pert buttocks peering over her towel. She was sure each contact with her back was lowering this scanty protection a few centimetres with each rub.

"H'mmmmmmmmm!" Emma purred languidly. Save for the towel, she was totally naked and could not recall another time she had been this intimate and vulnerable with anyone.

The sounds of Rosemary's masseur furiously pummelling the woman's prone body vaguely registered. She had paid for the evening's treat on Emma's birthday. The parlour was situated down a side street in the city just off the main shopping thoroughfare. Its cheap neon lighting, above the glass door, appeared tacky and lowbrow. Rosemary was clearly familiar with the staff at the reception desk as she paid their joint fees. She led Emma into the changing rooms where they quickly undressed. Emma had packed a one-piece bikini and insisted on taking it into the massage room tucked into the capacious pocket of the dressing gown. Once inside the room, she had stripped off her gown discreetly and lain upon the massage table waiting for the attendant to arrive, breasts squashed into the flat surface. By contrast, Rosemary had discarded her gown with an ease she would have shown in her own bedroom and idled on her own table.

This was the first time Emma had seen Rosemary nude and it was all she could do to repress her awe. The woman was as toned as a professional dancer and moved with the natural elegance of one. Her full breasts were starting to sag with the advancing years, but were still impressive. Emma could only hope she looked as good as she at her age.

Her tan was all over and no indications of bra straps or panty lines. Its swarthy hue contrasted sharply with the pale of Emma's own exposed flesh and her apple-cheeked glow. It even put the tans of the two male masseurs who entered the room after a polite wait to shame.

Emma almost dozed out, narcotised with tactile pleasure, and awoke in time for the end. She thanked her masseur and clambered off her table to scamper across for the next stage – the Jacuzzi.

Clad in her one-piece bikini, Emma reclined in the circular tub amid the fizzling water. The whirlpool currents spiralling around her lithe young body replenished her. She leaned back and closed her eyes to savour the feeling.

"That look's inviting." Rosemary's upbeat voice cut into her reverie. Emma blearily opened her eyes and was suddenly very awake.

Dressing gown slung over her shoulder, the American woman was totally naked. She stood proudly and without a trace of self-consciousness over the tub. There was no trace of vulnerability about her state, Emma likened her to some fantastic goddess from antiquity. She looked formidable, yet entirely feminine. Two red spots burning her cheeks, Emma tried to avoid her bright eyes which seemed to penetrate into the very core of her being. The younger girl muttered something polite and made room for the women to clamber in.

Emma could not help noticing how Rosemary made every act into a feat of provocative posing. Now, exulting in the swirling torrent of water, she arched her back and leaned back on her two arms as if in the throes of orgasm.

"Rosemary?"

The woman did not alter her expression. "H'mmm?"

"How do you get into this business?"

"Spend several years studying at Harvard and Yale."

"Be serious."

"Why so curious? Interested?"

Emma blushed slightly. "Not sure I could just do it cold with any fellow."

"You might not have to. I didn't." Rosemary adjusted her position a fraction. "Most women start off girl-on-girl to break in gently, and develop it from there."

Emma gave it serious thought. Rosemary seemed to sense an advantage to press home. "Women make the real money in this game, Emma. Jenna Jameson's as famous as any film star. Nobody gives a hoot about the guys. They're interchangeable."

Rosemary briefly descended into the water up to her shoulders, only to rise to her full height. The water stiffened her breasts to an unnaturally perfect degree that it was all Emma could do to stop gawping at them.

Rosemary brushed her hair back in a severe widows peak. "It's a well-known scientific fact, Emma. Men don't have sufficient blood in their bodies to work their brain and their dicks simultaneously."

The nervous tension broke. Emma collapsed into a fit of giggles. "That's true." Relaxed, she realised how ridiculously overdressed and prudish she must look alongside Rosemary. Without any prompting, she peeled off her outfit and carelessly tossed it outside the tub. Their eyes locked and Rosemary ran an appreciative scan over Emma's body. She liked what she saw. Emma lounged back on her underwater seat and surrendered to the spell of the water coursing around her body. It felt so natural.

Emma could scarcely keep her mind on her everyday minutiae the following week. About one tenth of her focus was devoted to her shopwork. People engaging her in small talk found her distracted – but curiously elated. Even on the Friday evening as she settled back in her bed, she harbored vague trepidations about going on and wondered if it was not too late to phone in and call it off. But then, Emma knew she would have gone the rest of her life regretting what might have been – and Rosemary had teased her with a lingering French kiss as she dropped the younger girl off, and tantalised her further by running her elegant fingernails along the underneath of her breasts more more expertly than any gauche male at the local dances.

Surely, at least, Sammy and the rest of the lads suspected something. After all, they were already doing something identical. She self-effacingly withdrew into the background much more than previous and had almost crumbled inside when Nick had casually asked what Rosemary was doing tonight, but Kevin had shrugged it off by replying that the woman was having a night out with friends. If only he knew.

Emma managed to get through the next seventy minutes before Kevin withdrew her in favour of John Swales. It had not been one of her memorable performances and had helped that Denbymoorside were so leery of Thormanton's reputation for brutality that they were half-beaten before kick off. A routine three-nil triumph with goals from Cooke (2) and Myers put Thormanton into their very first league cup final.

Emma had not tarried around amid the horseplay and joshing in the changing room afterwards. The chorus of "Scarborough! Scarborough! We're the famous Thormanton and we're going to Scarborough!" rang in her ears.

Emma was showered and changed and ready to be picked up by eight that night. She knew that it was pointless getting made up for where she was going. She had bustled downstairs and outside with a mumbled "Bye, Mum. Dad" before disappearing like a wisp through the front door.

The large-breasted woman named Sasha had picked her up in her car. She knew Kevin had hardly stopped raving about her but Emma, while not openly disliking her, felt she was a bit of a slapper and he could have done better.

"Nervous?" asked Sasha.

"Not sure," replied Emma. "I'll be glad to get it over."

"Oh, don't be like that," reproved Sasha. "I'd be doing a lot more if I didn't like dick too much."

From the outside, it looked just like another grey stone country house to Emma. The cars parked outside were considerably more cosmopolitan that normal. Sasha treated her like a princess and opened her passenger door to usher her inside.

Normally, she was told, the lads took turns operating the sound and lighting equipment. Respecting Emma's nerves, Rosemary had dragooned the girls in tomorrow's shoot as an ad hoc film crew. The sounds of their last-minute concerns twittering away from upstairs carried down to Emma as Linda made her up with a fastidious eye. Linda found the break from a load of indifferent guys a refreshing change as she found a willing pupil for her make up tips. It reminded her of dressing up a dolly when a child. Afterwards, she promised Emma she could keep a few items to take home. Emma already felt much better for the experience, as most was it was upmarket names beyond her meagre income.

Linda whisked off the towel around Emma's shoulders with a theatrical gesture. "Ta da!" A lingering gaze into Linda's hand mirror seemed to hold time in stasis. Emma was still recognisable but in an almost parallel universe way in which innocence, a knowing sophistication, budding sensuality and her usual perky, can-do nature all vied for focus.

"Ready, down there?" Rosemary's voice fractured her back into the present. Linda winked and gave the girl a "thumbs up" sign. Emma took a deep, quaking breath and skipped lightly upstairs to her destiny.

Made up and dressed as a precocious schoolgirl, Emma sat tight-legged at the verge of the bed on the studio. Sasha peered down the viewer of the digital camera and made a last-minute adjustment to the angle.

"I swore I'd never spread my legs in this industry again. At least for a guy."

Rosemary shed her dressing gown to reveal her leather bra and thong and stood over Emma. "I'm honoured," said Emma, glad to bring some levity to the situation.

"Action," intoned Rosemary and nodded at Sasha to activate the camera. Emma took a deep breath and braced herself.

Rosemary sat down beside her and recited the lines for her "older woman" character's seduction of "young, innocent" Emma. Emma, never a natural actress, woodenly responded – though she was aware of half-gabbling and stumbling over her dialogue. In a curious way, it took her mind off what was to follow.

Then, before she knew it, Rosemary had gently cupped her face in her hands and kissed her languidly on the lips. Emma froze for a millisecond. It could have lasted an eternity but, as Rosemary's tongue worked her magic, Emma felt herself responding in spite of herself. Hungrily, she worked at Rosemary's mouth and was gratified to feel the older woman abate for a moment and allow her to take command.

Eventually, they parted and Rosemary nibbled her neck as she gently eased her backwards onto the bed. For Emma, having a magnificent pair of breasts thrust in her face was a new experience. It was the first time she had a pair to toy with that weren't her own. She flapped her hands at them excitedly, like a maladroit teenage boy.

Between them, both females stripped off as teasingly as they could for the potential audience at home. Sasha switched the camera off and changed position to resume at a better angle as Emma and Rosemary, now both naked, settled into their former positions. "Action."

Rosemary started gently on Emma's pert young breasts. She cupped them delicately, traced them lightly with her fingers and ran her tongue around the aureola. Emma was already halfway into some dream dimension before Rosemary seamlessly segued into suckling them. Rosemary's free hand ventured down her writhing body and Emma obligingly parted her legs for access.

Even Rosemary was surprised by the decisiveness by which Emma grabbed her hand and placed it between her thighs. Rosemary began gently rubbing the pubic mound. Encouraged by Emma's inarticulate moans, she switched her focus to the labia , the perineum and ultimately the clitoris.

"Oh, fuck! Don't stop. Yes, there!" It was impossible to believe Emma capable of such passion. Rosemary concentrated on the areas the girl was most responsive to. Her touches became more rhythmic by rubbing a finger back and forth.

Rosemary was totally in charge of Emma's body. She was a conductor making the girl's cries retort as surely as a well-honed orchestra.

Lube had been suggested, but Emma scarcely needed it. Rosemary slipped her fingers further inside the girl's squirming body. Deftly, her fingertips located that spongy area of tissue inside the front wall of Emma's vagina and started drumming against it.

"Oh, fuck!" Emma had hardly ever uttered the word with such anger before. "Fuck me! Just fuck me!" When she finally detonated, she was sure her screams rattled the filling in her teeth.

And then it was over. "Cut!" Sasha lightly tapped the monitor screen and the camera wound down to silence.

Sasha discreetly went about her business while Rosemary and Emma lay catching their breath. The older woman seemed as exhausted by her exertions as the girl.

"So, innocent little Emma ain't a virgin."

Emma smiled while gazing up at the ceiling, lost in her thoughts. She felt oddly pleased that she had surprised this wordly woman. "Just the one. Must be over a year now. Nothing to write home about."

Elsewhere, the Landlord of the Thormanton pub, the Spotted Cow, was telling his customers to be careful tonight as Harold Earnshaw knew police patrols were out keeping an eye open for reported poachers in the area. He was also puzzled why none of the local lads seemed to be packing out his bar, hogging the snooker table and darts board, and generally fortifying themselves for a night at the clubs in town. Kevin was conserving his energies for the shoot tomorrow with an early night after watching Match Of The Day, as indeed were the majority of his team mates. Back home, Sammy seemed oddly restless to his parents who were pleased that their daughter was at least out enjoying herself with her friends. Little did they suspect that those same friends were baffled by her absence which did not seem to follow any real or imagined slights on their part.

Back on the bed, both performers lay still. No words were exchanged. They would have been redundant. Rosemary knew from long experience that some first-timers needed a period of contemplation to recover their wits. She had been one such novice once. As she had personally forsaken any guy-on-girl scenes for herself, she treated her sparing appearances as a special event. Little Emma needed scrupulous care and attention. She had potential. But Rosemary was also a businesswoman.

Sasha had reset the digital camera and indicated that it was ready. Rosemary rolled onto her back and rendered herself as vulnerable as she ever had. "Your turn to show me what you can do."

Emma had an unsettling feral glint in her wide eyes as she assumed the dominant position. "You're my bitch!" she growled.

"And action!"

Chapter Twenty Two

The black ball trundled down the bare polished boards of the wooden lane and cut a swathe through the white pins stood at the end of the bowling alley. Only two pins were left standing. Having executed the throw, Steven raised his arms in a pretentious gesture familiar from countless goals on the football pitch.

"Who's your Daddy, bitch?" he mocked Sasha, competing in the lane alongside him.

The girl said nothing, merely smiled seraphically and bowled her own ball with a practised ease to utterly demolish her own ten pins. "Not you!" she scoffed back at the nonplussed lad.

The Bowling club was situated in a block building whose neon illuminations provided the sole glimmer of individuality in the anonymous trading centre out on a limb from the bulk of the city.

Kevin had read enough soccer books – especially on notable coaches and managers – to realise the value of team-bonding exercises. "Anything you can't do?" Kevin asked Sasha as she drew her breath while the next rows of pins were established. "First snooker, now this."

"Practise," beamed Sasha. "We all used to go bowling together in LA."

"You oughta' have seen the faces of some of our opponents when we told 'em what we did for a living," added Rosemary.

"What do you think we do in our spare time?" said Sasha. "Shower together and paint each other's toenails."

Robert and Emma had formed their own duo. "Where's big brother, Emma? He's been in a bit of a strop these days."

Emma had changed significantly since the season started. It had been by small increments too minute to notice at first. But, over the months, Kevin could see how sleek and well-honed her body now looked. Her bell of hair billowed lustrously and radiated good health. More than a few of his teammates had remarked on the newfound tightness of her posterior. "Sulking at home."

"What's up wi' the miserable sod?"

Emma hesitated momentarily and exchanged a furtive glance with Rosemary. "Search me."

"Wanna' drink, Emma?" chimed in Nick from the bar.

"Just a mineral water for me, Nick," The girl's sweetly patronising smile was pure Rosemary.

"Nothing stronger?" asked Robert.

"I've been told it cleans out the pores."

"By who?"

"One of Rosemary's porn stars. Goes by the name of Angelina Croft. I helped her in make-up. She says she wouldn't be able to afford her car or a mortgage without the films."

"Oh, you've been around to Rosemary's while she's been, er.." began Kevin.

"Shooting her mucky movies, you mean, Kevin," laughed Emma, flinging her head back exultantly – an affectation reminiscent of Rosemary at her most flamboyant. "Yeah! Just for the one afternoon. Thought it would be good for a giggle. I always thought the women who acted in them were sad losers who'd been abused by their fathers, or druggies, but they come from all walks of life. One or two run their own businesses. They're just doing it for pin money."

"And they like having every orifice filled out like an application form by half a dozen blokes," added Robert. "Most women settle for classes on making chutney."

Like most changes in personality, what began as superficial affectations were gradually seeping into the core of Emma's soul to eradicate all her old mannerisms like some benevolent virus. Her unformed face was growing into the contours of the mask. The head-tossing and airy hand gestures were spontaneous and natural.

A paunchy middle-aged bowler sat a few aisles away was casting covert glances at Emma whenever he felt he was unobserved. Kevin squirmed in his seat. This dirty old man was lusting after a girl he considered in the same light as a cute best friend of a kid sister. Judging from the girl's languidly appreciative half-smile, she too was not unaware of the effect she was having. Like most socially subjugated people who suddenly become conscious of their power, the effect was intoxicating on her. It was physically repellent and exciting simultaneously – the fact he would be thinking of her whenever he touched himself intimately in his fetid, lonely bed.

"What are you gonna' do when the football season's over, Rosemary?" asked Nick.

Rosemary's attention was on sending her own ball spinning down the lane. "Move on. I'm earning enough from my website to buy my own place somewhere."

"Gonna' be a lot o' lads walking 'round Thormanton wi' long faces."

Rosemary surveyed the obliteration of her ten pins with hands on hips. "Question is, what are you gonna' do? Go back to having a meaningful relationship with your right hand?" It was meant as an impish joke but, for most of the lads, it was uncomfortably close to home.

"Or making Rosemary a rich woman by logging onto her website?" added Sasha.

A dull grey veil was cast over those lads in earshot. "Can't say I've given it much thought," rumbled Robert. "Going back to the bad old days."

"But things have changed since then," said Sasha.

"Doesn't all you've gone through fill you with any confidence?" inquired Rosemary off-handedly.

"With women," replied Nick. "You're either born with it or you aren't."

"Or it's something you develop," said Sasha.

"Did what's-his-name have it?" asked Kevin

"Ray?" Rosemary's face sobered briefly. "Eventually, yes. Unfortunately."

"I know plenty o' blokes walking around wi' fit wives and girlfriends I'd hardly call confident," said Steven, as he wandered back to his seat between sets.

"For all you know," laughed Robert. "They might have one as big as King Kong's thumb!"

Rosemary turned to face them. "It might be difficult for you to grasp, Steve, but that's not important."

"You're pulling my leg," said Robert.

"A woman's Holiest of Holies is only so big." Rosemary sounded oddly like some scientific expert. "It can only take so much."

"Besides, anything more than a mouthful is a waste of space." Sasha finished her last bowl for now with a flourish. All ten pins flew in every direction.

★ ★ ★

Louise gasped as she stared through eyes squinted with pain into her own face. Kevin squashed her up against the full length mirror on the clothes cupboard in Rosemary's bedroom. His hard cock slipped easily in and out of her supple arse and the liberal application of lube was causing a slightly queasy squelching noise that made it sound eerily like some prehistoric reptile eating.

"Like that, don't ya' whore!" Kevin could now ad-lib at will without the aid of a script. Rosemary scanned the pair of them through her digital camcorder mounted on a tripod. A jerry-rigged recording boom hung from the roof a few discreet feet away.

Kevin was gaining a taste for anal sex. Since that time with Rosemary, he had broached the subject with her, only to be met with a curt refusal. The woman made little secret of her loathing for it, but the business-like side of her brain acknowledged its popularity with male buyers. Louise had been saving up for a new car – her dayjob as a typist for an information storage and retrieval company paid her a pittance – and had replied in the affirmative when Rosemary emailed her. Unlike Rosemary, Louise positively welcomed anal. Rumour had it she did nothing else.

Rosemary and Kevin had got into a habit of filming him solo on the Saturday evening after a game. Rosemary had withdrawn from the actual performing and concentrated on her role behind the camera. Since the night with Harry, her relationship with Kevin had passed a crucial stage, and they invariably shared her bed on the Saturday night. Kevin tried to rouse his overworked genitals for a bout of lovemaking, but would mostly settle for using his tongue and fingers under Rosemary's expert tutelage. She guided him into rubbing the mythical G-spot to transport her into such a frenzy that she could literally ejaculate. For the rest of the time, they just lay in each other's arms, snug in their own sensual little world while the rest of the countryside went on its drab way outside. Occasionally, a girl performer they had just filmed would join them to sleep over for the morning. Not a word of this was said to the rest of the team. As far as they were concerned, Kevin had got there early to help Rosemary set everything up. Sandwiched between Rosemary and another gorgeous woman in a languid tangle of limbs, the few sounds of traffic passing by could have been indistinct transmissions picked up from Mars for all the impact they made. Life couldn't get better than this, he reflected.

Louise had showered and mentioned having something called a "vaginal douche" before travelling north. Kevin kept up a slow, steady rhythm out of respect for Louise's physical well-being, but it took supreme self-control. Louise's gasps and entreaties were a dangerous inducement to double his pace and jackhammer her anus to a bloody pulp. He recalled the sense of exhilaration and triumph, when he'd butt-fucked Rosemary. The man taking pleasure and the woman taking pain....

He was dimly conscious of a car drawing by outside, but was so engrossed in buggering Louise that he couldn't remember it pulling away. Locked into his own world, his senses focussed on the naked expanse of Louise's quivering back, Kevin found his concentration wandering to the pattern of freckles on the woman's back. It was a useful aid in forestalling him prematurely shooting his load.

Louise's buttocks were moving in time to his thrusts. She was no passive recipient. On the contrary, her vast arsehole and the pair of pale, wobbling cheeks in the dim half-light of the muted lamps resembled the lipless mouth of some bizarre alien creature undergoing cunnilingus. His cock seemed dwarfed by the immensity of it. The thought made Kevin redouble his efforts to assert his dominance. The accelerating pulse of his own tight arse assaulting Linda's had a peculiar similarity to one creature urgently pumping life into another.

Kevin and Louise both closed their eyes in unison. Linda's pained gasps were an alien mutation of agonised pleasure, Kevin's were those of pleasure and the final effort to complete some monumental physical exertion. Both blended into a discordant whole that was unsettling to hear. Utterly spent, Kevin clung to Louise for support, the fringe of his forehead drenched in sweat.

"And they say romance is dead! I'd give you seven out of ten, son!"

Kevin and Louise were suddenly very alert.

The door abruptly being kicked open preceded Ray's swaggering entrance into the room. Clad in a funereal black suit of an ominous sobriety, his mocking eyes swept across the tableau of Rosemary filming Kevin and Louise in flagrante. Behind him was an identically-suited man with a shaven head, well over six foot tall and so stocky as to be cubic, with a jutting, sharply-barbered beard angling his double-chin, standing with the intimidating calm of a man whose profession was violence.

Kevin and Louise clasped their hands over their exposed genitals. The girl scrambled off to gather up her clothes. Kevin felt as shamed and vulnerable as a youth caught blatantly masturbating by his parents. "What the fuck?"

"Put some clothes on, son" said Ray with a bleak smile. "Nobody likes a show-off!"

"Hi, Ray." Rosemary's calm self-assurance vaporized. She leadenly went through the motions of switching off the camcorder.

Louise was not completely dressed, but she swept up her discarded jacket and belongings and stumbled outside, past the mute hulk in the doorway, and rushed downstairs, fast as she dared without looking too craven. The sound of her car starting up and speeding off soon followed.

"Why don't you follow her example, and run along, sonny." Ray's tone was icily dismissive. "We grown-ups have things to discuss. I'm sure this was a welcome change from spanking your monkey, or whatever you retards do in Deliverance country, but it's time at the bar."

Kevin stepped into his boxer shorts and started to unfold his shirt. "How did you find out?" asked Rosemary, uncharacteristically submissive. Kevin had heard this note in her voice only once before. It had been the overheard argument at the porn studio which had terminated in her being slapped. The memory impelled him automatically across the room to remonstrate with Ray. "Now, look..."

The blow from the man hit him square in the solar plexus with a technician's precision. Kevin doubled up and slumped to his knees, choking for breath. For a moment, he felt as if all the air had been slammed out of his lungs. What was more chilling than the blow was the indifferent, matter-of-fact air the man had acted. There had been no warning or pre-amble, unlike the many brawls Kevin had witnessed in pubs and clubs. The fighters on those occasions were emotional and screwing their nerve up to act. Being able to perform the most horrendous violence was clearly this man's natural state. He had automatically punched out as naturally as anyone else reaching for a shelf.

Through watery eyes, Kevin saw Ray's expensive shoes plant themselves alongside him. "Take some fatherly advice, son. Never milk another man's cash cow."

"How did you find out?" he heard Rosemary saying.

"Ran into Teresa in her firm's car park. Last thing she wanted was a scene. Got her career to consider." A pause for effect, then, "Get packed!"

Kevin swung around as much as the pain in his guts would allow. "Rosemary! You're not leaving."

The woman would not meet his gaze as she shame-facedly opened a drawer to collect her belongings.

"Rosemary needs to be reminded of her obligations." sneered Ray. "It's contractual."

Kevin met his empty eyes with a courage borne of desperation. "Or what?"

Ray's smile did not reach his eyes. "I don't need to do anything except open my mouth. You think this hasn't happened before? And how old were you sheepshaggers when this started?" His voice adopted a patronising tone that was truly awful. "She's been a naughty girl in the past but she always has to come home in the end. Rosemary know's what sides her bread's buttered."

The realisation anaesthetised Kevin to the agony in his chest. He staggered to his feet to implore her but her face was averted with an ominous note of finality.

"It's all over, Kevin. Just go."

Chapter Twenty Three

"Christ! No wonder those sad cunts were so keen to bend over for you. Fuck all else to do 'round here." Ray's dead voice buzzed in her ears like static. "Sometimes, other people's lives scare the shit outta' me."

Ray's flatly mocking tone assailed her left ear. The leaden darkness of the North Yorkshire countryside, broken only by the odd pinprick of a light in the distance, dominated Rosemary's view through the car window.

Ray and his associate were driving Rosemary back to the city. She had packed the most basic essentials, including her filming equipment, into the boot of Ray's car. He had assented to calling back in the middle of the week to collect the rest, including her Porsche. Ray's sense of exultant triumph enabled him to make this small concession.

"Don was asking around for a shoot. A bukkake tour for your fans. We've got one or two hosts lined up and Gina says she'd be agreeable."

Rosemary nodded absently. Her life ahead stretched before her as endlessly as the terrain around her. The car jolted abruptly as it ran over a pothole in the single-lane country road. "Fuck me! Can't they afford to fix their soddin' roads?"

Rosemary was only faintly conscious of the red rear lights of the tractor plodding on ahead of them. Through the windscreen, she saw the machine chugging along. A wide farm implement was affixed to the back, a rotavator, she recalled John Swales calling it when he had glimpsed somebody working in an adjoining field using one during a Sunday session. Whatever it was, it extended along the width of the road rendering overtaking impossible. She idly wondered what the driver was doing with it, at three a.m. on a Sunday morning, when it slowed down to a halt. Something about the broad back of the lone occupant in the cab seemed familiar.

"Don't these sad bastards ever sleep?" spat Ray. His associate stopped the car and pulled on the hand brake. "Ask this fuckin' sheepshagger if he'd like to move on, Lou."

Lou, the minder, switched off the car, clambered out and strolled unconcernedly across the short distance to speak to the driver in the cab. "What's the problem, pal?" Rosemary felt a strange sense of déjà vu as the farmer turned slowly. An involuntary smile stretched her sensual lips as she realised it was the face of Robert Swales, half in shadow, illuminated by the harsh glare of the car headlamps.

"Yyyyaaaaagggghhhh!" A blood-curdling cry ripped off from some long-forgotten Hollywood war movie rent the air. Lou looked around wildly for the source, instantly alert like any pro. But he had not counted on his would-be attackers striking from above.

Sammy Patterson and Steven Cooke had been precariously perched on a thick tree limb waiting for this opportunity. Sammy let out the war cry as the signal for them to strike. They jumped into space and their combined bulk slammed into Lou's broad frame, felling him like a forest giant. Robert opened the cab door and jumped out in one swift, fluid motion to add his weight to their assault.

Confused, Ray looked around like a cornered animal. A throbbing hum announced the arrival of a second tractor coming up behind them, stopping right up against the rear of the car to hem it in completely. Robert's kid brother Richard was at the wheel.

Shadows fell across Ray's passenger door window. Kevin and the remainder of the male Thormanton players emerged from hiding in the bushes along the verge. Kevin brandished a heavy sledgehammer borrowed from the Fenwick's farm. He spat on his palms and swung the hammer in a savage arc. It shattered the glass into countless tiny shards. Chris Manby reached in to unlock the door and heave it open. Ray, more bemused than shocked, scarcely had time to move before several pairs of strong hands were at his collar, yanking him out of the car and pinning him down on the grass kerb.

Dextrous fingers undid the ornate buckle of his leather belt and slid Ray's trousers and underpants down to his ankles. Ray gasped as the chill night air hit his exposed genitalia. Nick Cammack held a lit torch into his snarling face, still more angry than fearful. Ray struggled to free himself, but their combined weight held him down firmly.

"Christ!" hissed John Swales. "It's like tryin' to hold down a bullock."

"And the resemblance won't end there, John." Kevin's voice was forebodingly calm.

"What the fuck are ya' playin' at?" cried Ray, still acting as if he had the upper hand, though he could see that Lou was equally helpless. "Are ya' that fuckin' desperate for a poke?"

"In case you're worried," beamed Kevin, "we're not gonna' ask you to bend over and squeal like a pig."

Kevin stood back and fumbled inside his jacket for something – a silver utensil with twin handles and a red rubber ring fastened around several grips at the other end. Ray was blind to its purpose until Kevin squeezed the handles and the ring was pulled in four different directions to increase its circumference. To drive the point home, Kevin hovered menacingly over Ray's vulnerable nether regions. The hole in the rubber ring was more than large enough to encircle his cock and balls. Kevin had used them earlier that year to castrate a five-day old bull calf. The mere thought made them visibly shrivel up as much as the cold night air.

Now, Ray knew fear.

"Wha'? No! Shit! I'm sorry. Jokes over. Lou! Do something!" Words tumbled out from a voice usually so languidly superior and patronising.

"Wha's tha' blubbin' about now?" jeered Robert. "I read somewhere that all our worries are summat' to do with sex. By the time we're finished, you'll be the happiest fucker alive!"

Ray felt emotions he hadn't experienced since adolescence. Anxiety clutched his throat. He felt something bubbling in his posterior than boiled over into a trickle down his legs. "Christ!" he heard John Swales exclaiming. "He's shitting himself!"

"You know, Raymond, I think they mean it!"

Rosemary stood over him, savouring the moment, surveying the scene like some exotic autocrat. From this position, Ray could see what her appeal had been as a dominatrix. "Rosemary! Call these little cunts off!"

The woman took her time. She straightened an errant lock of hair and idly examined the polish of her expensive high heels. "I'll think about it. That is, if you and your little playmate get the fuck outta' here and leave on the next flight back to LA."

"Bitch! I fucking discovered you. You'd still be waitressing at Starbucks, and giving blow jobs to casting directors, if it hadn't been for me."

"And you certainly got your money's worth, which is more than I ever did."

"I invested the time and effort."

"Then complain to your union." Rosemary's sweet smile could have frozen the Sahara desert.

"Smart-arsed bitch!" Time hung heavy in the ensuing pause. "Alright. You fucking win! Call your dogs off!"

The lads looked to the woman for authority. She drew out the moment for, what seemed to Kevin, to be the maximum level of sadistic amusement before inclining her head a fraction.

From the lads' angle this appeared a tense, dramatic scene. Only later did they appreciate how comic it looked when viewed from the side. The police car crawling around the corner of the road – concealed from view until the last minute by a tall, thick hedgerow – crept into view like a serruptitious interloper on a stage. Its dazzling headlamps illuminated a tableau straight out of vulgar farce as the pinioned Ray lay at the mercy of Kevin and his castration ring.

The car drew up to a halt. Everyone was too stunned to move. Even Ray forgot his predicament.

Police Constable Mark Allenby and his partner Paul West had already enjoyed a productive evening. In the back of the car with his Lurcher dog and a dead hare was Graham Noble – an 33 year old unemployed former warehouse worker from South Shields. He and his mates were frequent visitors to this area – especially at night time with lamps. Caught with his prey on Harold Earnshaw's 5-acre fallow field, he was being driven back to Salton Police Station to be charged with hunting wild mammals with dogs and possessing a lock knife. None knew this was merely the prelude to a night which would see this felony consigned to a footnote in the scandal to come.

Allenby stopped the car and clambered outside with a deliberate slowness. The gaping maw of his shocked mouth seemed carved into his face. Behind him, West and Noble exchanged shocked expressions like comrades in a foxhole as opposed to prisoner and captor.

The embarrassed pause seemed to last an eternity. In truth it was only twenty seconds. Kevin forced a fixed grin.

"Er, it's not what it looks like!"

Chapter Twenty Four

"Right, Kevin. You've just seen me remove the seal on the disc and place it into the DVD recorder. Is that correct?"

"Yes," intoned Kevin woodenly.

"Right, it is my duty to inform you that this interview is being audibly recorded and may be tentative evidence if your case is brought before a court. We are in Salton Police Station and I'm WPC Helen Pritchard attached to the Salton Police Station." The latter sentence was one of the few times the woman did not consult a laminated sheet in front of her.

DVD's! Kevin recalled a DVD showing an old black and white film of LORD OF THE FLIES IN English literature class at school. He had wondered about the authenticity of the climax when the feral schoolboys had been on the verge of lynching the young hero when the presence of an adult naval officer had abruptly terminated everything. The world beyond their primitive horizons had interceded to diminish their life or death drama to the level of a petty squabble. At the time, he thought it a bit far-fetched. Now he knew how it had been rooted in reality.

The police interrogation room was as utilitarian as one would expect. Kevin's Mother sat to his left trying not to look utterly pole-axed by this sudden turn of events. The woman officer advised her that she was not just here in an advisory capacity but to report whether the interview was being conducted properly and fairly. Her answers had been barely above a shocked whisper as the scale of Kevin's depravity came into focus. Although Kevin was made clear he had access to free and independent legal advise, he had waived the right. In a way, he wanted it off his chest.

Kevin was not brief. With very little prompting by the two officers, he narrated the full story from the collision with the white van to the sordid climax down the country lane.

"Didn't it worry you that anybody could have accessed this porn site?" asked the woman detective.

Kevin shrugged. It had worried him but, for a horny teenager, the advantages seriously outweighed such drawbacks. "Well, as long as I wor' getting' paid."

"Including family and friends," intoned the second, male detective. He sported the kind of bushy moustache that Village People had long rendered ridiculous as symbols of masculine virility. Kevin had recited his whole involvement with Rosemary from beginning to end for their benefit. He was too dispirited to even attempt to lie about his motives or sense of guilt. From time to time, as he recalled some particularly erotic episode, Kevin was gratified to see the stony features of the two police officers register a flicker of astonishment, and not a little jealousy.

"I doubt whether my Mother would be interested in such things. As for my Father, he's otherwise engaged…"

The first detective exhaled deeply, as if expelling all pre-existing conditions as to how people behaved. A discreet knock at the door broke the moment.

The woman detective broke off the interview and relayed this technical information into the tape recorder before clicking it off.

As she rose from his chair to answer the door, Kevin flexed his tired muscles. The woman exchanged urgent whispers with a uniformed colleague just out of earshot. Despite both maintaining a professional stoicism, it was clear from their body language that something unexpected had occurred.

Kevin hardly dared turn his head to see how his Mother felt. The woman detective trudged back into the cell.

"You're in luck. We've just spoken to the gentleman you and your mates pinned down."

"Oh."

"He's decided not to press charges. For someone who makes a living using his bollocks, he didn't seem too concerned about potentially losing them."

Kevin closed his eyes. His Mother somehow found her voice. "Why?"

"Shit scared, more likely," rumbled the male detective. "About what we might find out about him."

Kevin and his Mother rose almost groggily to their feet. Both were almost arthritically stiff from sitting for most of the past few hours. Somehow, they stumbled through the anti climax of the next few minutes as Kevin regained his belongings from the Custody Sergeant.

"How's the season going, by the way?" The voice of the male detective from the interrogation at his shoulder made him jump.

"Need a win this Saturday to win the league," gabbled Kevin in his desire to look a helpful member of the public, aware how easily he had got off. "Then we've got the cup final 2 weeks later."

"They normally play it at some neutral ground," added the policeman. "I had a nephew played in one a few years ago."

"Aye, Boro!

The detective rubbed his chin. "And, you say you finished last season bottom wi' no points!"

"Aye." Kevin pocketed his belongings and signed a form to complete the transaction. Then, he gathered up his resolve to ask the one thing he was truly curious about.

"Er, Rosemary? The woman who....well, you know?"

The woman detective strode past forcefully and barely spared him a glance. "We had a discreet word with that lady."

Kevin wavered in limbo as the woman marched off down the adjoining corridor. "And?"

"You ever watch old westerns, son?" asked her male colleague. Kevin nodded. "She's been advised to get outta' town! No questions asked"

* * *

Kevin's Mother drove him home in an air of baleful silence, she was forced to pull into a lay-by by a disturbing procession trundling past on the road.

A convoy of khaki army vehicles sped past with ruthless intent. Kevin could guess their destination.

In the gently setting sun of the early evening, Kevin kept catching the odd pop and crack from the direction of Fenwick's farm. Although disease free, it lay in the three kilometre buffer zone. Tom Fenwick looked up from his dinner to see a convoy of army vehicles draw up in his yard and a squad of armed men disembark, all clad in white overalls with matching hood. At the head of this group was a balding, middle-aged, bespectacled man who marched bumptiously up towards Fenwick's front door and pressed the buzzer. Tom reluctantly put his tea on hold and answered. The newcomer told him he was a Ministry of Agriculture, Fisheries and Food vet and produced a piece of A4 paper which he handed coldly to Tom.

The impersonal print said his farm was being served with an "A Notice". The words "contagious cull" had been scrawled across it. "I'm afraid all your stock has to be destroyed," the vet intoned.

"But they're not infected," protested Tom. "They're all perfectly healthy."

"I'm sorry, but the law is the law."

Harry lurched across the yard to lend support "Bollocks! Suppose we have a word with our solicitor?" he rasped. "Or the police."

"I am obliged to warn you both that should you obstruct our activities, you will end up looking at a bill for legal costs of thousands of pounds." The vet's eyes were invisible behind the glint of the sun on his glasses. "And your animals will simply end up being killed, regardless."

To Kevin, the reports of gunshots lasted for hours. The soldiers were very thorough. All the Fenwick's three hundred cattle were systematically murdered with captive bolts on the straw bedding they had been existing on for the past few months.

Once it was over, the soldiers searched outhouses and smaller sheds to ensure no strays or pets were hidden to save them from the wholesale slaughter. There was only one. It was an undersized calf born prematurely who had been abandoned by its mother. Every time it had attempted to suckle at her teats, the Friesian cow had indifferently kicked it away. For it to continue would have resulted in physical damage and malnutrition. So Tom and Harry had temporarily rigged up a secure shelter in a small shed with a bed of straw and access to rolled barley. silage, and water. First thing on a morning, and last thing at night, powdered milk diluted in warm water was hand-fed into its clumsily sucking mouth in a rubber bottle.

The calf resembled Bambi as it innocently looked up from chewing its food. It seemed to cock its head at an angle to appraise the newcomer in the unfamiliar white garb. Then, the soldier levelled his bolt gun at a point between its eyes and pressed the trigger.

Chapter Twenty Five

The buzz of Kevin's motorcycle sounded unusually muted as he pulled into the Fenwick's yard. Even for a Sunday, it was abnormally quiet. One of the cars – the family hatchback – was vacant from its slot in the garage for the first time in weeks.

Kevin tried the front door but there was no response. A cursory glance through the kitchen window confirmed that the house was empty. It was his first visit to the farm for weeks and it was surprising how drab and seedy it now looked.

Dare he look? The cattle shed was situated around the corner from the straw barn. Silently, fearing that his presence would arouse someone's wrath, Kevin picked his way along the tarmac path and pulled back the spring bolts that held the metal door in place.

The stench hit him like a physical blow even before he swung the door open. Foul odours were nothing new to one who laboured on a farm but this was something else. It was a sickly-sweet musk that assailed his nostrils and made his throat dry retch. Steeling himself to breathe through his mouth, Kevin plunged into the stygian darkness of the cattle shed.

The corpses of the cattle – prize bull, cows, heifers and calves alike – were gathered together in a rough mound.

Heads lolled at grotesque angles. Tongues protruded from open mouths. Unnaturally opaque eyes stared sightlessly ahead. One moment, they had been placidly grazing heedless to all going on around them. Then, the strange men had pulled up and all hell had been let loose. Could their limited minds have had any conception of what was happening to them?

Kevin recognised the calf he had delivered the night his motorcycle had been hit by the white van. He had felt a genuine sense of accomplishment when he and Tom yanked it struggling from its mother's womb, watched it grow uncertainly, ever watchful that, with its birth history, was probably predestined to an early natural death. Once it had reached a certain point of physical maturity, Tom felt they could breathe a sigh of relief. It was now felt sufficiently strong enough to survive.

Now, it lay upside down, head bent back, trapped between its mother and another cow in a tangle of limbs. Its expression was one of unendurable torment.

"Mornin', Kev!"

Tom's flat voice made him jump. It sounded leeched of all energy. His eyes having grown accustomed to the darkness, Kevin saw the man stood atop the pile of corpses like some ghoulish mountaineer.

"Christ! I didn't see you up there, Tom." Kevin looked around him. "Where's Harry?"

"Gone wi' t'missus, kids, and me Mother for a day out. Felt they needed to get away after all this."

"I don't blame them. Why didn't you go with them?"

Tom seemed abstract. "Had things to do."

An almost palpable miasma hung over the pile of corpses. To Kevin, it seemed the ghosts of the massacred cattle were marshalling themselves to summon forces of vengeance. Kevin still found the stench was rippling his throat, threatening to make him throw up any minute. But there was another smell lingering on the air. It took a moment for him to recognise it, but there was no mistaking the near-addictive aroma of diesel. Its source was difficult to pin down, but was very close.

"Still going to university, Kevin?" It seemed an extraordinary question to as in the circumstances.

"Aye!" replied Kevin. "Touch wood."

Tom's voice became inward and reflective. He must have been rehearsing this conversation most of his life. "I could have gone to University. Got seven O levels. I always did well at science."

The sun was directly behind Tom, and Kevin was forced to squint into the glare. It was difficult to make out details, but there was something about Tom's appearance. "Aren't you afraid o' catching summat' up there?" he called up to the man. "Can't be very healthy."

"Whenever I thought o' another job, I wor' always laughed at. 'Stick to farming. Thou'd be lost anywhere else.'"

Kevin sniffed the air as much as his stomach dared. The smell of fuel was stronger the nearer he got to the heap of bodies, and Tom. "Someone been spilling diesel?"

"Farming's not a job. It's a fucking life sentence."

Kevin stood at the foot of the pile of cattle. It was possible to discern greater details this close up. Tom's hair looked slicked down to the scalp. His work overalls looked drenched in something too. "You slog your guts out all hours of the day – build summat' up from nowt'. And its wiped out in a day!" The flatness of his voice had an obsessive quality. It was building up to a pitch. "What's the point, Kev'? What is the fucking point?"

Kevin put two and two together at the last possible moment. What occurred next confirmed it. Tom Fenwick produced a cigarette lighter from his pocket and lit it. With a trance-like deliberation, he ran the flickering flame over his overalls.

Kevin saw, almost in slow motion, the farmer ignited in an orange flare. Whether he felt any agony, Kevin could not tell from the stoical expression on his face. There was a near apologetic shrug of the shoulders as the flames engulfed him. The fire spread to the cattle and, within a few short moments, it was impossible to distinguish Tom's stumbling body from his stock.

Kevin made a token attempt to clamber up the hill of corpses but the incredible heat drove him back. Eyes watering, and not just from the inferno, Kevin shielded his face from the flames and backed outside the shed.

Cursing his cowardice at not wishing to witness Tom's final conflagration, Kevin slammed the door shut behind him and fumbled for his mobile. He dialled the emergency operator and gabbled out a plea for the fire brigade, somehow managing to recollect Tom's address after so long.

He automatically started back as a spurt of flame burst through the roof. It seemed to possess some life of its own and was breaking down barriers like some imprisoned beast. Kevin cast an anxious glance at the Fenwick's family farm house a short distance away. Had Tom intended this? Was it some subconscious attempt at wiping the slate clean? In the final moments of sanity, had he gained a sudden clarity at how fragile were the constructs he had built his life on. The reality – the bedrock of his life – that he took for granted had been the flimsiest of film sets. It could be dismantled in the snapping of a malevolent god's fingers. In eradicating all traces of his existence, Tom had merely been trying to help along a process already well advanced.

Kevin was wondering how best to keep the fire away from the rest of the farm and its flammable straw and sileage when he caught a flashing blue light on the periphery of his vision. It was a convoy of red fire engines – as relentless as the army land rovers a day earlier, but mercifully swifter.

They turned down the Fenwick's farm track and sped efficiently towards the blazing cattle shed like gliding beetles. There was no need for Kevin to give elaborate directions – the flames were visible for miles.

★ ★ ★

"We have gathered here not to talk about Tom but to pray for him. We believe that our prayer here can help Tom where he is now. We know that prayer is powerful and we believe that we can help the departed by praying for them. The best gift you can now give to Tom is to pray for him. There is no better gift you can now give Tom. There is nothing that you could now do that would be more helpful and beneficial to him than praying for him. When we lay a wreath in someone's honour the flowers will wither but the prayers we offer for someone will never wither. If you say just one prayer for Tom, it will last into eternity. Prayer has lasting value."

The words of the Reverend Gordon Hill (M.A. Exeter College, Oxford) droned on in Kevin's ears as he bowed his head respectfully. It had been years since he had been inside a church. The few funerals and weddings of relatives had not seen fit to invite him, or had been held at registry offices.

The pitifully small congregation for the village meant that the vicar had to divide his Sunday's between three villages within a five mile radius of each other. Many of his Thormanton teammates had evaded church for so long, they had lost track of who the current vicar was. The most St. Gregory's parish church figured in their consciousness was a tale that had passed into urban legend. It was a few decades ago when, during the reign of a blind previous incumbent of the vicarage, a particularly bold lad had entertained the others, during a dull Sunday School, by taking out his penis during hymn singing.

"We do many things during life that in a sense, in the light of eternity, are a waste of time. What really matters in life is putting God first. Jesus said in our Gospel that He is the Way, the Truth and the Life and if we are not living our lives in union with Jesus then we are not on the way and if we are not on the way we are lost."

Harry, his Mother, wife, and family were at the front of the congregation, their eyes red with weeping. Harry had been given first choice to be one of the pallbearers, but had been too grief-stricken to bother. Instead, Kevin, along with Robert and Richard Swales, and three other neighbouring farmers were bearing their melancholy load on their shoulders down the aisle to Tom's final resting place in the graveyard. Black and brown suits, that had not seen the light of the day for ages, had been laboriously donned for the occasion. Kevin reflected how odd everyone looked in formal dress out of their usual ragged farm or work wear.

"On one occasion Jesus said, "Seek the kingdom of God first and all these other things will be given you as well." When we do that, when we seek the kingdom of God first, love the Lord our God with all our heart, soul, mind and strength, and our neighbour as ourselves, then we are on the way, and not wasting our time."

Tom was carefully lowered into the newly dug grave. Kevin rubbed his shoulder from where the heavy coffin had been digging in remorselessly and idly turned to the open gateway. He glimpsed many more of the local villagers lining the single street to pay their last respects. In his darker moments, he often wondered if anyone would turn out for his.

"Ashes to ashes. Dust to dust."

Chapter Twenty Six

Norman Helmsley hung up his stained butchers smock and cap in the usual place for his wife to collect and wash and gathered his sports bag for the short journey across town. The shop, which had been in the family for nearly eighty years, was located just off the High Street in Norbury town centre, within sight of the recently-built Morrison's that threatened to usurp it.

Now in his mid-fifties, Norman was fast approaching retirement age for a referee. Even in the less rarefied environs of the Norbury and District Under 18 football league, there had to be guidelines. In his prime, Helmlsey had run the line at top European club ties, as well as refereeing routine league encounters, albeit outside the Premiership. He had never really aspired to those heights, being quite content to amble along at a reasonable level. It endowed him with a certain local celebrity at the assorted local sports committees he attended, that had ancillary benefits for his business through the contacts he made. He had also developed a well-honed repertoire of anecdotes about the various major and minor sports celebrities he had fleetingly encountered.

Still, he liked to keep his hand in, and maintain some involvement with the sport he had been obsessed by as a boy, but never talented enough at to even make his school's first eleven. The shortage of young men willing to take the arduous first step on the rung of becoming a qualified referee by starting out at local junior level was also responsible to a degree.

Leaving his shop in the capable, and impatient for his retirement, hands of his eldest son, Norman Hemlsley clambered into his reliable Vauxhall Corsa, flung his sports bag into the back seat, and drove off sedately for the short excursion across town to Mill Road sports ground.

Norbury Town's senior non league side were away for a meaningless end of season fixture at a Nottinghamshire club, but the junior eleven still subsisted in their metaphorical shadow. A mere thirty or so spectators had turned up – mostly relatives of the players or the odd pensioner with nothing better to fill his time.

Norman parked his car in the space reserved for officials and marched at a brisk pace to the changing rooms. He exchanged pleasantries with his two linesmen, both familiar to him from countless previous engagements, and quickly changed into his newly laundered kit.

He glanced at his watch. It read ten minutes to three. He was a man of neat, punctilious habits by nature and liked everything just so. Norman reflected that was why he had never cut the mustard as a footballer – that, and his general lack of talent. Time, he thought, for a pre-match chat with both teams – just to let them know who's boss.

Norbury Town was the first changing room down the short corridor. He knocked twice on the door and stepped inside. Norbury were fully changed and fretting impatiently for the game to commence. "Alright, lads," he said, "I know there's a lot at stake today, but try and keep it clean. Okay?"

"*We* will," retorted the Captain, a curiously ominous emphasis on the first word. Norman briefly took in Colin Adkins sitting on the bench seats.

"Thought you played for t'other lot, lad?" he queried.

"I did," said Colin. "Though I'm not sure if I made the right move."

Norman bid them good luck and made the short walk to Thormanton's changing room. The moment he entered, the tense atmosphere hit him square in the face.

The Thormanton team were all arranged in attitudes that made it impossible to read their faces. There was no sense of jokey camaraderie among them as there was in other teams, even struggling ones. They hardly seemed capable of looking each other in the eyes. Norman scented trouble, but felt it was nothing he could not master. He had come across some genuinely nasty pieces of work in his officiating career, and had developed certain strategies for dealing with them. He repeated his early admonishment as he had to Norbury. It barely merited a grunt of acknowledgement. The youth he had recognised as the Captain and Coach of this miserable collection was standing apart from the rest at one end of the room. The space between him and his peers was considerable and looked too distant to be accidental.

A flushing toilet heralded the entrance onto this grim tableaux of Emma. Her bright-as-button eyes, and nervous smile, were the first sign of chirpiness Norman saw in this grim place. With a final "good luck", Norman turned his back on them and lumbered out of the changing room.

In the numerous reports of the match that ensued, many of the commentators noted that the game started in a nondescript fashion, with no hint of what was to follow. Norbury won the toss and elected to kick off first. The opening first minutes saw both teams bogged down in an ill-tempered midfield scuffle with chances on goal at a premium. The greatest difference was that, while Norbury were yelling and shouting instructions and warning to each other, Thormanton were sullenly silent. They seemed as indifferent to one another as in their changing rooms.

Finally, the ball came to Kevin, wide on the wing, who chipped the ball in for a cross – only to see it safely caught by the Norbury goalkeeper. Steven, who had been lurking in the penalty area, turned on him with murder in his eyes.

"Can't you cross any fuckin' better than that?" he snarled across the pitch.

Kevin contemptuously turned his back on him. "Piss off!" he snorted back, dismissively.

"Steady on, lads!" interceded Norman Helmsley. "Watch the language!"

Three minutes later, Kevin floated in another cross only to see it go harmlessly wide for a goal kick. Steven rounded on his Captain. "How the fuck am I supposed to get on the end o' that?"

"Try working for a change, instead o' just prancing about like a fart in a trance!"

Steven froze at Kevin's venom. "What did you say?"

"Steady on, lads!" Helmsley was growing alarmed at the game's emotional temperature. But he sensed this was nothing to do with football. "It's just a game." Like many involved in sport, he never truly believed that.

But their words had stirred up something deeper, more primal. The Thormanton players were staring daggers at Kevin, the Norbury team were ignored bit-part actors in this drama.

"Ignore him, Steve," Robert butted in. "Twat's not worth it!"

"What's your problem shit-for-brains," said Kevin.

"You're the cunt wi' the problem!" Robert shot back.

"What?"

"I dunno' what to think anymore," Steven erupted, sounding close to the edge of sanity.

Although the Norbury goalkeeper had retrieved the ball, the match had stopped in its tracks. Thormanton were ominously encircling Kevin, while Norbury hovered around in a kind of limbo. They stood mesmerised by the spectacle. As usual with men who are goal-orientated and obsessive, when something outside occurs which breaks into the everyday ritual, the Norbury players were like actors who had stumbled onto the wrong play.

The sound of her brother's voice at her shoulder made Emma jump. She was astonished to see he had wandered yards out of his goal, heedless of the danger. "If I'd've known, I would've..." he began.

"What?" interjected Kevin. "Said "no?". Who the fuck are you tryin' to kid?" He took them all in with one contemptuous sweep of the pitch. "None of you would. For all your big-man talk, we were all in the same boat. We would've jumped over a fuckin' cliff if she'd said."

Robert had screwed his nerve up long enough. His meaty hands clutched for Kevin's throat. Kevin knocked it to one side, but Steven took advantage of his vulnerable posture to weigh in with a left hook. It caught Kevin neatly on the jaw and sent him staggering. Robert leapt upon him and wrestled him to the ground. This was the signal for the rest of the team to pile on top of them.

All thoughts of the game forgotten, Norbury looked on. Emma flapped about pathetically, trying to assert calm. "Stop it, Sammy! He couldn't help it!"

Red card poised for holding aloft, Norman Helmsley waded in to impose some authority. "C'mon, lads! I can't allow this. You're going to have to..."

He made the mistake of laying a firm hand on Robert's shoulder. In the heat of the moment, the hot-blooded lad shrugged it off and swung around with his right fist bunched up. Secure in his position, Norman had left his head open to such a strike.

It caught him a sickening crunch on the side of the cheek and felled him like a forest giant. Norman did not even have time to fling his hand out to protect himself as he hit the turf. It was like a switch had been pulled. The assault on Kevin ceased abruptly. The jeers of the spectators died in their throats.

Eyes blazing, Norman Helmsley pulled himself to his feet and fixed the Thormanton players with a basilisk glare.

"Champions! Champions!"

Even the victory chorus of the triumphant Norbury players had a muted, half-embarrassed air about it as they held the silver championship trophy aloft for a parade around the pitch. The time was four twenty seven p.m. on the final Saturday afternoon of the league's season, and the match had been decided before it had barely started. The Referee had abruptly stopped the game and awarded the fixture, and the title as a result, to Norbury Town by default. The Thormanton team did not make even a token attempt to dispute the decision. The fortunes of a meaningless sports event seemed trivial suddenly.

"Absolute disgrace! In all my years of refereeing games, even in Europe, I've never had to put up with this before!"

Robert, Steven, and the rest were sitting dispiritedly on their benches in the changing room as Norman Helmsley, with his two linesman and a League Official, who had been present on the day with the trophy, backing him up for moral support, read them the Riot Act.

"We're not only docking you points, you'll be damn lucky if you're allowed to play in this league, next season! You can be bloody sure you haven't heard the last o' this!"

With that, he turned on his heel and marched outside, the others following in his wake. The Thormanton players stayed in their slumped positions for several minutes. They looked as if they hadn't even been aware of the tirade. The silence was disturbed only by the sounds of Emma's sobbing. Kevin was not present. He was, even now, been speedily conveyed by ambulance to Salton General Hospital.

Chapter Twenty Seven

Kevin lay flat on his back in the men's ward. His Mother had paid him a visit a few hours earlier and departed, satisfied his injuries were minor. An elderly man with a few lank wisps of grey hair and a bushy moustache was in the bed next to him, almost comatose and linked up to a saline drip. Screens had been hurriedly erected around his other neighbour and the Nurses on duty were conversing in urgent whispers, the clacking of their high heels providing its own aural illustration of their activities. Everyone else in the six-man ward was quite nondescript, apart from the wizened old man taking frequent gulps into an oxygen mask linked to a tankard-like machine standing at one side of his bed. Half his neighbours looked as if they wouldn't be leaving Salton General Hospital in anything other than a coffin.

Kevin tried to move but the livid bruise running down his spine was a physical migraine that held him in its sway. He found himself in a dreary limbo, too exhausted to stir and too agonised to sleep. Time lost any meaning as he lay there.

Something about the male nurse stood out for Kevin as he spotted him loitering in the open doorway. The ones he had seen throughout his evening in hospital had been tall, young, well-built, and, on at least one occasion, gay.

This one was pushing fifty, grey-haired, red-faced through too many liquid lunches, and with a prominent paunch overhanging his ill-fitting trousers. He was casting his eyes nervously around the room, trying to look inconspicuous, but Kevin could sense, as he had long ago realised girls did at dances, that the man's covert attention was focused on him.

Visibly screwing up his courage, the man tried to act as if he had every right being there, as he strode across to the side of Kevin's bed. "Hello, Kevin, isn't it?" The false tone of politeness put the lad on guard.

He nodded absently, beginning to sympathise with all those girls at dances and night clubs he had approached in a similarly nervous, gauche manner. "Keeping well, are you son? You took quite a beating, they say."

"They felt they had a genuine motive," he replied through gritted teeth

"I've not heard the full story. Just snippets. Mind filling me in on what really happened, son?"

That was it. Kevin was now certain. "You're not a male nurse, are you?"

The man smiled, almost with relief. "No, son. Didn't know it was that obvious. No, actually, I'm a journalist." He fumbled inside his trousers and withdrew a creased and tattered business card. Kevin scanned it as best he could from his awkward position.

"What have you heard?" asked Kevin.

"Some fight over a woman," came the breezy reply. "But whispers about porn. Everyone else is keeping schtum about it. But they all agree you were the ringleader, Kevin. So I was wondering, like, if we could get your side of the story?" Seeing the mute resentment in Kevin's eyes, he added, hastily, "I could make it worth your while. And nobody would need to know you talked."

"Draw the screens up," said Kevin, after a pause. The male nurse wheeled the portable curtains around the bed and sat down expectantly, a pocket tape recorder with a full cassette primed to monitor everything.

"Well, it all began with this accident I had with a white van....."

* * *

Kevin was discharged the morning after and picked up by his Mother in the Hospital park for an ominously silent drive home. He retired to his bedroom, to catch up on the sleep he had missed in his ward, as soon as he arrived. The rest of the world could wheel its merry way in his absence and he could hopefully wake up to a brighter dawn. Kevin barely staggered through the following days. Despite the sun glaring down from a clear, early spring sky, all seemed bleak and gloomy. Even the grass seemed lank and lifeless, with the odd dead shoot visible. The absence of work gave Kevin an excuse to wallow in his hollow-eyed depression by retiring to his bedroom, under the pretext of being ill, and stayed there for several days, the door locked.

It is amazing how dark and overcast the world looks when one is unemployed. One is confined to a dark, reclusive place that even the brightest sunshine cannot penetrate. When the mask of employment is whipped away, one sees the world in all its dreariness and futility. Kevin felt himself losing his old vim and sparkle. Like some insidious stain, its shadow soiled the zest he once gained from captaining Thormanton.

Friday came and went with its promise of socialising, and he still had plenty of cash from his filming, but Kevin remained stubbornly reclusive. He awoke at two in the afternoon to a torpid curtain of rain that rendered his surroundings into a semi-monochrome panorama that mirrored the bleakness of Kevin's soul. He managed to dredge himself up from his bed and prop himself up in front of the television for the rest of the afternoon. Around eight, he could stand the inertia no longer and forced himself into a shower to revive his depressed spirits. The spray and the gel, between them, invigorated him and he buttoned his best shirt and jeans on with a new resolve.

The door was unlocked and Rosemary's rented house eerily empty. A pair of skid marks on the gravel drive bore testimony to the hasty departure of her Porsche.

Kevin idly wandered through the deserted rooms searching for…what? Something tangible to remember the bittersweet experiences he had endured here? He knew it was a futile, but still he found himself climbing the stairs to the studio bedroom.

Almost reverentially, Kevin peered in through the open doorway. All that remained was an unmade bed and mattress with a few stains discolouring its surface. Hard to imagine the muted lighting of the arc lights lending an exotic air to the setting, nor the sweaty, frenzied coupling. Sasha, Kath, Linda, Teresa, Joanna, their names rolled off his tongue like the lyrics of a popular nursery rhyme. He closed his eyes to imagine the heady musk of their naked, perfumed bodies. He could recall every inch of their lovely faces distorted in the throes of orgasm. Women he would never have dreamt of having a chance to even talk to, let alone fuck.

He sat on the edge of the bed and ran his hand over the ribbed contours of the mattress. It had conveyed him through times he dimly guessed he would never experience again. Kevin stood up, walked out, paused in the threshold of the doorway for a last, lingering look, then slammed the door shut and strode briskly downstairs.

Within two minutes he was roaring away from the house on his motorcycle without a backward glance.

Chapter Twenty Eight

The barrenness of his local village pubs held fewer appeal for Kevin than usual so he mounted his motorcycle and sped off the few miles to Salton. The majority of pubs in town were invariably orientated towards the youth market, with most having a disc jockey at weekends. However, even Fridays were sparsely attended, and Kevin could only dimly guess how they made ends meet during the week. Three had already closed during the past few months. It was the type of pub where decrepid old men dropped sulphurous farts like mustard gas.

Now, hunched morosely over his pint in the bar of The Fox and Rabbit off the main street in Salton, Kevin stared into the deep, dark dregs of his pint glass. The thirty-something disc jockey was duetting with an overweight bottle blonde of around eighteen (but could easily be younger) with a tuneless rendition of the old karaoke reliable "Paradise By The Dashboard light." The man made a decent stab at emulating Meatloaf, but the girl (who threatened to overspill the tight, low-cut outfit that seemed a size too small for her) lagged a beat behind her lyrics as they flashed up on the screen.

Three pints in, Kevin regretted ever having come out tonight. The disc jockey's attempts at stoking up a party atmosphere had a note of desperation about them in a bar with around eight customers scattered listlessly about, and he looked faintly pathetic and creepy hugging the bottle blonde long after their song had finished.

"New face here?" queried the forty-something landlady, not unkindly.

"Aye. Not exactly welcome in my local," answered Kevin.

The Landlady glanced expectantly at his empty glass. "Can I get you another?"

"No, it's alright. Long past my bedtime," said Kevin as he lurched out of the bar. The cold air hit him like a chloroform mask the moment he was outside. Donning his helmet, Kevin mounted his motorbike, kicked it into life, and, betraying the odd, uncertain wobble, glided off down the main road out of Salton.

The rutted, pot-holed back road had since been tarmacked over by the council, but would have tried the patience of many motorists, worried about the welfare of their car. Knowing it was off the beaten track, and that police on the lookout for drunk drivers would disregard it, Kevin had long grown into the habit of automatically using it as a route home.

He saw the glow of an oncoming van's lights bathe the grass verge from the opposite direction as he neared a blind corner. Kevin slowed down in anticipation of his befuddled senses not being sharp enough to react, but the white van was almost on top of him before he could swerve. The driver was heedlessly cutting the corner and almost at Kevin's side of the road. It caught his wing mirror and snapped it off. The bike was caught a glancing blow. It bucked like some metallic steer and sent driver and machine rolling over a steep bank on their side of the road in a tangle of flesh and iron.

As before, the van roared on with no thought of the carnage in its wake. For all Kevin knew, it could have been the same vehicle. Several seconds passed with him lying on his back, not daring to even wiggle his feet in case he felt no response. The motorcycle's engine still buzzed mutedly like some dying beast.

Kevin somehow staggered to his unsteady feet and switch off his bike. Another car was smoothly gliding down the road towards him, and Kevin felt a strange sense of déjà vu. Something about its whispery silence and the sleek brutality of its lines was hauntingly familiar. Then, he realised. It was a Porsche – like Rosemary's.

It drew up a few feet ahead of Kevin's accident and the purr of its motor wound down to silence. After a pause, which seemed to indicate an uncertainty on the part of its driver, the front door swung open. Kevin blinked in the harsh illuminations of the head lamps. For an instant, he thought that Rosemary had returned to take him away from all this, for he recognised the registration number of the license plate. The slender figure in form-hugging clothes, the bell of fine, soft hair, the skittish toss of the head, all were eerily alike.

Then, the girl stepped into the light, and even before her face was revealed, Kevin could see she was a fraction smaller than Rosemary. Emma's soft, questioning features seemed enhanced by her make-over. There was no sense of an awkward fit. One reason could have been that Emma's personality had undergone incremental changes since the two had first met. Kevin had never seen her face creased with a mockingly-amused smile before – a smile that indicated a maturing worldview and sense of irony.

"Going my way?"

★ ★ ★

Strange how one did not sense the cold after a while. The Porsche was parked in a pull-in a short distance away with the stricken motorcycle strapped to the roof. Kevin and Emma were spread-eagled out under the reflected earth-light of a full moon casting its blandly benevolent gaze upon them. Their vantage point atop the grass pasture sloping down Box Hill afforded them a marvellous view of the surrounding North Yorkshire countryside sprawling away into the dark horizon.

Emma reflected how amazing there were so many lights twinkling away around them, mocking the dark of one a.m. on Monday morning with a garish, artificial day. She could dimly imagine what dramas were been enacted out behind those banal exteriors, especially after her recent experiences.

"The keys came in the post, with a letter telling me where in York I could find it," Emma chattered gaily. "In the railway car park. Rosemary said it was all mine. She must've wanted to leave in a hurry and travel light."

"You've not seen her since?" asked Kevin.

Emma emphatically shook her head. "From what I've heard, she wasn't at her other house, either. That was rented too. Landlady said she'd done a midnight flit."

"Must've been prepared for summat' like this happening all the while," mused Kevin, his eyes distant and thoughtful. "Could be anywhere in the world by now. What's it been' like in the pub this week? It's not like I've felt like going, you understand?"

"Strange. Nobody's been talking about it. It's like they've been steering 'round the subject." Emma giggled. "Bit like an alcoholic relative at a family party. But you can tell they've been thinking about nothing else."

A pause, then. "How's your Sammy?" ventured Kevin.

"Still a bit pissed off. I think he suspected summat' odd wor' going on."

"Christ! What a fucking mess!" He sensed, Emma staring affectionately at him.

Emma managed a weary smile, her face drenched with sweat and her fringe plastered to her forehead, in spite of the chill, oddly like a child who had just completed an errand and cheerfully expected some payment. Then, she flopped down onto Kevin's broad chest and snuggled up against it, like a newborn calf against an adult.

Silence. Totally serene calm. The only sound was the steady munch of the sheep grazing on the lush grass. In spite of the intimacy, Kevin felt curiously compelled to keep it fraternal.

"Look, Emma, I'm sorry."

"For what?"

"For getting you involved in all this. And Sammy."

"Fuck Sammy! If he can't accept it, that's his problem!"

Emma purred and adjusted her position. No, Kevin and the others need never know. They need never know about Emma's overnight stays on Friday at Rosemary's rented house. They would certainly never learn about her semi-inebriated late night sleepovers. Drunken reminisces about men had inevitably turned to physical intimacy. Emma had lain back and exulted as, after an initial massage in baby oil by Rosemary and two of her star performers, the girl had been pampered and brought to a shuddering orgasm by several pairs of hands exploring every orifice. Her lithe body felt as if it were being tenderly conveyed by a powerful gust of wind to the furthermost reaches of the sky, soaring above the earth and its petty concerns, only to be gently brought back to terra firma with the gentlest of bumps.

No. There was no need for them to now this. Nor was there any need for them to know about she and Rosemary orally pleasuring Kirstie, the older woman taking the lead and showing Emma how to give maximum satisfaction, the two of them lapping at the girl's vagina like cats at a bowl of milk.

Emma felt a surge of power at bringing Kirstie to a peak of ecstasy. She felt a true sensual connection to the girl as she curled up alongside her and hugged her. Emma decided she had never slept as soundly as she had that night. The money Rosemary had given her would pay for her now heightened fashion sense. Emma could still smell Rosemary's body and her heady musk. On the whole, she still preferred guys, but it was nice to know the other option was there, and available, should she ever need it.

A few errant streaks of orange peered through the murky purple of the night. It would soon be dawn.

Chapter Twenty Nine

It broke with a vengeance on Monday. Robert clambered into the cab of a cattle lorry to aid the driver with directions to a smaller farm a few miles away their family owned. The driver had a red-topped tabloid tucked away in a glove compartment that Robert idly picked up to glance through to while away the journey. At first he did not think the headlines were about them.

"SEX FOR SUCCES UNITED! THE BOYS DONE GOOD! FARMERS' BOYS SCORE OFF THE PITCH AS WELL AS ON!"

"Fucking hell!" The involuntary exclamation made the portly driver turn in his seat. But Robert paid no heed. His perception of the outside world had shrunk to the limits of the scope of the report. Despite a few lazy errors, the basic facts of the story were accurate.

Like a series of carefully-timed booby trap bombs, the Thormanton personnel learnt of their newfound notoriety at separate junctures throughout that day. Some, like Robert, scanned a discarded newspaper, or had it pointed out to them by shocked workmates. Many were confronted by stern countenanced parents when they innocently ambled inside at the end of a working day. By five p.m., it had replaced the economy and various international wars at the prime subject matter on the hourly news bulletin on local BBC and commercial radio.

By noon the next day, a two-hour music and chat show on BBC local radio devoted the bulk of its running time to a phone-in discussion of the scandal. The anodyne woman presenter and her callers debated the topic with all the depth and insight of two old women gossiping over a garden fence, as indeed, they did every other subject. Like a virus, it spread uncontrollably into the national media. Some of the lads found themselves barricaded into their homes by the intrusion of sweaty, red-faced journalists and hollowly sincere female correspondents asking for five minutes of their time for their angle on the story. Parents were subjected to anonymous inquiries about their sons upbringing and whether they were aware of how they were spending their Sundays (and having their failings as fathers and mothers implied as a result). Some of the cannier victims ensured they gained some payment for this invasion of their privacy.

By Friday evening, the story had become so ingrained in the fabric of the nation that it had become a rich source of puerile humour for superannuated Oxbridge graduates and ageing students in mainstream comedy. Steven felt himself squirming in his chair and cursed himself for staying in that night to watch TV instead of boozing his Friday night away. More than one high profile professional football league manager had been jestingly queried whether he should resort to such motivation for his next match.

In the midst of all this, there was a league cup final to perform the last rites of this season. The minibus had already been hired weeks in advance and the Thormanton team, minus Kevin, were picked up from the pub car park just after one thirty p.m. to be inelegantly conveyed to their destination.

The journey was the most silent the team had ever known. Each member was alone with his or her own thoughts. The last thing they felt in the mood for was a football game.

Boro's football stadium was situated, like so many community facilities, on an industrial estate of the northern outskirts of town. Stadium was a grandiose title for what actually awaited them. It seemed to have been absorbed into the prevailing dullness of the estate. Only a welcoming sign over the main gate differentiated it from the surrounding carpet warehouses and superstores. Four spindly floodlight masts stood sentinel at each corner. The stadium was a drab rectangular construction composed of the crinkly tin usually associated with the surrounding DIY stores. The limited resources of the sale of Boro's original ground (which also helped in wiping out their mammoth debts) and assorted grants which funded its birth had combined to limit the club's pretentions to flamboyance. The ground held a capacity of six thousand, which was more than adequate for the club's average attendances.

It was such a familiar sight to hardened Boro supporter Peter Russell that, at first, he failed to spot what really was happening. Then, it struck him. "Hey! There's a lot of people going to this game. Is there another match going on?"

Everyone else saw what he was getting at. The pavements thronged with groups of casually dressed men decked out in scarves and bobble hats of their normal team. Liverpool and Manchester United supporters rubbed shoulders with York City and Whitby Town followers. Chris Manby and John Swales held an impromptu competition to spot the most obscure football team. Stevenage Borough and Woking vied for the first place.

"They can't all be for us," exclaimed Steven. "I heard last year, they barely got around twenty."

Robert pointed to the long lines forming impatiently at the sole turnstile opened for the event. "Well, that's where they're all going to!"

The minivan pulled up to an uncertain halt outside the main double gates and the team clambered out. Even before they were fully assembled, a tremor of excitement rippled through the line of spectators. Leering grins and lewd jeers greeted their arrival. As one of the stewards opened the gates to admit them, the Thormanton players ran a gauntlet of back-slapping, obscene gestures, and coarse remarks. Emma had never felt to nakedly exposed in her young life.

"Ta!" said Robert, bringing up the rear as the steward locked the gates shut behind them.

"They've been ringing up the ticket office all week asking if you wor' playing today," wheezed the portly middle aged man. "From all over the country. I reckon we've got more here than for Boro's last home game."

The steward directed them to the changing rooms and Thormanton beat a hasty retreat. Once they were ushered into there's – the away team's at normal matches – a not entirely welcome surprise was awaiting them.

"Now' then, stranger," barked Robert at the solitary figure seated on the bench seats of the changing room.

"You decided to turn up, then," replied Kevin, changed into his football kit.

"Nowt' else to do," answered Robert.

"You've got a fucking nerve!" spat Sammy.

Kevin looked unabashed. "I'm not here to beg for your forgiveness."

"Very wise," Steven bit back.

Chris Manby gestured down the corridor. "What are they all doing here? Anyone would think we wor' famous."

"We are," said Emma.

"You know what I mean."

They quickly changed into their newly-laundered gear and filtered out down the corridor in dribs and drabs for the pre match kickabout. As soon as Steven and Richard, the first two, emerged from the tunnel, a huge cheer went up from the audience crammed into the home supporters "Spion Kop" end. It was the same for every Thormanton footballer who wandered onto the pitch. Once they started going through the motions of limbering up to get warm, the spectators started to cheer their every move. Soon, some of the less bashful Thormanton players got into the spirit of it. Always the poseur, Steven mimicked the postures of several Premier League stars as he intercepted passes from the wing to volley home past Sammy in goal. Gathered like vultures behind their goal were a pack of press photographers who loosed off snaps like sub-machine gun fire. They made a particular bee-line for Emma, who vamped up their attention to the manor born.

Clustered forlornly around their goal at the opposite end were Colin and the Norbury team. They made a token attempt to limber up, but it gradually ebbed away as they became aware of their status as bit-part players in their opponent's drama.

Kevin drew closer to the home supporters end to retrieve a loose ball, and took time to study the faces on display. They were mostly male, but, in spite of a variety of ages and backgrounds, there was a quality common to them all.

Each had an unfulfilled air about them. Life had not panned out as expected, each were leading make-do lives, many were just filling in time until death. Suddenly, on virtually their doorstep, were these everyday lads who seemed to have unwittingly gained the secret of sex and the social power it conferred. Now, as if they could absorb this mystique through osmosis, they had turned up to view for themselves like acolytes at a religious festival. It was a heady sensation for Kevin. Less than a year ago, he had known only too well what their crushed lives had been like. Kevin had been one of their number. Now, through the beneficence of a casually cruel goddess, they had been elevated to this idolatry.

Ten minutes before kick-off, Thormanton pulled themselves away from this intoxicating attention and follow in Norbury's wake down the tunnel back to the changing rooms. Once back inside, they all sat around on the bench seats, nobody daring to break the mausoleum-like silence. Overwhelmed by feeling they could barely comprehend, conflicting emotions raged inside them.

"Fuck me!" snorted Richard Swales. "Who'd've thought there were that many sad bastards in the world!"

"Not so long ago, we'd've been among 'em," conceded Steven.

"Aye," added Richard. "But those sad buggers haven't turned up just to see a footie match!"

"People only respect power and success in this world. And they don't care too deeply how you come about it." Kevin spoke like he was reciting a half-remembered poem.

"Come again," asked Chris Manby.

"Summat' Rosemary said to me once. At the time, I wondered what she meant. Now, I think I know."

"Why not," rumbled Robert. His assent gave the others all the authority they required. They drew into a circle.

Kevin extended his arm rigidly. "For the last time." One by one, they similarly raised their arms until their hands met in the centre. It was as if they were channelling some intangible supernatural force.

A joyous whoop went up. They took their places behind Kevin as their captain as they filed out of the changing room. Norbury were already lined up behind the Referee and his two Linesmen. The Referee gave a signal of acknowledgement and he started to lead them outside.

The steady metronomic beat of their boots accompanied Thormanton's passage down the long, dark tunnel to the slit of light at the end, to emerge, blinking, into the open air.

Chapter Thirty

Kevin realised exactly when the moment he could scarcely contemplate. It was such an alien state of mind that it was like trying to contemplate being blind.

He was aware of the usual pre match butterflies as both teams lined up for the publicity photograph before some sweating, out of shape hack from the local rag. Then he politely endured the ritual of both teams shaking hands in a wooden act of gentlemanly sportsmanship. Having gone through the motion of limbering up, Thormanton assumed their 3-5-2 formation as, having won the toss-up, Norbury kicked off.

Kevin relished playing before an attendance that approached football league proportion. Some of the others seemed cowed by the atmosphere but Kevin had dreamed of an opportunity to perform on something resembling the grand stage many times while exerting himself before the meagre handful of local youth football. The only drawback was that, although it physically resembled a lower-league football crowd, it did not sound like one.

Most of the fans had no emotional investment in the outcome and had probably only heard of both teams in the preceding week. Even worse, the smuttiness of their rise to prominence infected the crowd's attitude. Emma, in particular, was subjected to lewd catcalls and lecherous cries whenever she received the ball far out on the right wing. Every jolt of her inhibited body language betrayed her unease. In goal, her brother Sammy made the best of a bad job by playing the mute fool to the crowd seated behind him whenever he retrieved the ball for a goal kick.

The trouble was that neither team had even the modest ability of the lower league journeymen these supporters were accustomed to. Too many passes went astray, too many basic moves were beyond their reach, the immensity of the pitch seemed to overwhelm their aggression and speed. It was football manqué – a hollow facade of the real Mccoy performed before an uninvolved crowd. This should have been the moment as Kevin finally realised he had reached his limits. But it wasn't. Not yet.

It was probably the unreal, uninvolving atmosphere that contributed to Norbury's first goal. Thormanton failed to clear a corner from the left and Colin picked up the loose ball and printed forward a few yards. Seeing Robert closing in for a tackle, he volleyed the ball in mid-stride goal wards.

Although scudding towards the far corner of the Thormanton goal, the diving Sammy had it safely covered. It was unfortunate that it struck Peter Russell's head in mid flight to deflect in the opposite direction and spin almost apologetically into Thormanton's net.

Thormanton were frozen in a tableaux of comic embarrassment – the gormless victims of some bizarre practical joke. Practically every Norbury player dived on top of Colin in a ruck. Deprived of any worthwhile football, the crowd erupted.

His fantasies of football glory curdling by the second, this should have been the moment for Kevin. But it still wasn't. Not yet.

It still wasn't the moment when, thirteen minutes later, Thormanton conceded a second goal. Galvanised by the goal, Colin and the rest of his Norbury colleagues steamed forward with renewed energy. Receiving the ball in acres of space, Colin had the time and talent to float in a near-perfect crossfield ball into Thormanton's penalty area. Norbury's centre forward timed his vertical jump to perfection to tower over Robert at a crucial moment. At full stretch, Sammy half managed to palm it out but a lurking opportunistic Norbury striker prodded it back. Covering on the goal line, Chris Manby interposed his body to block it but knew instinctively his time on the pitch would be summarily curtailed as he did so even before he felt the ball slap against his hands.

No, the moment was not the Referee awarding Norbury a penalty and theatrically brandishing a red card to dismiss Chris. The near tearful youth trudged off the field with something like relief, scarcely acknowledging the commiserations of Emma and the rest. As Colin strode up to slot the penalty home, sending Sammy completely the wrong way, with the predictability of a car crash, Kevin still felt an emotional involvement in the game.

Even the third goal for Norbury failed to dampen his ardour. Inevitably stretched urging forward for a goal in reply, Thormanton left acres of space at the back for Norbury to exploit. Colin latched onto a half hit through ball from his sweeper and surged through the centre of Thormanton's defence like an ice breaker through the Antarctic. Sammy dithered in the limbo between his line and the penalty box – uncertain whether to commit himself – and paid the price.

Colin executed a perfect chip straight out of the text book that looped mockingly over Sammy' head. The keeper made a backward contortion that was almost painful to watch as he despairingly tried to block the descending ball. To his credit, Sammy's outstretched fingers managed to gain fleeting contact and divert the ball from its trajectory. For an instant, it looked like he had pulled off the save of a lifetime as the ball trickled to rebound off the goal post. But the execution was merely being postponed. Another Norbury striker following up had an elementary task in side footing the ball into the net.

The remaining fifteen minutes of the first half ticked away with a visible sense of winding down and, when the Referee blew his whistle to signal half time, the Thormanton players trooped off down the tunnel as if seeking sanctuary in a hostile foreign clime. A section of the crowd had already started to barrack the fare on offer with a derisory chant of "what a load o' rubbish!"

One could have certainly been forgiven for thinking Robert Swales had had such an epiphany. "Well, it's fucking obvious we can't play unless we're on a promise to pop the ferret through the furry hoop afterwards!"

But Kevin was still away from the moment. "Aye! That's the whole point. We can play much better than this!"

Steven paused between guzzling his slice of orange. "In case you hadn't noticed, Sir Alex, our film careers are down the shithouse!" The surgical whiteness of the changing room walls made this talk resemble an autopsy.

Kevin had never stood taller and more erect – fatigue notwithstanding – than in the seconds he surveyed his battle weary troops in a tight semi circle. Later, he wondered if this was the last glow of the fluorescent light bulb before it burst. "So, the only way we can motivate ourselves is if we're starring in some old perve's wank fantasy! Is that it?"

"It obviously helps!" muttered Steven.

"To coin a phrase, we didn't become bad players overnight," said Kevin, dredging his considerable memory bank for managerial clichés.

"We always were bad players," said Sammy.

"But we only narrowly lost out on the league title through our own fault. And we battled through to this cup final. Now, come on! We've already beaten this fucking lot once this season," said Kevin.

"But now we're down to ten men," whined Peter Russell.

But Kevin was on a roll and the momentum could not be arrested. "We're giving Colin too much time on the ball. It's high time we made the twat pay fer' thinkin' he wor' better than us. Rob! I want you an' Steven to man mark him like you did Rothwell. Remember, he's not half the player Rothwell was."

Robert sighed wearily. "Wharraboutit, Steve? Think you can go a whole half without goal hanging?"

Steven's face looked noncommittal. "I've nowt' else to do."

"And another thing I noticed, their right back is as slow as a snail wi' piles. An' this bigger pitch is gonna' expose him. So everyone funnel their passes down that flank and we can trust Emma to beat him wi' speed."

Kevin paused with the precision of a natural orator and mimed listening to the faint hubbub of the crowd down the adjoining tunnel. "There must be over a thousand who've come to see us. When will any o' us ever play in front of an audience like this again?"

Without waiting for a reply, with no certainty that they would even follow him, Kevin marched purposefully down the tunnel and back onto the pitch. He did not gaze back over his shoulder until he was ensconced back in his familiar central midfield berth.

Kevin was marginally encouraged by their upright posture as they trooped out of the tunnel to join him. All were lined up in time to await Norbury as they filtered onto the pitch a few minutes later. Colin and his colleagues paid them little heed as they sloppily assumed their positions. The indifferent murmur of the crowd abated somewhat but the match itself seemed to have become something of an afterthought to the spectators, many of whom were still queuing for their half time refreshment.

The callous background hubbub did not abate as the balding Referee raised the whistle to his lips, comically ballooned out his ruddy cheeks and blasted the shrill note that heralded the final forty-five minutes this team would ever play together.

That they had been rejuvenated by the interval pep talk was immediately obvious to Kevin. Robert and Steven had adopted the brutish sentinel duty familiar from their approach to Rothwell against Wellthorpe – so long ago now – and had fallen back into it like choreographed dancers. Some of their movements seemed almost identical to the earlier match – as if one were observing edited highlights in a greatest hits package.

Every loose ball Thormanton gathered was funnelled out down the right channel to the Emma whose speed on the turn was already threatening to publicly emasculate the lumbering Norbury defender opposite her.

The raising of the game's tempo by Thormanton flatfooted Norbury. A diving header by Richard Swales plucked out of the air by the full stretch Norbury goalkeeper should have served as a warning. But Colin and his team mates seemed to regard it as the last desultory gesture of defiance by a dying beast refusing to go peacefully into the dark night. The half-hearted corner kick that ensued and was easily cleared seemed to confirm it.

The game drifted into a deceptive lull for several minutes. It was as if it seemed indecisive about what path to take next as it stuttered around in a cluttered midfield void. Then, Robert Swales upended Colin in a hard, but legal, block tackle and Steven gathered up the loose ball in his path. He took it forward several paces before unleashing a low accurate pass to Emma – alert on the wing as a terrier. Beating her defender with a practised ease, she turned sharply and set off for goal like a hound on a scent. The scattered Norbury defence converged on her like predatory vultures on a graceful swan. Perhaps it was her self-effacing nature that caused what happened next. Emma looked, to Kevin, as if she might go on to score a solo goal. Instead, she obviously caught Richard Swales on the edge of her peripheral vision and neatly passed the ball to him. Emma released her side pass with split-second perfect timing. Richard steadied himself before hitting the shot after a momentary hesitation.

It was not a thing of beauty. If anything, it was slightly mishit and it travelled with an awkward bobble. But it was sufficient to elude the Norbury goalkeeper's outstretched fingers. The ball had scarcely settled in the back of the net before Richard Swales scooped it up to convey it back to the centre circle. They were all aware of starting a momentum it would be foolish to arrest.

Norbury kicked off – their every blasé body movement betraying how much of an irritating minor inconvenience they regarded this goal. The tempo of their play was a fatal beat slower than Thormanton's. One of their midfielders fatally dallied on the ball and Robert's full length tackle aw the ball squirm loose to Kevin.

Kevin probably felt the first intimations of the Moment then. Normally emotionally-invested in a game, often to the detriment of all reason, Kevin was aware of a curious coolness seeping into the fabric of his soul. Rather than react instantly, he trapped the ball calming the pandemonium around him, glanced upwards, and effortlessly floated a cross field pass that hung unnaturally in the clammy afternoon air. The Norbury central defenders were formidably squat and burly but had the turning circle of an oil tanker and Emma had already demonstrated she had the beating of them in a straight race. She cut infield and sped off for the Norbury goal like a beautiful comet with the duo of Norbury defenders trailing behind like flotsam caught up in her tail.

As the Norbury goalkeeper lumbered off his line to narrow the angles, Emma paused mid stride in an almost provocatively teasing gesture. Her confident sexuality mocked the lumpish, unformed masculinity of her adversary as she dared him to advance closer. Rosemary's influence was absorbed into her being like creosote into timber. She made a deft feint to go one way, then unleashed a rasping low drive.

It was doubly emasculating for the goalkeeper that it comically nutmegged him between his chunky legs on route to the back of the net. Emma's goal celebration looked impishly regal as she fell into the arm of Steven and Peter racing up in support in time to congratulate her.

The shellshocked aura that descended on Norbury like a mantle acted like a pool of blood for the basking sharks of Thormanton. Only Colin seemed galvanised into urgency by the growing crisis. He pointed at an imaginary watch on his wrist.

"Only ten more minutes! Come on! Don't pack in now, sit back and defend!" All pretentions at footballing elegance had been trampled underfoot.

But the tide of events were against him. As Kevin casually took his position in central midfield for the restart, something about the immediate atmosphere niggled him. The aura around him seemed to have imperceptibly altered and he wondered what it was, until the obviousness of the answer almost made him laugh aloud.

The crowd were no longer ironically cheering and hooting what was happening on the pitch. Although there was still an undercurrent of mocking humour, their cheers and groans of theatrical agony were authentic. They were genuinely engrossed in the drama of the contest. Thormanton's fight back from oblivion had tamed their recalcitrance and yanked them by the scruff of the neck into the roles of committed observers.

Thormanton poured forward like locusts ready to devour a field of barley. Steven, freed from his onerous man marking duties by Colin deciding to drop back to act as sweeper, darted onto a pass from Paul Myers only for the Referee to acknowledge his frantically waving linesman and blow for offside. But there was to be no respite for Norbury. It had been the brief reprieve of the boxer virtually out on his feet under a relentless pummelling from his opponent.

Two minute later, Paul Myers was adjudged to have been shoved in the back by the Norbury Captain as they both went up to head a high clearance. The Referee blew for an indirect free kick five yards outside the Norbury penalty area.

Richard Swales was the picture of perfect balance as he chipped the dead ball into the Norbury box. Kevin looked as if he had mistimed his leap as he rose to head it. But it was deceptive. The ball struck him on the back of the head to fly into the net past the bewildered goalkeeper.

All square. And that was the Moment. Football had occupied the percentage of Kevin's brain not otherwise engaged with sex or ambition. But, as he clambered to his feet to a fusillade of hug and back slap from his fellow players, Kevin felt oddly purged. No, not purged – empty. He felt quite indifferent to the whole game now. For all the unbridled enthusiasm of the Thormanton players, Kevin could have been an adult relative having proved himself to a group of youngsters playing some juvenile game he himself had outgrown. For a second he seemed momentarily at a loss as to how to continue, then he trooped dutifully back to his half for the restart.

It was probably just as well there was less than two minutes to go as Kevin feared his enveloping indifference would make him a liability to the rest of the team. For the rest of the match, Kevin felt as if he was watching someone else going through the motions. He brutally robbed the Norbury Captain with a crunching two-footed tackle that sent the ball spinning loose. Richard Swales gathered it up and looped a long, diagonal ball for Steven to chase. The impetus gave his legs fresher energy than the Norbury player challenging him and he left the youth trailing in his wake. Cutting inside the penalty area from the right at an acute angle, he faced a one-on-one with the burly Norbury keeper.

It was a situation seemingly tailor-made for the goal hanging glory hunter and Kevin wasn't the only one there who anticipated Steven succumbing to the temptation of trying to dribble around his opponent to score. Instead, he astonished everyone by neatly side-footing the ball to Emma on his right. Not even breaking her stride, the girl accepted it as gracefully as a flower from a lover and toe-poked it into the back of the net.

Four-three with marginally less than thirty seconds to go. The Referee impatiently waved on the Thormanton celebrations so the game could quickly restart for Norbury's and sportsmanship's sake, but it was the most token of futile gestures. Colin had barely passed it five yards into the Thormanton half when the final whistle blew.

A thunderous roar echoed around the rudimentary stands. Steven sank to his knees, anaesthetised by exhaustion. Paul Myers' face muscles sagged with relief, making him look nearer thirty than twenty. Emma looked dazed with happiness. Sammy, virtually a bystander during the second half, seemed impelled to impress himself on events by soliciting the approval of the crow behind his goal as he retrieved his belongings. Robert pulled his shirt over his head to mop a brow saturated in sweat. Richard Swales tottered around like a zombie, his body a frail twig buffeted by the backslapping of his comrades. Chris Manby, still clad in his playing kit, sprinted at full pelt from the Manager's Technical Area with an energy and fitness painful to watch, encumbered as they were with aching limbs and joints. Peter Russell simply flopped onto his back and lazily extended his arm for high fives from the other.

Kevin regarded it indifferently. It was nice it had happened and they had something tangible to show for this momentous season. But it had all the allure of a discarded chrysalis to a butterfly in flight. Colin and his Norbury colleagues had already slunk off the pitch down the tunnel back to the sterile changing rooms. They had no desire to be bit-part players at someone else's festivities.

The League Officials bumbled down from their privileged seats in the Directors' Box to hurriedly set up a table in front of the Main Stand for the Presentation. Every stilted move betrayed their growing self-consciousness at holding it in front of such a large gathering.

Kevin fidgeted impatiently as the portly middle-aged men finally erected the trestle table with the recently polished trophy atop. The Thormanton players lined up expectantly for Kevin to march forward for the presentation but he dithered somewhat.

"Aren't you gonna' collect it?" asked Emma, indicating the Official hovering over the trophy.

"You collect it, Emma" said Kevin, flatly. "I can't be bothered." Emma opened her mouth to protest but Kevin forestalled her. "I think you deserve it." The pop-eyed girl needed no further prompting and took his place at the head of the line. The Official overcame his confusion and went through the motions of reverentially handing the trophy to Emma. The girl gripped the side handles and brandished it over her head – the body language for doing so having been memorised from countless televised cup finals. The crowd even had the good taste and manners to cheer.

As the trophy was handed around, Kevin was the only member of the side not to touch it. He was already heading down the player tunnel without a backward glance.